SURLY COWBOY

A COOPER BROTHERS NOVEL, SWEET WATER FALLS FARM ROMANCE BOOK 3

ELANA JOHNSON

AEJ
CREATIVE WORKS

SURLY COWBOY

CHAPTER ONE

L ee Cooper pulled his shirt over his head and tossed it in the general direction of his bed. It landed short and fell to the floor, but he didn't bother going to retrieve it. As frenzied as his mind was, the one thought he landed on was *No wonder Ford is a slob. It's genetic.*

He ripped open the closet doors, everything inside blurring for some reason. Probably because he hadn't taken a proper breath in the past minute. Maybe two. Fine, ten.

Lee closed his eyes and slowed down. He dropped his hands to his sides and took a long breath in through his nose. He watched a morning affirmation channel online every day, and the woman who led the group did breathing exercises like this.

In through the nose, he heard in her voice. *Hold it. Longer. Really take a moment and slow down your mind. Your heart. Release those muscles. Okay, out with me.*

Five, four, three, two one, zero.

Lee opened his eyes when he got to zero, and the shirts took on individual form in the closet. "Okay," he said. "You're fine. Ford is fine. His teacher just wants to talk to both you and Martha on a weekday evening. It's not a big deal."

He'd gotten off the phone with his ex-wife ten minutes ago, and he'd hurried to finish an email that had to go out today. Then he'd dashed home, and he wasn't any worse off by taking twenty seconds to center himself again.

With a bright red shirt covering his upper half and a peanut butter sandwich in one hand, Lee dashed back out the front door of his cabin and down the steps to his truck. The old girl had started to show her age, with rust wearing through around the wheels and the engine chugging to life like it would rather not.

Lee knew how she felt, and he patted the dashboard. "I'll let you retire soon, okay? But Ford needs us tonight."

He had no intentions of buying another truck, though he had plenty of money to do so. Lee rather liked this one, and he saw no reason to spend money on something when he already had one that worked.

The drive to Sweet Water Falls passed in a flash, and

Lee had no idea where his mind had wandered. He blinked, and the dark-haired image of Rosalie Reynolds flashed in his mind. Ah, so he'd gone down *that* path again.

He hadn't been brave enough to drop by the woman's office, even when she was expecting him to. He'd sent Will instead. *Begged* was a better word. The proper word. Familiar loathing and disgust built within Lee, and it was all directed at himself.

His heart pounded right now, though Rosalie wasn't anywhere near him physically. He wasn't sure why she affected him so thoroughly, only that she did. They'd only met the one time. He'd only spoken to her twice, once in person and once on the phone. He'd looked at her picture plenty of times on her website, and he was taking that knowledge with him to the grave.

He didn't need to add "stalker" to the list of names he'd been called over the years. Grumpy, sure, he could own that. Short-tempered, yes. What Cooper man wasn't? He could hardly be blamed for that one. It was genetically inbred in him to get angry or frustrated at the drop of a bale of hay or the first sign of oil leaking from a tractor.

Meticulous, he actually counted as a compliment. Anal-retentive was a bit of a stretch, but Lee didn't even mind that one. He worked with a lot of papers that held a lot of numbers, and someone had to be detail-oriented and obsessive about checking them to make sure things got done correctly.

Money in, money out—Lee took care of that.

Paychecks due, new orders received—Lee took care of that.

New clients and their contracts, established accounts and their renewals—Lee took care of that.

Lee ran Cooper & Co almost single-handedly these days, and most of the time, he let an inch of pride into his heart at how proud Daddy was of him. At how much Daddy trusted him to take over the generational operation that had been supplying milk to the people in Southern Texas, Louisiana, and Arkansas for over a century.

He pulled into a spot at the elementary school, spying Martha's car a few spaces over. She and Ford weren't in it, which meant Lee was late. His ex-wife would give him the stink-eye for that, but he'd come as soon as he'd been notified of tonight's meeting.

As he jogged toward the entrance of the building, he tucked in his shirt and he dang near pulled off the door as he opened it.

"Dad," Ford said, jumping to his feet from a cement bench across from the entrance.

Lee's whole face lit up, and he couldn't be mad at his son no matter what. He opened his arms to him, glad when Ford flew into his embrace. He always wanted Ford to be able to come to him for help, for the good, the bad, the anything.

"Hey, buddy," he said. "What am I doin' here tonight, huh?"

"Your son got in a fight," Martha said, and Lee looked over Ford's head to meet her eye. She didn't look too terribly upset, and Lee kept hold of Ford in one arm as he leaned forward to touch his lips to Martha's cheek.

He settled awkwardly back on his feet, even putting another few inches between them. "I got here as fast as I could."

"We've got five minutes still," she said, nodding down the hall. The three of them started that way at a much slower pace than Lee had used coming inside. He'd loved Martha once-upon-a-time, and sometimes when he looked at her, he only saw the good things they'd experienced together.

It didn't take long for him to remember the things that had driven them apart, and he certainly wasn't interested in getting back together with her. Lee simply took a long time to forgive—himself and others—and he wasn't sure he'd ever be able to get over infidelity.

Something about it just cut him right to the core, and even now, he worked against the feelings of betrayal and mistrust of all women.

Ford's teacher—a Miss Bair who was easily a decade younger than Lee—stepped into the hall. She smiled at Ford and then Lee and Martha. Lee didn't want to be in her shoes, and he gave her a smile back so she'd know they were going to agree with her.

Lee was, anyway.

"Evenin'," he said when no one else spoke. "I hope you weren't waiting long for me. I live pretty far out."

"Not at all," Miss Bair said. "Come on in."

Martha went first, then Ford, and Lee held the door for the teacher and entered last. She'd set up some chairs around her desk, and he sat in the last one.

"Did Ford tell you what happened today?"

"I heard most of it," Martha said. "Lee hasn't gotten much information. I didn't find the note or hear the message you left until about forty minutes ago."

"Ford?" Miss Bair prompted.

The boy squirmed in his seat, and Lee put his arm around his son. "Hey," he said real quietly. "Remember the roof? And the stars?"

Ford looked up at him, his innocent eyes so wide and so beautiful. He nodded, and Lee smiled at him. "Go on then." He ignored Martha's questioning gaze and glanced at Miss Bair.

She smiled at him, but Lee felt no spark of attraction to her. She had dark hair too—his preferred type—and nothing. Absolutely nothing like what he felt when he looked at Rosalie.

He had to call her again. Stop by her office. Something. Travis's wedding was in ten days. Could he ask

Rosalie to go with him? Maybe he could offer to pay her, or pay for her dress, or something.

Nope, he told himself. *You're not paying a woman to go out with you.* Either she'd say yes or she wouldn't.

But not if you don't ask.

"...so I told Simon to leave her alone," Ford said.

"Wait," Lee said, coming back to the conversation at hand. He really couldn't let his mind wander in situations like this. "Simon Alvarez?"

"Yes."

Lee glared at Ford and then Miss Bair. "I thought Simon and Ford weren't going to be allowed to be together."

"It was lunch recess, Dad."

"I don't care," Lee barked. "You're not supposed to be near him."

"He was teasing Lily," Ford said, his eyes welling with tears. "He had her up against the kindergarten fence, and I helped her."

Lee opened his mouth, but nothing came out. He looked at Martha, and she stroked Ford's hair off his forehead. "But you hit someone, baby. That's not how you solve problems."

"Your mother's right," Lee said, swallowing afterward.

"But it got Simon to leave Lily alone," Ford said, looking from him to Martha and back. "And then I was able to help Lily to the office. She was having a panic attack."

"Whoa," Lee said. "What?" He looked at Miss Bair, who wore a look of sympathy on her face. "Is she okay?"

"She's asthmatic," Miss Bair said, giving Ford a maternal smile too. She wasn't mad at him, Lee realized, though she certainly couldn't condone him hitting another student. "Once the nurse got her inhaler, she calmed right down."

Lee nodded, suddenly so tense. "So now what?"

Miss Bair leaned forward and put her fingertips on Ford's knee. "What did we decide, Ford?"

"That I won't hit people," he muttered. "Whether it's to help someone or not."

"That's right," she said. "Instead?"

"Instead, I try to get Lily away from Simon, or I start yelling for help from the sixth grade aides or the recess monitors." He hung his head, as if this option was the worst thing imaginable.

"Simon won't have lunch recess for three school days," Miss Bair said, pulling her hand back. "Unfortunately, I have to do the same to Ford."

"No suspension?" Martha asked.

Miss Bair shook her head. "I can't do that," she said, and while she couldn't say more, Lee heard it all. She actually agreed with Ford, and she'd do what she could to protect him. She looked from Martha to Lee. "Any questions?"

"No, ma'am," Ford and Lee said together, and they looked at one another and laughed.

"I think that covers it," Martha said, and the three of them stood. Lee took his son's hand in his as they left the classroom, but he waited until he was all the way outside before he crouched down in front of his eight-year-old.

"I don't think you should hit people, bud," he said. "But I'm so, *so* proud of you for standing up for Lily." He grinned at Ford and nodded once. "Okay?"

Ford nodded and reached out to touch Lee's cowboy hat. "I don't want to tattle to the recess monitors."

"Just stay away from Simon."

"But what if he's hurting someone?"

"Ford," Martha said, kneeling down in front of him too. "You'll get suspended next time, I promise. You can't hit other children."

He nodded again, his chin so low.

"Hey," Lee said. "Chin up, son. Look at me."

Ford did, and he seemed so lost and looking for Lee to guide him. "Do you want the other kids to think of you as a bully?"

"No."

"You can't hit other kids, not even if you're standing up for someone." He smiled and tapped Ford's nose. "Plus, if you get suspended, I'll work you like a dog on the farm. Is that what you want?"

Ford grinned too. "Can Queenie come with me?"

Lee laughed, realizing that his "punishment" for his

son getting suspended wasn't a punishment at all. He exchanged a glance with Martha.

"Come on, Ford," she said. "Give your daddy a hug. We have to get going."

Ford wrapped his skinny arms around Lee, and he held his son just as tightly. He whispered, "I love you, son. You be good for your momma, and you obey your teacher."

"Yes, sir," Ford said.

Lee stood and watched Ford link his hand in Martha's. She met Lee's eyes, and so much was said between them. Then they went to their car, and Lee went to his truck.

He drove back to the farm alone. He made dinner for himself, and he ate it alone. He hated being alone, and he wanted to do everything in his power to change his single status.

He got out his phone and let his thumb hover over the icon for the dating app he'd once used. He couldn't tap on it; he just couldn't.

He only wanted to go out with one woman, and she was Rosalie Reynolds.

Therefore, the following afternoon, Lee went through a similar routine as the previous night.

He changed his shirt. He washed his hands. He loaded himself into his truck. He drove to town.

Everything blurred around him, because when Lee focused on something, it was all he could see. All he could think about. All he could taste. And right now, that was a certain curly-haired brunette with gorgeous eyes. She'd rendered him mute once, and he was determined not to let that happen today.

He swallowed as he flipped on his blinker, scanning for the Curious Kids office. A small sign sat on the roof announcing the location of his destination, and he dang near stomped on the accelerator to get away.

"No," he coached himself. "You've come all this way. You're just going to go in there and tell her how stunningly beautiful she is, and then you're going to ask her to your brother's wedding."

The pit in Lee's stomach roared at him, but when a break in traffic presented itself, he made the turn into the parking lot.

No one sat in front of Curious Kids, and Lee took the spot directly outside the door. He killed the engine. He got out of the truck.

It was almost like his mind was moving through a checklist. *Do this. Do this. Do that.*

Go inside, check.

Find Rosalie, check.

She stood from the smaller of two desks, off to his left. With a smile on her face, she said, "Lee Cooper," in that melodic voice he couldn't get out of his ears.

Ask her to the wedding.

Wait.

Tell her how gorgeous she is.

No.

Say you can't stop thinking about her.

Creepy.

Do some*thing.*

Lee couldn't do anything. He felt like he'd entered the presence of an angel, and he stood there, frozen and mute.

CHAPTER TWO

Rosalie Reynolds had never been happier for her self-imposed dress code when she came to the office. She currently wore a pencil skirt that fell just below her knees, and she felt every inch of herself as Lee Cooper's gaze moved from her low heels and up along her skirt to the bright candy apple red blouse she'd chosen this morning.

She wasn't sure why she'd gone with red. Maybe she thought it accentuated her lips, which always seemed a bit too pale pink to her. Or maybe she'd been told a time or two—or twenty—that red complimented her darker skin tone and hair. She wasn't sure.

What she knew was that her phone blared at her again, the sound of an airhorn she hated but had also set. It was her sister, Natasha, and Rosalie's heart bobbed in her throat. She'd been texting her sister about perhaps joining a dating app now that James had made the move to California and he was good and truly gone from her life.

The face of her sweet daughter flashed through her mind. James would never be good and truly gone, but Rosalie also wasn't dealing with him on a daily basis anymore. Part of her languished in indescribable sadness, and the other part kept urging her to move forward with her own life.

Maybe with Lee Cooper, she thought, her face burning as the cowboy's eyes finally latched onto hers. His were just as foresty as she remembered, and she itched to see some of that deep, red-gold-brown hair.

"Can I help you?" she asked as professionally as possible. After all, he'd shown up—unannounced—at her office. The last time she'd seen a Cooper, it had been his brother, William. He'd been the one to bring back the faulty game and make the trade. "Is everything okay with your new disk?"

Rosalie cocked her head as her phone yelled at her again. She honestly didn't have time for Handsome's staring. Her heart told her not to send him away, but she wasn't sure what else to say. Natasha's notification went off again, and Rosalie swiped her phone from the edge of her desk. She tapped out a quick, *With a customer. I'll text you right back*, and looked back to the gorgeous, if not a little...strange, cowboy.

Strange wasn't the right word. It almost looked like he'd fallen into a trance.

"Lee," she said, really snapping out his name.

He blinked a couple of times and looked around the office, as if he'd driven here while asleep and just now realized where he was.

"Are you okay?" Rosalie took a step toward him, but when those delicious eyes came back to her, she paused. "I was just about to leave, so is there something I can do for you?"

He cleared his throat, and praise the heavens, she was going to get to hear that low, growly voice of his again. "Yeah, I was just thinking about something."

"Okay," she said.

He folded his arms, something shuttering over his face. "Ford doesn't really like the game I bought."

Rosalie blinked now, his statement a complete surprise to her. "Oh," she said, her brain whirring quickly. She wanted satisfied customers, but her return policy didn't include "didn't like it."

"Well," she said smoothly, her policies flying into place. "You're outside of the thirty-day, no-questions-asked refund period. So...I'm sorry."

"You're sorry?"

Rosalie squared her shoulders against this surly cowboy. "Yes," she said. "I can't just refund everyone's money because they don't like something."

"He hardly plays the game."

"I'm sorry about that," she said, breaking her eye contact with him and returning to stand behind her desk. She looked down at the papers there, but her concentration had broken completely. Handsome had a way of making her feel like the only woman in the world, and Rosalie hadn't felt like that in a long, long time.

She dared to look at him again, the frown between his eyes making him even sexier. She wondered what it would be like to kiss him when he wore such an unhappy look, and she could imagine a fight ensuing between the two of them for the control of *that* kiss.

She shook her head and muttered, "Keep it together, Rose," at the image of Lee pressing her against the very wall behind her and kissing her senseless.

"What?" Lee asked.

"Nothing." She looked up at him again, her phone blaring out at her again.

"What is that awful noise?" he asked. "It's happened like five times."

Rosalie could handle her company being insulted. Fine. Not everyone liked her games. She understood that from a consumer standpoint. She could even handle a critique of her personally, though she worked hard to keep her imperfections concealed behind the closed doors of her house.

But no one, not even Handsome, would criticize Natasha.

She took one step toward him, feeling every cell in her

body light up with fire. The angry kind. "That is my notif-ication for my sister," she said, hearing the danger in her own voice. "She has some special needs, and I need to be able to hear my phone whenever she texts." She had a similar notification sound attached to her daughter's babysitter, as well as her neighbor, both of whom helped Rosalie with Autumn now that James was gone.

"So if you don't need anything, *Mister* Cooper, I really have more important things to do than stand here and be insulted by you." She'd taken several more steps toward him, and he hadn't backed up an inch.

The man was muscle from head to toe, and she'd seen him soften before. She really wanted him to back down now too, because then she'd feel powerful and strong. At the same time, her eyes dropped to his mouth, and wow. That was what power and strength looked like.

She yanked her eyes back to his, and even through the lenses on his glasses, they fired at her. "Or stared at," she added.

"I wasn't staring," he said.

"You've been here for at least five minutes," Rosalie said, lifting her chin. "And have said twenty words."

"You know what?" Lee asked, but he didn't finish his challenge. He simply growled—yes, growled—and spun around. He stalked the three steps to the door and went out onto the sidewalk. As the glass door swung closed behind him, Rosalie's heartbeat shook through her veins.

He yelled something as he got in his truck and

slammed the door. Rosalie stayed very still, wondering why she wanted him to come back inside. He reminded her of a feral cat—skittish, unsure, but oh-so-wounded. She wanted to help all the strays in her neighborhood, and she couldn't help wondering if Lee had strayed into this part of Sweet Water Falls specifically so she could see him.

She sure had been thinking about him a lot. She'd almost called him after he'd gotten the second disk to make sure it worked. At the very least, she'd wanted to make sure he'd gotten it from his brother. Deep down, Rosalie knew both of those were covers simply to interact with Handsome again.

Lee didn't pull out, and Rosalie turned away from the door. Her legs shook as she returned to her desk. She still had some work to do, but it would be there waiting for her tomorrow. It always was.

She bent to get her purse from the bottom drawer, and she dialed Natasha while her eyes darted back to the front windows. Handsome's old, rusted truck still sat outside, and Rosalie wasn't sure she wanted to leave all of a sudden.

"Rosie," Natasha said in her thick tongue. "You're working?"

"Yes," Rosalie said. "Always working." She wiped her hand through her hair, but her fingers always got caught in her curls. She wasn't one of those women with the perfectly straight hair that shone like sunlight off snowfall. She'd been trying to grow out her curls, but they never made it much further than her shoulders.

"Mom says I can come visit this weekend," Natasha said, and that made Rosalie smile. "She said I have to ask you first."

"This weekend is great," Rosalie said, already feeling tired. But just like she couldn't say no to Autumn, she wouldn't deny her autistic sister her first trip to the beach. At least this year. "Maybe you could come stay with me this summer."

Rosalie had an extra bedroom, and Autumn loved Nat. James was gone, and why not? Rosalie didn't have anything else going on in her life. Her parents might enjoy the break, and Nat would get to go to the beach every day. Truth be told, Rosalie could use a beach day every week too.

"Don't tell her things you can't do." Mom's voice came through the line, the Jersey accent still thick though she'd lived in Texas for almost three decades.

"I'm not, Mom," Rosalie said, smiling as she pictured her mother. They had the same curls, and Rosalie loved her parents with everything she had. "I miss you guys. Will you stay the weekend too?"

"If we can come," Mom said.

"She said I can come," Nat said, her argumentative tone strong.

"I know what she said," Mom shot back. "But she really needs to think about it. So think about it, dear."

"Okay," Rosalie said. "I'll check my calendar when I get home." A quick glance toward the windows showed her that Handsome still hadn't left. What was he waiting for? "But I don't think there's a conflict."

As she watched, Handsome opened the door on his truck and got out again. Rosalie's heartbeat went wild, and she said, "I have to go, Mom. Nat, there's a customer coming in."

"Text me back about that picture," Nat said.

"She has to go," Mom said, and the call ended just as Handsome yanked open the glass door again.

Rosalie took a moment to stuff her phone into her messy purse, and she tugged on the zipper. It wouldn't quite slide, because she might have stopped by the store and bought Autumn a couple of packages of new underwear. Princess style, so the girl would remember to stop playing and go to the bathroom when she needed to.

Her face heated as the zipper caught on the plastic, the sound unmistakable. She abandoned the idea of closing her purse and faced Handsome.

His chest lifted and fell in the way it would had he just run a couple of miles. "Rosalie," he said, and it sounded like a bark. "I don't care about the game. That was just a stupid thing I said, because I couldn't figure out how to say what I really wanted to say."

Rosalie's pulse fell to the soles of her feet, but she still managed to ask, "What did you want to say?"

Lee took another breath and blew it out. "My brother is gettin' married next weekend. The fifteenth?"

Rosalie did know the date, so she nodded.

"I was wonderin'... See, the thing is, Rosalie, I've been thinking about you since that blasted math night months ago. Then I started thinking maybe you and I could go to the wedding together."

Whatever she'd been expecting him to say, it wasn't that. She opened her mouth to reply but ended up simply fishing her mouth closed and open. Closed and open.

I've been thinking about you since that blasted math night months ago.

Warmth slid through her, and the brightness of the sun started to fill her when she thought about being on this cowboy's arm at his brother's wedding. Her mind misfired about when Nat was coming, and what date the wedding was on, and if she could really go out with a man right now.

A smile touched Lee's mouth, and he cocked one eyebrow. "Who's staring now?"

The fire inside Rosalie flared, and she folded her arms the way he had several minutes ago. "Really, Lee?"

The smile fell from that mouth. "No, ma'am," he said, lifting his hat and smoothing back his hair. "You stare all you want."

She would, thank you very much, and she let her gaze drip down his bright coral shirt, past his belt buckle, and along his jeans to his cowboy boots. His hat was the same dark brown one he'd worn to math night a couple of months ago, and it made the saliva in Rosalie's mouth turn to sand.

Her eyes came back to his, and he raised his eyebrows, a silent *Well? What do you think? Will you go to my brother's wedding with me?*

She opened her mouth to answer, feeling more alive than she had in twenty months and so many things streaming through her mind that she couldn't sort through them fast enough to find the words she wanted to use.

CHAPTER THREE

L ee wondered if Rosalie could see through clothing for how long she stood there staring at him. He felt every inch of her appraisal, and at one point, he tucked his hands into his pockets as if that would save him.

His impatience grew with every breath he took, and he was reaching a point where he was either going to explode or stomp back to his truck again. He'd called Cherry, his older sister, from the cab of his truck, because she was the only one who knew Lee had left the farm early today specifically to ask Rosalie to Trav's wedding.

Lee Howard Cooper, she'd lectured. *You get out of that truck right now and do two things. One, apologize. Profusely. Two, ask her to Trav's wedding!*

Cherry had not been happy with his invented reason for stopping by Curious Kids, and Lee had fumed in the driver's seat, wondering if Rosalie would leave with him parked right there. He didn't think she would.

Even now, a hint of wariness sat in her eyes.

He lifted one eyebrow, his sister's words still echoing through him. *I asked someone to accompany me to the wedding, Lee*, Cherry had said, plenty of venom in her voice. *If you don't ask her, you'll literally be the only one dateless.*

When he'd demanded to know who she'd gotten to go with her, she'd refused to tell him. *After you ask Rosalie.*

So Lee had hung up with his sister, gathered himself together, and come back inside.

"Well?" he asked now, because he figured that was better than growling or exploding. The impatience in him meowed and settled down. "I'm sorry, Rosalie," he said, his voice quiet now. He hadn't apologized upon re-entering the store, and he should've. It would be the first question out of Cherry's mouth. "I didn't mean to interrupt your day, and then act...grouchy about the game. That was..."

Stupid came to mind.

Rosalie watched him, her head tilted slightly as if she didn't want to miss anything he might say.

"That was me just gettin' in my own way," he finally said with a nod.

"Mm." Rosalie took a couple of steps toward him, which sent everything male inside him back to blasting off like a cannon. "Here's what I think, Mister Cooper."

"It's just Lee," he said, reaching up to push his cowboy hat a bit further forward. She was going to say no. Right to his face. Most women who wanted to go out with a man didn't start with, "Here's what I think."

Lee knew that much. He studied the tips of his boots for a moment, Rosalie's heels bringing her closer and closer to him. Her feet entered his sphere of vision, and Lee couldn't help himself. He literally couldn't keep his head down. He looked up and right into the woman's eyes, and he felt things he hadn't felt in years.

His first thought was to kiss her, and he narrowly stopped himself from that humiliation-fest. "What do you think?" he asked instead.

"I don't think our first date should be at your brother's wedding."

Lee's brow furrowed. "You wanna go to dinner tonight?"

Rosalie smiled and reached up to brush something from his shoulder. Electricity arced through him, and Lee felt sure the shock would render him frozen and mute all over again.

"Dinner's not a bad idea," she said.

"My family just eats leftovers on Thursdays," he said. "Will's doing this huge thing for Gretchen's birthday party tomorrow night. We could go out Saturday, or you could come out to the farm for Sunday lunch."

Lee swallowed, unable to even imagine walking into the farmhouse where he'd grown up with Rosalie

Reynolds on his arm. She was definitely right, because his family needed to be eased into the idea of him showing up with her at Travis's wedding.

Ten days. It was only ten more days, and now that Lee had asked Rosalie, he didn't feel such darkness hanging over him.

"We'll come back to a lot of what you just said," Rosalie said with a smile. "Because I didn't understand most of it."

Lee gave her a small smile too.

"Do you eat dinner at restaurants?" Rosalie asked. "Or are we talking a big, family meal every night?"

Lee realized what he'd said, and he shook his head. "Sorry, I...I've been out of this dating scene for a while."

"Ford's what? Eight?"

"Almost nine."

"How long have you been divorced?"

"Six years," he said, a horrible thought blitzing through him. "You're not married, are you? I suppose I should've asked that first." His chest heated, and he took in a big breath. "No boyfriend?"

Something shivered across Rosalie's face, and she turned away from him. "No," she said. "No boyfriend. Not married." She flashed him another smile, but it held more pain than her previous ones.

Lee cocked his head then. "I sense some stories."

Rosalie laughed lightly. "I do have some of those." She met his eye again, a boldness in her face he sure did like.

Around the farm, Lee had to make quick decisions sometimes. Everyone looked to him to be the boss, and that
was no easy weight to carry. "Lee, I'd love to go to dinner
with you tonight. I just have to make a couple of phone
calls first."

"Sure," he said easily, his breath practically
whooshing out of his body. He held it back just in time,
and covered his long, relieved sigh with a smile. "I know
what it's like to always have one more thing to do at
work."

Rosalie looked over to the rack of games that
stretched as tall as he did. "Yes," she said absently. "But
these are personal calls. I need to talk to my mom and
sister about coming this weekend."

"So no dinner on Saturday."

She smiled at him. "Probably not. Tonight, I need...I'll
have to check with my babysitter or arrange for a different
one if she can't stay."

Lee didn't miss a beat. "How many kids do you have?"

"Just one," Rosalie said, reaching to tuck her hair. Of
course, the curl didn't stay. "A little girl. She's four."

Lee nodded, so much understanding pouring through
him. "I can hang around town for a bit. It's thirty minutes
out to the farm, so it doesn't make much sense to go back
and then drive in again." His eyebrows went up. "How
long do you need?"

She raised her arm and looked at her watched wrist.
"Let's see...it's almost four-thirty." She looked up, a ques-

tion in her stunningly beautiful eyes too. "A couple of hours? Six-thirty?"

"Sure," Lee said, though he had no idea what he was going to do in Sweet Water Falls for two hours.

"You sure? You'll just hang around here?"

"I can go see my boy," Lee said, deciding on the spot. Martha didn't care when Lee stopped by, as long as he let her know he was coming. "Call my daddy and see if he or Mama needs anything from town. I'll be fine."

Rosalie nodded and turned back to her desk. "All right. I'll be ready at six-thirty." She picked up her phone and faced him again. "Want to give me your number, and I'll text you my address?" She met his gaze again. "You are going to come pick me up, right?"

"Yes, ma'am," he said, rocking back onto his heels for a moment, then righting himself. He rattled off his number, sure he'd entered some dream world through an ordinary storefront door-portal. He hadn't gotten a woman's number in forever, but as his phone chimed, he now had Rosalie's.

"That's me," she said, smiling still. Lee couldn't quite believe that either. Questions screamed at him again, but he silenced them all. He had her number now, and they were going to dinner in just two hours. He could ask about her divorce—or if she'd been married to her daughter's father at all—her age, everything later.

Much later, a voice told him. His sister's voice. Both of them combined in his head, tormenting him with things like, *Be nice tonight, Lee. Don't ruin anything tonight, Lee. Don't ask her hard questions tonight, Lee. It's a first date, for crying out loud.*

Through Clarissa's and Cherry's voices, he managed to hear Rosalie say, "Okay, well, I have to get going," which was her obviously telling him to get his feet moving toward the exit too.

"Right," he said, pulling his hands from his pockets. "Okay, I'll see you soon."

"Yep," she said, and Lee turned smartly on his heel the way soldiers did and left Curious Kids. Outside, the air went down like soggy paper towels, but Lee didn't care. He felt like jumping up and touching his heels together, then congratulating himself for finally, *finally* asking Rosalie to be his date for the wedding.

Instead of doing any of that, he got behind the wheel of his truck, started it, and backed out of the space. He left the parking lot completely, thinking an ice cream cone sounded like a fine way to spend at least ten minutes of the next one hundred and twenty.

Perhaps he could take a nap too. He never had much time off from the farm, and as he waited in the drive-through line for one of the famous Rock House cement-thick shakes, he tapped out texts to Daddy and Mama and Martha.

He didn't tell anyone that he'd successfully asked out Rosalie, and he collected his orange chocolate chip shake from the window and headed down the street to a shady parking spot alongside a park.

Only then did he take a bite of the sweet treat. Happiness soared through him with the fruity chocolate, and he grinned as he tapped the screen to call Cherry for the second time that day.

"You better be reporting the success of the tasks you were assigned," his sister barked at him.

"Yep," Lee said, mimicking Rosalie's last word to him.

"Lee," Cherry said, her voice mostly a gasp. "You did? You asked her to the wedding?"

"Yes," Lee said, taking another bite of his treat.

"Well, what did she say?"

He looked up and out the windshield. "She said she thought we should go out before the wedding," he said, some of his joy freefalling now. "So we're goin' to dinner in a couple of hours."

"You're kidding," Cherry said.

"No, why?" Lee didn't like her theatrics, and his irritation with his sister grew. "Is that bad?"

"No," Cherry said, her voice too high now. "Not bad at all."

"But..." Lee prompted, scooping up another bite of ice cream, this one with a nice load of chocolate chips. He put the whole thing in his mouth, which had started to grow freezing cold.

"Did she commit to the wedding?"

"She said—" Lee cut off, trying to think back through

the conversation. It took him several moments, and not even the chocolate in his mouth helped settle him. "She said she didn't think our first date should be at the wedding."

"So she didn't commit to it."

"No," Lee said darkly. He stirred the melting edges of the shake into the thicker middle part. "Not that I recall."

"But dinner tonight is good," Cherry said with a false brightness to her voice. "Where are you going to take her?"

Lee looked up again, this time plenty of alarm streaming through him "I...have no idea."

Cherry laughed, but Lee didn't find anything funny. He lived out on the farm, and he only came to town to collect Ford on Friday afternoons. He drove him back to school on Monday mornings. He might stop by the drugstore then, or pick up some essential groceries for the weekend on Friday. But he didn't have friends in town, and he didn't socialize with anyone outside of the men and women who worked at or came to Sweet Water Falls Farm or Cooper & Co.

"I'll look up some places for you," Cherry said. "And text you."

"Thank you," Lee said. "My brain feels like it's gone on vacation." He shook his head. "Every time I'm around this woman, I fall apart."

"Well, that's good, right?" Cherry asked.

"How is that good, Cherry?" He shook his head again.

No, falling apart around the gorgeous Rosalie Reynolds was definitely *not* good. Jeez Louise.

"It means you feel something for her," Cherry said. "It's sweet."

"I just end up looking like a fool," he muttered. "Nothin' sweet about that."

"Just remember that she said yes to dinner," Cherry said. "She must see something she likes already."

"I can't imagine what," Lee said, actually looking down at his shirt. Perhaps Rosalie liked bright colors on cowboys.

"Come on, Lee," Cherry said. "You're a handsome man."

"Okay," he said, a new blush crawling into his face for absolutely no reason. "You promised to tell me who you asked to the wedding if I went inside and apologized and asked Rosalie, and I did all of the above."

Cherry remained silent for a few moments, and then she cleared her throat. "Fine," she said in her ultra-refined voice. The tone she used whenever she talked about her job in the city, as if Sweet Water Falls was way beneath her. "I asked Charlie, and he said yes."

Lee forgot about ice cream and video games and his own name. "You asked Charlie?"

"Yes," Cherry said, plenty of haughtiness in her voice. "I don't need a lecture from you about him."

"You don't?" Lee asked, dumbstruck. "Cherry...the

man broke your heart. He's the reason you won't come home."

"Not entirely true," Cherry said. "There are many and varied reasons I won't come home."

"He's the biggest one." Lee pictured the tall, tan, talented Sheriff's deputy. Charles Hooper had dated Cherry for years. Three or four or six, Lee wasn't sure. He hadn't wanted to get married until he'd achieved a certain rank in the Sheriff's department, and Cherry wasn't going to be a perpetual girlfriend while the man built his career.

They'd broken up, and Cherry had fled Sweet Water Falls in favor of San Antonio.

"But he's still just one," Cherry said, sounding tired now. "Listen, Lee, I have to go. I'm so happy you asked Rosalie. Are you happy?"

"Yeah," he said slowly. "Do you think I should press her about the wedding when we go out tonight?"

"I think...wait and see how it goes. If it goes real well, you can ask her when you drop her off. Just be like, 'so...I didn't really hear if you said yes or no to the wedding. Should I be lookin' for another date?'"

Lee chuckled as his sister laughed. "I do not sound like that," he said, though she'd gotten his accent pretty spot-on, even the "lookin'" was exactly right.

"Sure," Cherry said, still giggling. She sobered in the next moment. "Lee, not a word about Charlie to anyone, especially Mama."

"No, ma'am," Lee said, his spirits quieting. "But you'll

tell them, right? I hate keeping secrets. I'm no good at it, and they knot me all up."

"I'll tell them," she said. "Soon."

"When?" he pressed.

"As soon as you tell them you'll be at the wedding with Rosalie," she said, nailing into his heart with those words.

"You know what?" Lee asked, but he didn't have anything to follow it up with.

"What?" Cherry challenged.

Lee shook his head and stirred his shake as a couple of boys ran out onto the grass near him, a soccer ball going back and forth between them. "I don't know what," he said. "But one day, I'm going to have something really amazing to hold over *your* head. See how you like it then."

Cherry laughed again, and Lee allowed himself to smile. "Call me later, little brother," she said. "I want to know how the whole date went."

"Send me some places to take her," he said quickly. "*Nice* places, Cherry."

"You got it." With that, the call ended. Lee sighed and took another bite of pure perfection. He nursed the shake until it was gone, and then he checked his phone.

Another sigh pulled through him, but this one carried a lot more weight. Mama and Daddy had texted, both needing items at different stores. Martha had also responded and said Ford finished his piano lessons at five-thirty, and Lee could come by any time after that.

"Can't sit around eating ice cream," he muttered to himself as he flipped his truck in reverse and backed out of yet another parking stall. If he timed everything just right, he could run his parents' errands and see his son before he had to be on Rosalie's doorstep for dinner.

His stomach trembled, and Lee told himself it was just the orange chocolate chip ice cream causing havoc with his guts. But really, he knew it was because he'd have to somehow find a way to charm, chat, and chuckle with the gorgeous Rosalie Reynolds...without making a complete idiot of himself.

He really didn't want to come up short this time, and he honestly hadn't felt half as excited about a woman as he did Rosalie. He'd never believed in love at first sight before, but when Rosalie was in the room, Lee couldn't even *see* anyone else.

"Slow down, cowboy," he muttered to himself as he turned into the organic grocery store lot. "She might be the one for you, but that doesn't mean you're the one for her."

He applied the brakes in his truck as he came to a stop in a stall, and he could do the same for his thoughts about Rosalie. It was their first date. He'd just see how things went tonight, but as he walked inside to get Daddy's sprouted wheat bread, Lee prayed that this dinner would be amazing for both him and Rosalie.

CHAPTER FOUR

Rosalie worked very hard not to roll her eyes as Nat continued to talk about the colorguard competition she'd watched last week. "Nat," she said. She'd been sitting in her driveway for ten minutes already. "Nat?"

"...it's just so hard to watch, you know?"

"Yes," Rosalie said automatically. "Honey, I'm sorry, but I'm home now, and I have to go inside and talk to Autumn."

"Okay," Nat said cheerfully, and Rosalie wished she was like her autistic sister sometimes. "Mom said I could text you when we left tomorrow."

"It's on Saturday," Rosalie corrected gently. "You're driving here on Saturday."

"In the morning," Nat said

"Yes." Rosalie gathered her purse and reached out to touch the button that would turn off her car.

"Love you, Rose," Nat said, and those words filled the world with love.

"I love you too, Nat." Rosalie ended the call and got out, the Texas evening heat assaulting her as she quickly went toward the house. She opened the door with a "Hey, everyone," and stepped over the gate keeping Thumper from escaping.

Right now, she didn't see the white rabbit, and she didn't have time for him anyway. Charity poked her head up from behind the small island in the kitchen. "Hey, Mrs. Reynolds."

Rosalie didn't correct her on the Mrs. part. She hadn't gone back to her maiden name after the divorce, because she wanted to have the same last name as her daughter. She wanted them to be a family, and for a while there, she could admit she'd hoped James would come around and come back to the two of them.

"Autumn's in the back yard." Charity stood with the broken pieces of a glass in her hand. "I just dropped this glass, so be careful."

Rosalie stopped where she was, taking in the shards of glass. "I can help," she said.

"Don't worry about it." Charity gave her a smile and tucked her stick-straight blonde hair behind her ear. Hers actually stayed, and Rosalie envied her that. "I'll get it cleaned up, and then I have to head out." She wore a sympathetic smile now. "I'm sorry I can't stay tonight. Is it something really important?"

Rosalie wanted to gush her guts to the college student who had a steady engineering-major boyfriend. She held back, telling herself she was this woman's boss and she didn't want too many lines blurred.

"It's fine," she said. "I asked Tess if Autumn could come over there."

"Oh, good," Charity said with a smile. "I have this huge study group for our finals next week." She ripped off a couple of paper towels and got them wet.

"Of course," Rosalie said, glancing down the hall toward where her bedroom sat. She wanted to change out of her pencil skirt and blouse, but she couldn't decide if she should go with another dress or choose slacks instead. Lee had been wearing jeans and a bright peachy-orange shirt, and he'd said he didn't have time to go home.

Maybe she should go with jeans too. She could pair them with that bone-colored wrap-around she'd ordered online last week...

"...Mom." Autumn touched her arm, and Rosalie blinked her way out of her wardrobe. Her beautiful daughter stood in front of her, her dark eyes alight with something.

"What, baby?" She bent to pick up the girl, her feet protesting the extra weight in her heels. "Did you have a good day today? Did you show Charity your pet rock?"

She'd painted them at preschool earlier this week, and her teacher had let Autumn bring the pet home today.

"Yep," Autumn said, putting her arms around Rosalie's neck. She hugged her, and Rosalie embraced her back. She loved her daughter with everything she had, and she could not imagine moving to California the way James had. Didn't he miss Autumn? How could he stand to not see her as often as he once had?

"Come see the house I built for him and Thumper," Autumn said, pulling back and wiggling to get down.

"All right," Rosalie said, shooting a glance toward Charity. The college student smiled and waved to her, because she knew that once Rosalie stepped foot in the back yard, she'd be there for a while.

Rosalie knew it too, and her eyes next landed on the microwave, which showed her the clock. It was just after five. She had time. Her nerves still bounced through her veins, because she wanted to look perfect for Lee tonight. Absolutely perfect. Presentation perfect.

She wanted to be princess-beautiful for him, and she thought of herself in a yellow gown like what the princess wore in the movies, and she pictured herself dancing with the beastly Lee Cooper as the moon rose higher and higher in the sky.

It was a nice picture, but the heat outside ruined it. A gown like that would only make her sweat, and Rosalie didn't have anything princess-like about her.

"Look," Autumn said, crouching down in front of a

semblance of a structure made of twigs and grass. "Thumper likes it."

Thumper was eating his house, but Rosalie didn't say so. "It's great," she said. "What did you name your rock again?"

"Stone, remember?" Autumn looked up at her with child-like innocence in her gaze, everything so unassuming and so happy. Rosalie wished she could feel like that again. She wanted to believe in the goodness in the world again, and she told herself she had to *choose* to see the positive.

James had left, yes. *It was twenty-one months ago,* she thought, and she pasted a smile on her face too. "Stone, that's right," she said. Autumn had been naming things what they were since she was old enough to talk, and Rosalie should've remembered.

Had Lee not stopped by her office, she would have. "Listen, honey," she said, crouching down in her heels. "Mommy has to go out again tonight. Tess said you could come to her house and play with Baylor. Doesn't that sound fun?"

Autumn looked at her with hope and wonder in her eyes. "Can I wear my penguin costume?"

Rosalie grinned at her daughter. "I don't see why not."

Autumn whooped and ran toward the house. "I'm going to go change right now!"

Rosalie let her go, but she sighed as she stood. She kicked off the offending heels, having enough of them for one day. She'd put all the proper pieces together again tomorrow, even though it was Friday, and she'd go into the office where she worked alone.

She was so tired of being alone. She didn't want to be the only one in charge of Autumn, or the house, the yard, Thumper, the car, all of it. The weight of that responsibility crushed her, and she wished James had not left Sweet Water Falls.

At the same time, she couldn't help thinking that if he hadn't, she wouldn't be as ready or as excited to go out with Lee Cooper as she was.

With a jolt, she turned back to the house. She didn't have time to stand around in the yard and contemplate her life. She had a hot date with a handsome cowboy to get ready for.

"I don't know how late," Rosalie said, giving her friend and neighbor a smile. "I brought her pajamas, but she can honestly just stay in the costume." She smiled at her daughter, who'd run right over to Tess's five-year-old, Baylor. He wore a superhero costume, and no one in the house seemed to think adding a penguin to the mix was a problem.

Gratitude for that, for Tess always saying yes whenever Rosalie asked her to babysit Autumn, and for all she had swept through her.

"Who are you going out with?" Tess asked.

Rosalie swallowed, not sure why she didn't want to say Lee's name. At the same time, she knew exactly why. Tess was a stay-at-home mom who got together with a lot of other stay-at-home moms. They talked. They fueled the rumor mill in a small town like Sweet Water Falls, and she didn't want to be the subject of it.

"Uh, can I tell you after? Maybe it'll be terrible." She smiled as if she really expected the forthcoming date to be simply awful. Besides, all Tess had to do was stand at her front window and watch to see who pulled into Rosalie's driveway in only ten minutes. Then she'd know. Then the whole town would know.

Panic poured through Rosalie. She needed to cancel this date. At the very least, she needed to call Lee and tell him she'd meet him somewhere. Anywhere but her front porch.

Tess gave her a sympathetic smile. "Sure, hon. You tell me after." A crash sounded in the kitchen, and Tess's attention got diverted in that direction. "Benji!" she yelled, already hurrying toward the white cloud of flour as it lifted high enough to be seen over the countertop. "I told you to stay out of that flour!"

Rosalie took that as her cue to leave, and she quickly slipped out the front door while Autumn was playing happily with her best friend. She'd already kissed her, as well as given her explicit instructions to listen to Tess and her husband Frank, and to go to bed on time. They had to be at the office in the morning, and if she didn't go to bed on time, she couldn't come with her.

Autumn loved coming to the office with Rosalie, so she didn't expect any problems. She crossed the lawn between their two houses and hurried inside. She still had to feed Thumper, who stomped his foot at her angrily for leaving for five minutes.

"I know, bud," she said to him. "Your turn. I'll leave the light on for you tonight. Don't worry." The rabbit didn't like being left home alone, and certainly not in the dark. He refused to go in a cage, and Rosalie had often wanted to install a video camera so she could see what the bunny did in her absence. He wasn't a killer rabbit or anything, and he didn't chew shoes or furniture. She honestly thought he probably hippity-hopped into Autumn's room and took a nap on her bean bag.

She opened the fridge, sure she had some carrots and celery for the rabbit. As she opened the produce drawer, she knew there wasn't anything inside. "What happened?" she asked. She'd hurried inside after Autumn and found the girl wrestling with her penguin costume. Charity had already gone.

Once her daughter was ready, Rosalie had taken her into her bedroom and put a movie on for her, and Autumn had snuggled into her bed to watch it while Rosalie proceeded to try on several different combinations of clothing. This jacket with those jeans? These slacks with that blouse?

In the end, she'd settled on an animal print faux wrap-around dress that showed her wild side. Rosalie didn't really have one of those, but she sure did like a fake leopard print, especially when the spots came in a deep navy blue and not black.

She hadn't eaten, but she'd fed Autumn a peanut butter and honey sandwich and a cut-up apple. She stepped back from the fridge and looked in the sink, finding the remains of a veggie bowl there. "Did you already get fed?" she asked the rabbit.

He stomped quite vehemently that he had not. So Autumn had had the baby carrots with ranch, as was now drying in the sink. Rosalie sighed, but she couldn't be angry with Charity or Autumn for eating vegetables.

She simply didn't have anything to feed Thumper, and she couldn't just leave him. "I'll see what I have in the pantry," she said, yanking open the door at the same time the doorbell rang.

Thumper stomped three times in a row in quick succession, almost like he was the one standing on the front porch knocking. Rosalie turned that way, her mind clearing of every other thought.

Lee was here.

An alarm on her phone chimed, and sure enough, the hour had struck six-thirty. She hurried toward the door, her first inclination to remove the gate so he could come in. At the very least, she wouldn't have to step over the gate in her knee-high skirt. Humiliation filled her at the thought. She really should've arranged to meet him somewhere. Everything seemed to be tilting sideways tonight, and if this date went bad, she didn't want it to be her fault.

She opened the door, and she wasn't surprised to find Lee standing there. He wore the exact same clothes as before, but now he held a couple of items in his hands.

"Howdy," he said, quite pleasantly too. He lifted a box of candy. "I had some help at the grocery store, and someone told me your daughter likes lemon drops."

Rosalie's eyes traveled to the yellow box of candy, a brand-new door in her heart opening wide. It was just big enough for this cowboy to walk through.

He lifted the other hand, which held a plastic grocery sack. "And a little birdie told me that you had a...wily rabbit who might like these things."

Rosalie almost burst into tears. She took the bag from him, still trying to control her emotions. He'd brought the perfect gifts—not flowers, or chocolate, or stuffed animals, but cabbage, carrot tops, and red leaf lettuce.

She looked up, wonder running through her. Whoever he'd run into at the store was her guardian angel. Or else Lee Cooper was.

"Can I come in?" he asked, and Rosalie stepped back, her mouth still unable to form words.

CHAPTER FIVE

Lee couldn't describe how he felt as he lifted his leg and stepped over the knee-high gate keeping him from Rosalie. Shiny, maybe. It was almost like light beamed from him—his smile, his eyes, his very soul—as she stepped back to make room for him in the aisle she'd made between the wall and the couch she'd placed facing into the living room.

He'd never been happier to run into Karyn Harlow at the organic grocery store. He didn't even care that that the baby carrots had cost twice as much as he ever would've paid. Seeing the wonder and gratitude on Rosalie's face had been worth every penny.

"Just in here?" he asked, moving past her and toward the kitchen at the back of the house. Her home smelled like powder and perfume, and Lee ducked his head and smiled to himself. That wasn't her house. That was *her*, and he sure did like it. He liked the scent of her a whole lot.

His heartbeat scampered through his whole body, but he managed to lift the veggies to the counter just as something thumped loudly to the right and behind him. Surprise tugged at him, but he turned and looked.

A white rabbit sat right at the end of the hallway. Anyone who hadn't run into Karyn would've thought it was the cutest little family pet. His little pink nose wiggled, and Lee wondered if rabbits were like dogs. Could he smell the cabbage?

Lee chuckled and tugged the head of greenery free from the bag. "Do you just chop it up, or...?" He glanced over to Rosalie, who'd come a little closer to him. She currently pressed her palms together, a nervous look on her face.

That gave him pause, but she wiped all of her emotions away in the next moment, her brilliant, professional smile appearing on her face. "Sure," she said, finally speaking. "I can do it."

"I know how to chop things," he said smoothly, a blip of irritation firing through him. He turned in his cowboy boots, looking for a knife block next to the stove. Rosalie had set up her kitchen like most people, and he pulled the large chopping knife from the wood smoothly.

She bent and pulled something from a lower cabinet, then set the cutting board on the counter next to his unpacked vegetables. "You cook?" she asked.

"Yes," he said, trying to decide how much to tell her. Lee didn't like putting too much out there too soon, which was why he'd preferred the online dating apps in the past. "Every Wednesday for my whole family, actually." He gave her a ghost of a grin and sliced off a huge chunk of cabbage. "How much to you feed him?"

With her standing so close, that sexy dress hugging her waist and curves, Lee could hardly think. The dark blue leopard spots sat against a cream background, and she wore a pair of off-white sandals on her feet. She made his mouth water, and he couldn't think about anything but dropping the knife and taking her into his arms.

The rabbit stomped again, sending three loud booms through the house. Rosalie giggled—another kick to his defenses—and moved behind him. "Thumper, knock it off. You're being rude. He's making your dinner."

"Thumper," he repeated. "Sounds like the perfect name for him."

"Autumn named him," she said. "His full name is The USS Thumper, but she allows us to call him by Thumper."

"Like a ship?" Lee made quick work of the cabbage and carrots, still not sure how much to make for the rabbit. He did seem unusually large, and Rosalie didn't frown or complain when Lee slid everything into a big bowl he'd found in a cupboard beside the fridge.

"Yes," Rosalie said, placing the bowl on the floor for Thumper right where he sat. She straightened, her eyes blazing out dark fire as she met Lee's. "Her father is in the Navy."

"Ah." Lee nodded and watched the rabbit chow down a long string of cabbage. He nodded to the lemon drops. "Well, those are for your daughter. I have something for you in the truck."

The fire turned into dancing lights. "Is that right?" Rosalie took a step toward him, seeming to realize as she did that maybe she didn't want to. She halted after the single movement, and Lee really didn't want tonight to be stilted.

He cleared his throat, so many things running through his mind. He didn't normally just let words come out he hadn't thought about thoroughly. "Rosalie," he said, reaching out one hand. She moved toward him then and slid her fingers between his. He watched as their hands joined, something kicking and screaming and firing through him.

Nerves. Desire. Fear.

He looked up at her, seeing all the same things in her expression too. "You're not going to be the CEO tonight, are you?"

She blinked those long lashes at him, confusion running through her eyes now. "What?"

"Earlier, a minute ago," he said. "You seemed real... nervous, and then you just wiped it away like it was nothing." His brain told him to stop talking, and stop talking right now. Instead of listening to the very rational side of himself, he kept going. "I'm nervous too, but I don't want to go if it's not going to just be...real."

Rosalie started to tug her fingers back, but Lee held onto them. She stilled. The air quieted as the air conditioner in her house switched off. Even Thumper had taken a break from his feast.

"I'm a little nervous," Rosalie said. "I haven't been out with anyone since the divorce."

Lee nodded, a smile creeping its way across his mouth. "I've seen you polished and perfect, Rosalie. You're flawless. Tonight, I want to go past that." He brought his gaze back to hers. "Do you still want to go? I've got reservations at Montague's."

Her eyebrows went up. "You do? How did you manage that?"

He grinned fully at her. "My sister has some connections." Cherry really had come through for him. Karyn had too. Lee felt like the Lord had stitched everything together just right for tonight, except for maybe Lee himself.

"Flawless, huh?" she asked as if seriously considering canceling on him. Lee could see she wouldn't. She'd taken great care with her clothes, her hair, her makeup. She *wanted* to be flawless, and he stopped himself just in time from thinking she'd done so for him. She probably felt more confident when she wore her hair back on the sides the way she did and put on just the right dusting of pink powder on her cheeks.

"Perfectly flawless," he confirmed.

Rosalie tilted her head and stepped toward him, turning at the same time. She linked her arm through his. "All right, Mister Cooper. I suppose I can stomach dinner at Montague's with you if I'm flawless."

Lee continued to shine as he walked with her toward the front door, because she hadn't sneered out the word *Mister* this time. In fact, it sure seemed like this woman was flirting with him. Lee had been out of the real dating pool for a while, so he wasn't going to jump into the deep end yet. He was simply going to beam sunshine from every pore in his body.

They both stepped over the gate, and Rosalie pushed the door closed behind her. "What about you?" she asked, sliding her hand along his forearm and sending shivers down his hip and into his leg from her touch. "Have you dated a lot in the past six years?"

"No ma'am," he said. "I wouldn't say a lot."

"What would you say?"

Lee exhaled as he went down the steps. Free from the roof over the porch, he looked up into the brilliant Texas sky, evening still a ways off as summer came closer and closer.

"I'd say I've struck out," he said. They continued toward the truck, and Lee saw all of her imperfections as they approached. He'd never minded, but he suddenly wanted a golden chariot to escort Rosalie everywhere.

She didn't say anything as they rounded the hood.

Not until he'd opened her door for her and stepped back did she even look at him. "I'm not sure what you mean by *struck out*."

"I mean, I've been out with three women in the past six years," he said. "And every relationship was a disaster."

"Three women in six years?"

Lee ducked his head. "Well, Rosalie," he said, trying to think of something funny and flirty. He was probably going to fail spectacularly. "We can't all be flawless, and we don't all regularly get out into schools to meet surly cowboys who won't clap for us after a perfect presentation." He looked up, his hope soaring toward heaven.

Her smile already sat on her face, and she reached one hand to slide along the side of his jaw. "You're not surly," she said.

"I assure you, I am." Perhaps he shouldn't take her to dinner tonight. Someone was bound to have some problem he'd have to deal with, which would absolutely put him in a foul mood. He couldn't hide how he felt very well, and most of the time, he didn't even try.

"I would've said handsome," she said. "There's a reason I noticed you weren't clapping. Have you thought about what that was?"

"No ma'am," he whispered, his skin burning with her touch. Her fingertips touched his earlobe, and Lee wanted to lean into her hand with everything he had. He fought against that movement and stayed very still.

"Hmm." Rosalie pulled her hand back and stepped to get into the truck. Lee closed the door behind her, released the breath he'd been holding, and told himself not to mess up this date as he went to get behind the wheel.

Over and over and over, he begged the Lord to, "Please help me tonight," he murmured at the tailgate. "Please."

He managed to curtail his pleas before he got in the truck, and he gave the old girl a pat the way he always did. She started right up, which was why Lee didn't much care to get a new one. He was comfortable in this truck, despite the rusting spots and the boxier shape compared to other pickups.

"Did you just give your vehicle a little pat?" Rosalie asked.

Lee's face burned, and he focused on flipping the gear shift into reverse. "Maybe."

"Does she have a name too?" The woman was teasing him. Teasing.

Lee had no idea what to do with that. "No," he said, reaching the road and getting them moving in the direction of Montague's. "Do you name your cars?"

"I did when I was in high school," she said airily, as if all girls of such an age did such a thing. Lee wouldn't know. He'd worked the farm six hours a day in high school, on top of everything he had going on academically. "I had a cute little two-door sedan we named Peanuts."

"We?" Lee asked.

"My sister and I," Rosalie said, her voice turning a bit quiet as she looked out her side window. "Her name is Natasha. She and my mother are coming to visit this weekend."

"You were texting with her earlier," Lee said. He hadn't gotten any information about her family from Karyn. Only the bit about the lemon drops and the angry rabbit who liked to bolt the moment the front door opened.

"Oh," he said before Rosalie could respond. "Your present is sittin' right there." He kept both hands on the wheel as he nodded with the brim of his hat toward the package on the seat between them. When he'd dated Martha, she'd scoot all the way over and ride with her thigh pressed against his. Lee wondered if Rosalie could scoot in her dress, and even if she could, if she'd want to sit so close to him.

His jaw tingled where she'd touched him minutes ago, and he steadfastly refused to look as she picked up the brown paper baggie. "This looks like a penny candy bag," she said.

Lee said nothing, because she'd already guessed what the bag held. He held his tongue as the paper rustled, and then she made a very feminine squealing sound that forced him to look over at her.

"Lee Cooper," she said, drawling out his name as she reached into the bag. "Where did you get these?" She pulled out the plastic bag of sour grapes, now the one with sunlight pouring from her face. She looked at him, and Lee wanted to make her smile like that every day of the week.

"There's this little shop out on the highway," he said. "Sweet Water Taffy? My brother's girlfriend—fiancée—" Lee cleared his throat, because Gretchen was definitely Will's fiancée now. He'd asked her to marry him, and she'd said yes. By Christmas, Lee would be the only single Cooper in Texas. Cherry would never come home for good, and he didn't want to live out on the dairy farm with all of his siblings and their joyous relationships.

The very thought made his mouth turn down and his mood sour.

"Your brother's fiancée," Rosalie prompted.

"Right," Lee said, flipping on his turn signal. "She owns it, and she can order anything. She had those in today, and I said I wanted them for you." He came to a stop behind a couple of cars lined up at the red light, the weight of her gaze on the side of his face like a metal safe filled with bricks. "What?"

He met her eye, and she wore wonder in her expression. "How did you know these are my absolute favorite candy?"

"I didn't," he said. "There's cherries in there too." He'd taken a stab in the dark on the candy. Karyn had said that Rosalie liked sour candy more than chocolate without any more specifics, and Lee had called Gretchen from the parking lot of the grocer.

"I had to swear Gretchen to secrecy," he said, easing up on the brake as the traffic started to move. "No one knows about this date but my sister. The one who lives in San Antonio."

"How many sisters do you have?"

"Two," he said. "You? Just the one?"

"Yes," Rosalie said. "Just the two of us. She's far younger than I am, but we're very close."

"That's great," Lee said.

"Are you close with your family? You must be if you make dinner for everyone every Wednesday."

"Yeah," Lee said with a sigh. "Too close sometimes." He couldn't name how many family dinners had turned into shouting matches, nor how many times he'd wished he'd just stayed home and eaten cold cereal for his evening meal.

"Too close?"

"Yeah," Lee said. "Don't worry. You'll see what I mean when we go to the wedding." He glanced over to her to gauge her reaction. "Which you never—" He cut off as a horn blared in his ears. He instinctively yanked the wheel to the right, narrowly missing a car coming into his lane.

"Moron!" he yelled, forgetting where he was and who he was with. His heartbeat raced along his ribs again, this time from the adrenaline and not from the nearness of Rosalie.

Oh. Rosalie.

He cleared his throat and glanced over to her. "He almost hit me," he growled.

She gripped the handle above the window, nodding. She clearly knew they'd almost been in a collision.

Lee gripped the wheel with both hands, feeling like the Lord had just done what Lee should've expected Him to do—abandon him on this date with the only woman Lee wanted to impress.

He pulled into Montague's and found a spot relatively easily for the hour. He came to a stop, put the old truck in park, and sighed. "I'm sorry," he said. "I did try to warn you."

She didn't move either, and Lee honestly felt like putting the truck in reverse and taking her home. He moved his hand to do exactly that, hoping Cherry hadn't had to do anything too terrible to get him this reservation. He'd never be able to call her and tell her about the past twenty minutes. He'd never tell anyone. His brothers didn't know where he was tonight, and no one ever had to know.

Then Rosalie asked, "Why are you not getting out? Are we early?"

CHAPTER SIX

"Do you still want to go?"

Rosalie had a hard time making sense of his question. "Yes," she said, almost guessing.

"My default is yelling," Lee said, his voice barely loud enough to be heard. His shoulders lifted and raised again. "I still want to go eat if you do."

"I'm hungry," Rosalie said, reaching for her seat belt. She didn't mind so much that Lee had yelled at the other driver. In all honesty, she might have too. She'd just needed a minute to breathe after the near-accident.

"Stay," Lee said, his voice louder and more commanding. "I'll come help you down."

She did what he said, watching him as he jogged around the front of the truck. He pulled open her door, and she turned her legs together so her knees pressed into one another. She reached out, and his gloriously warm hand took hers.

Rosalie seriously contemplated falling on purpose in that moment, just to feel what it would be like to be held again. It had been so long since she'd stood in the arms of a man, especially one as tall and strong as Lee Cooper.

In the end, she slid from the truck with relative ease, adjusted her skirt, and looked up into his dark, deliciously green eyes. Asteroids could've hit the Earth a meter from her and she wouldn't have noticed. He tucked a curl behind her ear, saying, "That bit has come loose, baby."

She automatically reached up to fix her hair, as she'd tried to tame the curls by pulling back the sides and clipping them into a barrette on the back of her head. Sure enough, the left side had come out already, and Rosalie sighed as she removed the barrette entirely.

"I hate my hair sometimes," she said, trying not to sound too whiny. "Thank you." She tossed the barrette onto the seat of the truck and bravely lifted her chin to face Lee again. "Anything else I need to fix?"

"I'm afraid I erased your smile," he said, bringing back part of his. "Can we maybe erase the drive here and just pretend it didn't happen?"

"No," Rosalie said, smiling at him as she stepped out of the doorway and linked her arm through his. "I learned you have two sisters on the way here and at least one brother, the latter of whom is engaged. That, and you have access to really great candy, and that you think your family is a little too close sometimes."

Lee chuckled, sending vibrations into the air and right down into Rosalie's lungs. "Wow," he said. "All I learned is that I need to remember not to yell names at people when they almost hit me."

"And that I have one sister," Rosalie said.

"And that you love sour candy," he added, giving her a sly look out of the corner of his eye.

Rosalie couldn't argue with that. "You have to tell me," she said as they walked toward the entrance to Montague's. "Who told you about Thumper?" Maybe they'd told him about her love for sour grape penny candy too.

"Karyn Harlow," he said. "She said she lived down the street from you. She knows Trav and Will—I have two brothers."

"Ah," Rosalie said. "I assume you're the oldest."

"The oldest brother," he said. "My sister in San Antonio is actually the oldest child." He opened the door, and Rosalie stepped past him to enter first. She kept her questions to herself as Lee gave the host his name and it took several long seconds of conferring between the host and the hostess as to where they could possibly put Lee and Rosalie.

Finally, the man said, "Right this way," as he flashed a tight smile.

Rosalie slipped her hand into Lee's as they walked

past the other diners to their cozy booth near the back of the restaurant. The simple act of holding his hand made her feel more connected to herself, as well as to him. She missed the soft touch between two people who loved each other, and she craved the ability to be close to someone.

At their booth, a huge window sat to her right and showed the park across the street. Happiness flowed through Rosalie as she slid onto the bench, and she picked up her menu as the host said who their waitress would be.

"Oh, really?" Lee asked. "Can we, uh, sit somewhere else?"

Rosalie lowered her menu, sure she hadn't heard him right. It had nearly taken an Act of Congress for the pair at the podium to agree on this table. Lee shifted in his seat, his eyes flying all over the restaurant.

The host was as confused as Rosalie. "A different table?" He looked around too.

"One where Diane isn't the waitress," Lee said, sliding out and standing up. "Please." He didn't sound particularly sorry for not wanting Diane to be their server, and his plea wasn't particularly gentle either.

"Uh, sure," the host said. "I'll put you over here. Damon is in this section." His eyebrows went up, and Lee nodded. Rosalie followed them over to a table—not a booth—away from the windows and closer to the kitchen door, silent.

Once they had their menus and the host had left, she studied the options for a pasta feast. "You don't like Diane?" she asked without looking at Lee.

"Not particularly," Lee answered just as casually. "She was one of the strikes. I'd forgotten she worked here." He was mumbling by the end of the sentence.

"Your sister must not know about her," Rosalie said, plenty of teasing in her voice. She dared to look up at Lee, who shook his head.

"No," he said. "Cherry doesn't know about Diane."

"And no one knows we're on this date," she said. "Besides Gretchen, who's going to keep it a secret." She lowered her menu and folded her arms across it.

Lee shifted on his hard chair, his eyes studying the menu items. "That's right," he said. "I'll tell everyone when I'm ready."

"Is it going to be a big deal?"

He pulled his gaze from the menu and looked at her. "Probably," he said. "See, in the Cooper family, everything is a big deal. I may or may not have said things like I'm never dating again and the last thing I want is to ever be married again." He returned his attention to the flimsy piece of plastic listing all of their delicious choices. "So yeah. Me showing up at the Sabbath Day dinner and announcing I went out with a woman is going to be a big deal."

He didn't sound happy about that, but Rosalie secretly liked it. She liked that he'd tell his family about her, and she hoped his face would flush red then as it was now. "Maybe you won't tell them on Sunday," she said, unrolling her silverware and laying her napkin across her lap. "Maybe it'll just be a secret between us—and Gretchen—for a while."

"Gretchen won't tell," Lee said. "She owes me for a secret I kept for her."

Rosalie's eyebrows went up. "Is that right? You regularly keep secrets for your brother's fiancée?"

"It's not like that," Lee said, plenty of growl in his voice. He slapped his menu down on the table, some of that surliness he mentioned coming from him. Rosalie actually leaned closer to it, the danger of him exciting to her. "It's a long story, but she basically hired us for her cream providers at the candy shop, and she asked me not to tell Will. It was a few days at most. I'm just real bad at keeping secrets."

"Mm." Rosalie looked up as a waiter approached. He seemed frazzled and over-busy already. They put in their drink orders, and she looked back at Lee. "Sunday is only a few days from now. Maybe her limit will be reached by then."

Lee's eyes widened, which only made Rosalie laugh. "Come on, cowboy," she said, going for a term of endearment for him. He had called her *baby* in the parking lot. "Let's not worry about it tonight, okay?"

He swallowed and nodded. "All right," he said. "Tell me about how you got into the game industry."

He had no idea what type of Pandora's box he'd just opened, because Rosalie could talk about board games, video games, game production, and game conceptualization for hours. *Don't do that tonight*, she told herself sternly.

She did say, "I started making games for Natasha when she was little. She had a hard time learning the same things as everyone else, but she loves games. All kinds of games..."

A FEW HOURS LATER, LEE STROLLED UP ROSALIE'S WALKWAY, her hand held securely in his. "If you haven't been to a farm in a while," he said. "I'd love to show you around mine. It's real busy in the springtime, but we have huge apple orchards that need picking in the fall, and hayrides, and all those farm-family things. Ford loves it; I'm sure Autumn would too." He spoke with a level of easiness that Rosalie liked. Once she'd started talking, Lee had loosened up and brought back his charm and wit and gorgeous grin.

Rosalie smiled up at the moon before remembering she had to go next door to get Autumn. She didn't want to say good-bye to Lee at the bottom of the stairs, and she was having a hard time gearing up to let him go at all. Her own neediness surprised her, and she'd been telling herself for the past hour that she was simply lonely, and Lee had eased a lot of that.

"Thank you, Lee," she said when her foot touched the porch. "This was a mighty fine evening."

He chuckled and shook his head, his eyes on their still-joined hands. "That steak was mighty fine," he said, looking up into her eyes. "You should've dipped it in the spicy chimichurri."

"I liked what I tasted," she assured him. Silence dropped between them, and Rosalie had forgotten about this awkward part of dating. Was he going to ask her out again? Should she tell him she'd love to come to his brother's wedding with him?

Her mind blitzed around, and Lee had stepped closer and leaned down before she could make sense of it. An alarm screamed in her head that she couldn't kiss him. This was their first date, and she couldn't.

She sucked in a breath, and that soared through the sky, screaming the way big jets did when they flew over stadiums. Lee froze.

"Lee," she started, but she had no idea how to finish.

"Thank you for dinner," he said, pulling everything back in the two seconds it took him to speak those words. His hands left hers; he put a couple of feet of distance between them; he closed off all of the emotion on his face.

Without her saying anything, he turned and went down the steps, his boots making quick clickety-clicking sounds on the wood. He strode toward his truck like he couldn't wait to get away from her, and Rosalie sighed as she watched him go.

He didn't look back once, and she stood on her porch until the last growls of his engine disappeared from her neighborhood. Her shoulders sagged, and she ignored the loud thump from the moody rabbit on the other side of the door as she turned to follow Lee down the steps.

At the house over, only a low lamp burned in the window. Rosalie knocked quietly, and it took several long seconds before Tess opened the door. She clutched a robe across her chest, and the house was dark and silent behind her.

"Sorry," Rosalie said in a low voice. "I'm not too late, am I?"

"It's just after midnight," Tess said, and Rosalie's shock came out in a gasp.

"Tess, I'm sorry. I didn't know."

"Yeah, because you were out with Lee Cooper." Tess's smile said she'd already been in on the town gossip.

"It was just dinner," Rosalie said. She wasn't going to throw more fuel on the flames of the Sweet Water Falls rumor mill. Tess didn't need to know Lee had then taken her across the street to that park, and they'd fed the ducks and geese, watched the sun set and the stars come out, walked and talked and talked and talked, held hands, and then finally went back to his truck.

She should've known how late it was by how empty the parking lot at Montague's was. She should've known to look at her phone and check the time. Rosalie had been lost inside the magic that Lee put off, and she shivered now, thinking about going back to her house without him.

"Come in," Tess said, stepping back. "She's just here on the couch."

Rosalie collected Autumn into her arms, who woke for only a moment and then promptly laid back down against Rosalie's shoulder. She couldn't carry the girl for long, but she made it home and down the hall to Autumn's bedroom. Thumper hopped ahead of them, and once Rosalie had her daughter tucked in bed, she found the white rabbit on the bean bag in the corner. "No stomp-ing," she told him, then left the room, pulling the door almost all the way closed as she went.

She exhaled slowly as she made her way into her bedroom, her mind replaying the whole evening as she removed her makeup, her clothes, her jewelry, and all of the different pieces she'd put together to look amazing for the date. She caught sight of herself without any adorn-ment, and she paused, the lights in the bathroom so harsh.

"Why didn't you want to kiss him?" she whisper-asked herself. The truth was, Rosalie would happily kiss Lee, but there was a small piece of her heart that still belonged to James. She'd panicked less than a half an hour ago at the thought of kissing Lee, because she was married to someone else.

"You're not," she told herself, her shoulders coming up in her wispy pajamas. "You can kiss whoever you want." With that, she left the bathroom and turned off the light behind her. In the warm safety of her bed, she closed her eyes and fantasized about what it would've been like to feel Lee's strong mouth against hers.

Definitely like a fairy tale, she thought just before she drifted to sleep.

"ROSE!"

She turned from the back door, where she'd been standing as she watched Autumn lay in the back yard with Thumper. Natasha came barreling toward her, and the two sisters laughed as they hugged.

"How was the drive?" Rosalie asked as she stepped back. "Where's Mom? Did you leave her out in the driveway to get all the luggage?"

"No," their mother said, entering the house. Rosalie had taken down the gate in anticipation of their arrival, and she'd banished Thumper to the back yard so he wouldn't escape. "I left it for later."

"Mom." Rosalie wasn't sure why her emotions surged up her throat at the sight of her mom. She hugged her tightly, trying to hold on to everything raging through her. She hadn't told anyone about Lee yet, and she wasn't going to. The cowboy hadn't called her yet, and Rosalie knew that with every passing hour, she lost more and more ground with him.

She'd told herself all day yesterday that he was busy. That he owned a huge cattle operation, as well as a farm. He had a lot to manage. He was a single dad, and she couldn't expect him to call her first thing in the morning.

Or at lunchtime. Or dinnertime. Or before bed.

This morning, she'd reminded herself that she'd told him her sister and mother were coming for the weekend, and of course he wouldn't call and disturb their visit. That put her to Monday, and if he didn't call then... Rosalie wasn't sure what excuse she'd make for him then.

She also wasn't sure if she was making excuses for him or for herself. She'd enjoyed their date, and she'd thought he had too. He'd acted like he was going to kiss her—and then she'd rejected him. Deep down, she knew that rejection was why Lee hadn't called her yet.

She'd probably humiliated him, and for a man as proud and in control as Lee wouldn't like that.

"Are you okay, dear?" Her mom peered at her with curiosity in her expression, and Rosalie shook herself out of her thoughts.

"Of course," she said. "Autumn is in the back yard. Let's get her and go to lunch. I'm starving." She turned to get her daughter, noting that the sliding door had been pushed open wide. Nat had gone back there. Rosalie stepped over to the door and slid it shut, because she didn't need to be cooling the whole neighborhood.

She smiled at the scene in the back yard, because it was what slow, country mid-mornings should be like. Her sister had laid down on the ground beside Autumn, the white rabbit cuddled into her chest. Thumper adored Nat, and she was the only one who could get him to calm down when he was in the throes of a stomping fit.

"Look at them," Rosalie said.

Her mom came to stand beside her. "Let's leave them for a few minutes," she said. "Nat's been talking incessantly, and I could use five minutes of silence."

Rosalie looked at her mother, a strange mix of laughter and helplessness combining inside her. "I'm sorry, Mom," she said, sliding her arm around her mom's waist and squeezing her.

"It's fine," her mom said. "But let's just leave them for a few minutes."

"Yeah." Rosalie watched as Autumn tipped up onto one side, her face full of animation. She was probably asking Nat about something she'd seen on TV that Rosalie wouldn't let her watch. Nat loved reality TV and the sports channels that showed cheerleading competitions, band march-offs, and colorguard shows. When she wasn't working part-time at the shoe store their neighbors owned, Nat could be found singing at the top of her lungs or watching TV.

Rosalie turned away from the glass doors when her mom did and followed her the few steps into the kitchen. "How are you, dear?" her mom asked.

She sighed as she sank onto a barstool. "Fine, Mom."

She picked up the brown bag of candy Lee had brought. "What's this?" She pulled out the individual bags of sour grapes and sour cherries.

"My...a friend brought me those," she said.

Rosalie's mother didn't miss a beat. "A friend? Who?"

"Lee," Rosalie said, swallowing before she'd finished his name.

Mom nodded and picked a red sour candy from the bag. She popped it into her mouth, and Rosalie had just started to think she was out of the woods when her mom asked, "Is Lee a man or a woman?"

Rosalie took a moment to check her phone just to make sure it was on and held plenty of charge. No problems there. Lee simply hadn't called or texted. She looked up and into her mom's eyes, unable to lie to her. "He's a man," she said. "And we went out on Thursday night and now he won't call me."

To her mother's credit, she simply finished her candy and reached for another one. "Do you have his number?" Her eyebrows arched as she met Rosalie's eyes again.

"Yes," Rosalie said, her mind whizzing through possibilities now. "I mean, yes, I have his number." She wasn't sure why she'd repeated it, only that her mind seemed made of mush at the moment.

Her mom simply nodded, popped another sour treat into her mouth, and then moved to call the girls into the house so they could go to lunch.

CHAPTER SEVEN

Lee woke up on Sunday morning, the house dark and quiet. If he laid really still and held his breath, he could hear his son's fan blowing down the hall, even with both bedroom doors almost closed. When Lee lived in the cabin alone during the week, he closed his door all the way. When Ford was here, he didn't. He wanted to be able to hear more and get to his son if he needed to.

Nothing all that exciting ever happened around Sweet Water Falls Farm. Nothing that would require Lee to bolt straight up out of bed and go heroically rescue his son at least.

He opened his eyes, his misery shooting through him the same way a sharp pain echoed through his back. A hot shower would take care of one of those, and Lee hoped a huge breakfast of Dutch pancakes would ease the other.

As he scrubbed and then stood in the hot water to allow his muscles to relax, he knew breakfast wouldn't solve the silence between him and Rosalie. He'd told no one about her, not even Cherry. His sister had called a couple of times, but thankfully, Lee had been with clients both times.

He'd put her off by promising to call later or text after he got home. He'd done neither. If he was lucky, she'd call today instead of showing up on his doorstep, demanding to know what had happened on Thursday night's date.

He'd humiliated himself by going in for the kiss, that was what had happened. Lee had lost his mind for five seconds, that was all. It happened to other people, he was sure.

Every time he thought about Rosalie, it was of the weight of her hand in his. Or maybe the way she laughed at some of the corny jokes he'd told after dinner, while they'd been walking through the park. Or even maybe the way she leaned right across the table, her mouth open and waiting for the piece of steak he'd said she should try.

She felt fearless to him, and Lee wanted her in his life. "Not enough to pick up the phone," he muttered, giving the device a glare as he dried his hair with a towel. The sounds of life met his ears from down the hall, and Lee moved over to the door and opened it all the way.

"Ford," he called, and his son skipped into view wearing his pajamas. "I'm making Dutch pancakes for breakfast."

"Okay," his son said. "Can you make that blueberry syrup?"

"If there's blueberries," he said. "Check the freezer. Grandma put some in bags for us, I think."

"Okey dokey," Ford said, already skipping out of sight. Lee smiled to himself, so glad he hadn't had to wake up alone this morning. Not only that, but Ford always brought a ray of sunshine to Lee's soul, even if he was in trouble for falling asleep in the hay loft when he should be sweeping it.

Lee returned to his bedroom closet and got dressed. He wasn't going to church today, not that anyone would be surprised. He believed in God, but he preferred his own private way of worshipping Him. Lee wasn't sure how to hear the Lord. He talked to Him all the time, but it felt like there was some sort of muffler between Lee's lips and God's ears.

The date on Thursday only proved that completely, and when Mama texted Lee and told him that he and Ford could sit by her and Daddy in the pew, Lee would just send her a heart back. She invited him every week, bless her soul. Lee loved her back every week.

He didn't let his mind dwell on his mother. He should probably go to church with her every week so she could pass in peace, knowing her oldest son believed. Daddy had told him to follow his heart, and that he knew what kind of man Lee was. Lee wished he could sit down with his father again and ask him what kind of man that was. He hadn't quite dared to bring it up again, however.

He made it into the kitchen, where Ford had indeed found a bag of frozen blueberries in the freezer. He'd put the bag in a bowl and put that in the sink and had cold water running over it. He, as a person, wasn't there to make sure the sink didn't overflow. Not that it was even close to doing that, but Lee flipped the water off anyway.

"Ford?" he yelled.

"Out by the stream!" his son's tinny voice came back. Lee lifted up onto his toes and looked out the window that showed the back yard. There was no fence, and their cabin bordered woods and fields with a stream drifting right through the middle of it. In the fall, Ford could stand twenty-five feet from the back door and catch fish for dinner.

The boy crouched down at the stream's edge right now, peering at something. Lee wondered if he needed glasses, because Lee hadn't been much older than Ford when he'd gotten his spectacles. He adjusted his now and got to work in the kitchen. The syrup could wait until the cast iron skillets were in the oven, so he put together the Dutch pancake batter first, poured it into his individually-sized skillets, then slid them into the hot oven.

He'd just set a pan on the stove to boil the blueberries with a lot of sugar when the front door of his house opened. Ford had not come in from the back, and honestly, Lee expected to see Travis or Will walk inside. If someone came out to his cabin without a text or a call, it was one of his brothers.

This morning, it was both. Will wore slacks, a white shirt, and a tie, but Travis had on jeans, his cowboy boots, a plaid shirt in red, orange, and yellow, and a hat. He swept that from his head and nodded to Will.

"What's goin' on?" Lee asked, his heart starting to bob up in the back of his throat. If Gretchen sold him out, Lee was going to lose his mind. He'd kept her secret as professionally as a lifelong thief, and it had only been two full days.

He turned back to the stove with the sugar canister and didn't bother to measure. He simply poured some into his palm and then tilted it into the pan. He'd learned to cook from his mother and grandmother, and he hadn't seen a measuring cup until he was fifteen years old. Even then, it was only for candy-making. Grandma did everything else "by feel."

Feel the weight of that sugar, Lee? That's about half a cup. In it goes.

He did another half-cup and lidded the canister. Neither of his brothers had spoken yet, and that wasn't a good sign. He turned and set the sugar on the island, facing them in the process. "Is someone gonna say something?" He certainly wasn't going to give anything away.

Trav and Will exchanged another glance, and Lee

wished they all wore cowboy hats in the house. Mama
would kill them with her bare hands, cancer or not, and
Lee wasn't sure he could wear a hat indoors now at all.

"Rumor has it you went on a date last week," Will
finally said.

Lee's lungs iced over, making breathing difficult. "Is
that against the law?"

"Is it true?" Trav asked. He definitely possessed one of
the sharper tongues in the Cooper family. He made up for
it with the biggest heart.

Lee glanced at him and then back to Will. "What if
it is?"

Will sighed and moved to pull up a barstool. Lee had
two at the island, because it was just him most of the
time. With the smaller space, he didn't use a kitchen
table, and the computer took up part of the dining area.

"Lee," he said, but then he didn't go on.

"What?"

Trav moved to sit by Will, and Lee realized what was
happening. He was being intervened with. His first
instinct was to rage at them and tell them to mind their
own business. Right behind that, a quieter part of himself
reminded the hulking rage in his chest that he'd already
told Trav and Will about Rosalie. Way down deep, a voice
whispered that he should probably ask for their help.

He'd been the first Cooper to get married, years ago.
That relationship hadn't lasted long, and now Trav and

Will both had fiancées. Maybe they knew something that could help Lee.

He decided to listen to the whispering part of himself. "I went out with Rosalie on Thursday," he said, turning his back on his brothers.

"Lee," Travis said. "That's so great. Did you ask her to the wedding?"

"Yes," Lee said, stirring the simmering blueberries.

"Is she going to come?" Will asked.

"I don't know." Lee had tried to bring it up right before he'd almost been side-swiped. "She said we should go to dinner first, so we did."

"And?" Trav prompted.

Lee breathed in and out, turned up the flame beneath his pot of syrup, and faced his brothers. "And nothing. It was a great date until I embarrassed myself. So that's that. I'm going to attend the wedding alone." He thought of Cherry showing up with Charlie and how truly and completely miserable Lee would be by himself.

"Come on," Will said at the same time Travis asked, "What did you do?"

"It can't be that bad," Will added.

"Did you guys rehearse this on the way over?" Lee asked, looking between them. "How did you find out anyway?" He watched Will the closest, but the man gave nothing away.

"Shay heard some women talking in the store last

night," Trav said. "She told me last night while we were on the phone."

Gretchen hadn't said anything, and relief rushed through Lee. "What were they saying?" He held up his hand. "Never mind. I don't care."

"Did she ever say no to the wedding?" Will challenged.

"Have you been talking to Cherry?" Lee threw back at him.

"Yes," Will said without missing a beat. He didn't even blink.

Lee didn't want to argue with his brothers. He didn't want to defend himself. "Listen, I just don't think it's going to work out."

"You're not even trying," Travis said.

"Trav," Will said, and he shook his head a couple of times. He looked back at Lee. "I think we should do a poll at lunch today."

"Heaven help me," Lee muttered, actually looking up at the ceiling as he turned his back on his brothers again. "I think I've got work to do in the admin office this afternoon."

"Rubbish," Trav and Will said together. "You'd never miss a Sabbath Day meal. Mama would never allow it," Trav said.

Lee knew he'd never make his mother worry about him intentionally. "I think Ford has to get back early today."

"Liar," Will said.

Lee heaved a great big sigh, the syrup nowhere as interesting as he needed it to be. He fixed his best laser-glare on his face and turned around. "Why do you guys care?"

"Because you like her," Travis said, his voice turning a little needling.

"So what?" Lee asked. "I've liked lots of women."

"Lots?" Will repeated, his surprise right there on his face.

The back door opened and Ford walked in. "This needs to be over," Lee said.

"I'm doing the poll." Will got to his feet and opened his arms to Ford. "Get over here, Ford, and give your favorite uncle a hug."

Ford grinned and ran toward Will. Lee watched them hug and talk and laugh, and he did count his brothers as two of the biggest blessings in Ford's life. His too, if Lee were being honest.

A shrieking ring filled the cabin, and Will reached for his phone. "This is Gretchen. I'm headed to church."

"Take him with you," Lee said, glaring at Travis. His youngest brother simply put his palms together in a praying gesture and left the cabin with Will.

Lee enjoyed his breakfast with his son, and then they spent the morning outside near the stream so Ford could show him all the fishes and rocks he'd been finding that morning.

By the time Lee walked into the white farmhouse where he'd grown up, his heartbeat felt like someone had hooked him up to live electricity. It zapped him every few seconds, and then his pulse would skitter everywhere. He could barely get a decent breath, and when he did, he got the scent of caramelized onions.

Surprise bolted through him—which did nothing to settle his pulse—when he found Mama standing in front of the stove. "Mama," he said, quickly moving toward her. "What are you doing?"

"Making French onion soup," she said with a smile. She wore a tied scarf around her head, but her life still shone from her in her eyes. Her whole face today.

"Are you feeling okay?" he asked.

"Yes," she said, turning back to the onions. "I'm fine, Lee. You can set the table if you're concerned."

"Mama," he said.

"Sorry," she murmured.

Lee accepted her apology and got busy doing what she'd said. Daddy had been picking up the slack around the farmhouse for the past five years while Mama had been battling cancer. Today, Lee hadn't seen his father yet, and he kept glancing toward the arched doorway that led out into the foyer and then down toward the bedrooms on this level.

When he had the whole table set for ten, he returned to the kitchen. Mama finished pouring in the beef broth and stirred everything together. "I'm feeling tired," she said, handing him the wooden spoon. "Can you just babysit it while it thickens? Then we'll melt cheese over it under the broiler. Rissy can do it." She used the counter to steady herself as she moved away from the stove.

"Sure," he said, picking up the stirring where she'd left off. "Ford, help Nana out to her swing." He'd checked out there for Daddy too, but his father wasn't there. "Mama, where's Daddy?"

"He wasn't feeling well after church," Mama said, her voice growing softer as she moved away. "He went to take a nap."

Lee nodded, but Mama was already gone. Ford stayed right at her side, his hand in hers as they went outside. Mama loved Ford with her whole soul, and Lee wasn't surprised that she kept him outside in the swing with her. She could talk to him about anything and everything, and Ford loved his nana too.

Lee decided the soup wasn't going anywhere, and he left it to go check on his dad. Just as he stepped into the bedroom, his dad sat up. "Here you are," Lee said, trying to decide if Daddy needed help standing or not. He'd been in this bedroom a lot over the years to help Mama, though Will and Trav had been doing that more than Lee lately.

"Need a hand?" Lee fisted his fingers, hating how drawn and sunken Daddy's face looked. He'd always been the harsh taskmaster around the farm. He'd loved hard, but he'd worked his sons harder. Lee had wanted nothing more than to please his father growing up, and strangely, that hadn't changed for him as an adult.

"Yes," Daddy said, and Lee flew toward him. He helped his father to his feet and made sure he was steady before moving back. "It smells good."

"Mama made soup," Lee said, remembering he'd left it on the stovetop unattended.

"This is boiling over!" a woman yelled, and that would be his sister Clarissa. "Daddy?"

"Just stir it," Lee called as he moved toward the bedroom door. He turned back to his dad. "What do you need, Daddy?"

"I'll be out in a minute," his father said. "I'm okay, Lee. Just tired and a bit under the weather today." He gave Lee a smile, all of the glorious greens in his eyes lighting up when he did.

Lee left the bedroom and heard Rissa say, "You can't just walk away from French onion soup," in a disgusted tone. "Baby, put those rolls down. Will, get away from those treats!"

He braced himself to enter the kitchen, though the energy he'd find there actually drew him forward faster. Yes, his family was loud. They yelled at each other. Rissa would skewer him with a look that was ten times as loud as any lecture, and he didn't pity any child of hers.

At the same time, he couldn't wait to hug her and feel if her baby had started to bump out in her abdomen yet, and he'd even put up with Will's poll. He didn't think for a moment that his brother would let that go. In fact, he was quite sure Will had texted the entire family about it, and Lee better be ready for the Presidential inauguration of speeches.

He entered the kitchen and took a hard right, hoping to fly past the long table and out the doors at the back of the house. He hadn't even taken two steps before Shayla blocked him. "Sorry," she said, pressing herself into the wall behind her.

"Where are you goin' so fast?" Travis asked, stepping to the end of the table on Lee's side. "Will, he's here."

"I see 'im," Will said.

Lee eyed Travis and then Will. They wore identical expressions of half-regret and half-determination. He could probably get them to keep their mouths shut if he tried hard enough. Lee battled with himself, and then he lowered his head and waved his hand.

"All right," Will called. "Everyone listen up."

The chatter in the kitchen died down as Gretchen and Rissa turned toward the dining room table.

"Quick poll," Will said. "We just need a one-or-the-other. Lee went out with a woman last week and said something embarrassing happened that's preventing him from calling her."

"What happened?" Rissa asked.

Lee gave her a sharp look, but she gazed right on back. "Did you know the soup was boiling over?"

"Did you know Daddy isn't feeling well?" he shot at her.

Rissa blinked. "He said he was just tired."

"This isn't about Daddy," Will bellowed. "We just need a vote. Who thinks Lee should call this woman anyway? I mean, I had the nerve to go out with Gretchen even after my sister called the cops on us."

"You broke into my shoppe," Rissa said.

"I had a key," Will whipped at her.

"I went out with Shayla after I accused her of stealing her company," Travis said.

"The point is, we've all done stupid stuff," Will said. "Embarrassing things. And yet, here we are." He gestured around to all of Lee's siblings. "We all have someone who forgives us and accepts us as we are."

"How do you know she'll do that?" Lee asked.

"Because she went out with you in the first place," Gretchen said.

Lee glared at her too, silently begging her to not say another word. Only she knew he'd been out at all.

"I'm with Rissa," Shayla said slowly. "I think if I knew what the embarrassing thing was, I could make a better decision."

"You were going to be my favorite sister-in-law," Lee grumbled to her.

She burst out laughing, and that only fueled Lee's ire. He faced the room, glad his son was still outside with Mama. "Fine," he said. "Fine! I tried to kiss her after the date. She...wasn't ready for that, and I ran away. Okay? Are you happy now, Rissy?"

"Yes," she said, but her voice had lost its punch.

"Did she like, dodge, or just say something, or...?" Gretchen let her question hang there while Lee wished the floor would melt open underneath him.

"I think that's all we're gettin' from him," Travis said, stepping closer. "I think that's nothing, brother. I vote you call her."

"I'm with Trav," Shayla said.

"Big surprise," Lee muttered as she continued with, "So you want to kiss her. Big deal. She should actually like that. In fact, she's probably been kicking herself for not letting you."

"When did you go out with her?" Clarissa asked.

"Thursday," Lee growled.

"Oh, she's been kicking herself then," his sister said. She turned back to the stove like this was a done deal. Decided. Over.

"I'd call her too," Will said.

"Me too," Spencer said. "I mean, you still want to kiss her, right? That's not happening unless you call." Out of all of them, he had the best point, and Lee did like his sister's husband a whole lot.

"I'd call," Gretchen said. "Honey, she obviously likes you. She was probably just...nervous." She looked at Will as she walked toward him. "She's definitely been thinking about kissing you."

"She could call me," Lee said.

"Oh, boy," Travis said, but Shayla laid her palm against his chest.

"Honey," she said to Lee. "Let me tell you something about women." She laced her arm through Lee's, and he didn't want to shake her off instantly. He didn't like the way she looked at him, but he let her lead him to his seat at the table. "She's not going to call you, because she knows she made you feel bad. She *knows*, and she's probably desperate for you to call so the very first thing she can say is she's sorry."

"She doesn't know how to call you first," Gretchen said. "Trust me on that."

Lee looked up at Shay, and then over to Gretchen. Daddy entered the kitchen, surveying everything. "What's goin' on here?" he asked.

"Nothing," Will said, shooting a look at Trav. "Come sit down, Pops. You do look tired." He moved to help Daddy sit, and Lee stayed right where he was, letting Spence get his son and then help Mama into the house so she could sit beside Daddy.

He didn't say another word during lunch, and he was grateful no one shot him any glances to see if he was about to explode or not. He wasn't. He just needed some time to think.

Hours later, after he'd taken Ford back to his mother, and after he'd plucked his way through all of the songs he knew, Lee sat on his front porch, the last light of the day fading fast.

He set his guitar against the railing in front of him and pulled out his phone. "Now or never," he told himself as he dialed Rosalie's number.

CHAPTER EIGHT

Rosalie lifted her head from the armrest as the buzzing from her phone met her ears. It was probably another scam call, as she'd gotten several over the weekend. Her mom and sister had left that morning, and Rosalie had baked the rest of the hours in today away in her denial that she'd have to go back to work tomorrow, as well as sleep in her house alone tonight.

"Momma," Autumn said, and Rosalie glanced over to her daughter. A cartoon played on the television, which Rosalie had been facing but not watching.

"Yeah, baby?" The phone vibrated against the table down by Rosalie's feet, and she made no move to pick it up.

"Look at my horse." The girl held up a coloring page

that had been ripped from the book, her face filled with pride. She'd made the horse yellow and orange and brown, and Rosalie smiled at it.

"That's great, honey," she said, her stomach giving a vote of protest as she sat up. "Are you hungry? Do you want any dinner?" She'd eaten a lot of chocolate chip bread that day, as well as at least three cookies before she'd taken the rest next door to Tess and Frank.

"I don't know," Autumn said, and that was about the answer Rosalie had been expecting. She didn't usually rely on her four-year-old to tell her if she was hungry or what she wanted to eat. She fed her and took care of her.

Rosalie got up and moved down to the end of the couch, the blue light at the top edge of her phone blinking. "I'll make you a ham sandwich," she said. "Then you have to get in the tub, okay?"

"Okay."

She swiped on her phone, her eyes reading faster than she could comprehend. Her brain reacted, and the phone fell from her hands. Her heartbeat had also zoomed to epic speeds with the information from her brain, and she quickly stooped to pick up the phone, muttering, "Please don't be broken."

For Lee Cooper had called her.

Finally.

It had taken him almost seventy-two hours, but he'd called. She'd missed it, but he'd called.

Rosalie pushed her breath out of her lungs one ounce

at a time, noting that her phone had not cracked or broken. While she held the device, it started to vibrate again. Lee's name came up on the screen, and Rosalie dang near yelped.

Instead, she glanced over to her daughter, who now held a green crayon in her hand. "Baby, I'll be right back, okay?"

"Okay, momma."

Rosalie clutched the phone to her chest and practically sprinted down the hall to her bedroom. With the door only slightly ajar, she swiped on Lee's call. Running —or rather, the tip-toeing near-run she'd performed— had been a big mistake. Her breath felt stuck in her lungs, and she didn't want to sound like she was panting.

"Hello?" she asked, as if she didn't know whose voice would come through the line.

She did, and when Lee said, "Rosalie, I got you," she sighed right out loud and let all the tension sag out of her shoulders. "Are you okay?" he asked.

"Yes," she said, her brain trying to make sense of what "I got you," meant.

"Great." He let a beat of silence go by. "Listen, I'm no good at any of this, so I guess I'll just say it all, and then you can decide what it is you want to do."

"All right," she said.

He barely waited for her to finish with the last word before he said, "I had a great time the other night. I felt like you did too, so that's why I...I don't know. I think you're beautiful, and I haven't been able to stop thinking about you, and I know it was real presumptuous of me to think I could kiss you. I'm sorry about that, and I won't do it again, I swear."

Rosalie sank onto her bed, her smile warm and pleasant on her face. All of the worry and unrest that had plagued her since Lee had dropped her off on Thursday night simply evaporated. "It's okay," she said.

Lee blew out his breath. "Is it?"

"Of course," she said, lifting her head and watching the crack in the door. Autumn could color happily for hours with Rosalie half-asleep on the couch, but the moment she wanted to take a private call or go to the bathroom, the child suddenly needed her. "Well, most of it."

"Most of it?" He seemed genuinely confused, and Rosalie's guilt hit her right at the sternum. "I should've texted you," she said. "So you weren't worried all this time."

He said nothing, and Rosalie decided she better lay everything out between them too. "You were right about a lot of things," she said. "I did have a great time on Thursday. I'm glad to know you think I'm beautiful, because what woman doesn't want to hear that?" She gave a light laugh, beyond thrilled when Lee chuckled with her.

"I hope all the thinking about me is good thinking," she continued, trying to keep the conversation serious and not so flirty. "I think about you a lot too, Lee." She did, and she didn't see the point in trying to hide that fact. "There's just one thing you said there at the end I didn't like."

A couple of seconds went by, and then Lee said, "The apology?"

"No," Rosalie said, drawing the word out. "That was nice. Thank you for that. I don't normally kiss a man on the very first date, even if he has called me flawless and then takes me on a perfectly flawless date."

"I'm sorry," he said again. "I told you I haven't been out with many people over the years."

"One apology is enough," she said super-seriously. "I just didn't like how you said you'd never try to do it again." By the last word, Rosalie's chest felt like she'd poured popping candy down her throat. A whole vat of it.

"Kiss you?"

"Yes, Lee," Rosalie said with a giggle. "I definitely want you to try that again, maybe just not on the first date."

"There won't be another first date."

"Precisely."

Lee exhaled again, and Rosalie could feel the weight he'd been carrying over the past few days. "I should've texted you," Rosalie said again. "Or called you myself. I just...you seemed so upset when you left, and I didn't know what to say."

"You've said great things," he said quietly. "Am I to

assume that we have a date this weekend for the wedding? You never did say if you'd go with me."

Rosalie straightened her shoulders. "Yes, sir," she said, making her voice as cowboy-country as she could get it. "I'd love to go to the wedding with you this weekend."

"No other date to see how we get along?"

"If you'd like," she said. "I can consult my schedule."

"I'd love to see you," he said, his voice throaty and downright sexy. "Maybe tomorrow afternoon? I usually send someone to pick up our farm supplies at the IFA on Mondays, but I can do it if you're available." He broadcast hope in his voice, and that made Rosalie smile.

"Okay," she said without consulting anything. If she had a meeting or a call, she'd change it in the morning. She wanted to see Lee too and tell him everything was okay. They were okay. He could kiss her another time.

Her chest vibrated at the thought, because she still wasn't used to the idea of being single, where kissing a handsome cowboy was allowed.

"Say about three?" he asked. "You'll be at work then, right?"

"Yes," she said. "But I can plan to be done about that time if you have an hour or something. We can get ice cream or just sit in your truck and talk. I don't care."

"I'll think of something," he said. "Thanks, Rosalie."

"Lee," she said. "You don't need to thank me. I'm glad you called."

"Okay," he said. "Oh, and Shayla said to make sure

you know the wedding colors in case you care. Do you care?"

"Sure," Rosalie said, as she owned plenty of clothes and could see if she had something to fit in with the upcoming Cooper wedding. "What are they?"

"Forest green, eggplant purple, and dusky rose," he said. "I had to read that off a card, and I feel like an idiot." He laughed, and that made Rosalie's spirits soar toward the heavens.

She laughed too and said, "All right," she said. "I'll see what I've got in my closet."

"I'll let my brother know so they'll have a corsage for you," he said.

"I can't wait, cowboy."

"Me either. I'll see you tomorrow, baby." With that, Lee ended the call, and Rosalie said, "'Bye, Lee," in a whisper to only herself. Her phone rested in her lap while she tried to make sense of everything that had just transpired.

Then she jumped to her feet and strode into her closet, where one-half of it still sat empty. She hadn't moved her clothes over onto James's half yet, and she gave the empty clothing rods and drawers a good, long look.

She started leafing through her dresses, pulling out ones that seemed like the right color. She hung each of them on her ex-husband's side of the closet, slowly starting to fill up the space that had been empty for so long.

She thought of Lee's things here in the house, and such a thought would've normally scared her. Tonight, she didn't let the fear in, but thought about what it would be like to have a family again. She didn't want to raise Autumn alone, and Lee already had a son. He'd be a fantastic dad to a little girl, and Rosalie's eyes filled with tears.

Could she possibly have the future she'd always dreamed of? After the explosion that had hurt James and blown up her life, Rosalie had watched her future drain from her view.

Now, Lee emerged from the smoke and debris, and he offered family and fatherhood in the palm of his hand.

THE FOLLOWING DAY, ROSALIE PACED IN FRONT OF THE windows at Curious Kids. She'd changed her clothes four times that morning, and she'd just barely passed Autumn to Charity twenty minutes ago. Every one felt like a lifetime, because Lee still hadn't arrived.

She knew he couldn't stay long. After he'd called last night, they'd texted a little bit more, and she'd woken up to several more from him that had come in an hour before her alarm had gone off. She'd teased him about being an early bird, and he'd said that a dairy farmer had work to do at five a.m. no matter the season.

Rosalie wasn't great at text-flirting, and she had very few people she could consult for help. She'd called Charity and asked her to pick up Autumn a little later today, as that would allow her to stay later at work—or rather, out with Lee.

He likes you. Don't worry so much, Rosalie.

Charity's words bounced through her brain, but Rosalie didn't know how to stop worrying. She'd been a worrier for as long as she could remember, and part of that anxiety had bred her love of creating games. She'd been so worried about Natasha learning what she needed to learn so the other kids at school wouldn't make fun of her.

She'd asked Charity to read the text string between her and Lee, and while it had made her nervous and apprehensive, her nanny's words had helped calm her. At least for a few minutes.

A rusty truck turned in front of the windows and came to a stop in the parking stall. Rosalie let out a yelp and ran back to her desk, sure Lee had seen her eagle-eyeing for him through the windows. She reminded herself that the glass was reflective, and people couldn't actually see inside as she hurled herself into her desk chair.

She ran her fingers along her curls and pulled the nearest folder in front of her. She had no idea what it was about, but it didn't matter. Lee wouldn't examine her desk. Last time, he hadn't even come near where she spent hours of her time.

The bell on the glass door jingled as it opened, and Rosalie looked up as if she didn't know who she'd see there. Handsome walked in, and Rosalie smiled outwardly at him and inwardly at her nickname for him. With a mental jolt, she realized she should've been calling him that instead of cowboy.

"Hey." She slapped the folder closed and stood, feeling every inch of the flowy, loose fabric around her frame as she moved. She adored this jumpsuit made of fun, splashy flowers against a cream background.

"Howdy." Lee swiped his cowboy hat from his head in the most adorable gesture known to mankind. "Sorry I'm late."

"Can't control cows," she said as she walked toward him. He met her about halfway, and they paused just out of arm's reach of one another. Rosalie's heart boomed twice through her ears the same way Thumper stomped on the kitchen floor when he was hungry.

Then she said, "It's so great to see you, Lee," and stepped into his personal space. He put his arms around her, and Rosalie let her eyes drift closed as she turned her head and rested it against his chest.

This. This was what she missed most about being one-half of a couple. One-half of a life partnership. One-half of a marriage.

Lee had obviously not come straight from the farm and the "mess of cows" he'd texted about. His shirt smelled like the rainforest scent of dryer sheets, and it felt smooth beneath her cheek.

"It's good to see you too," he said, his voice stuck somewhere in his throat so that the words came out almost like a growl.

She stepped back, her smile still in place. "So what are we doing this afternoon?"

He glanced to the rack of games on his right and over to her desk behind her on his left. "You can play hooky?"

"I cleared my whole schedule just for you."

His eyes came back to hers. They burned with forest fires, and Rosalie wanted to lean forward and see if she could feel the heat. She didn't, and she simply let him soak her in. He scanned her down to her feet, where she wore a pair of off-white sandals that didn't add any height to her body.

"I like this...what is this?" He reached out and pinched the fabric of her sleeve between two fingers. "A jumpsuit?"

"That's right," she said, giggling. "It's a jumpsuit."

"I'm not great with fashion."

"Leave it to me," Rosalie said. "I adore clothes, and I could talk your ear off about them."

He looked at her again, his mouth curving up into a delicious smile. Rosalie had been thinking about it for days, wondering if she'd made the worst mistake of her life by not letting that mouth touch hers.

Her lips burned with want, but she sucked in a breath to keep herself from lunging at him. This second date hadn't even started, and kissing him now would be like doing so on the first date. "Let me grab my purse."

"I didn't see your car out front," he said.

"I let Charity take it." Rosalie turned back to her desk. "She's my nanny. She's with Autumn this afternoon, and she can stay as late as I need her to." She snagged the purse from the corner of the desk where she'd left it. As she faced Lee again, she said, "Well, within reason. She does have school tomorrow."

"How old is Charity?" Lee asked.

"Early twenties," Rosalie said. "She goes to college. I just meant I could stay out until nine or so pretty easily."

"Oh, I see," Lee said, his voice taking on a flirtatious quality. "You're trying to kill me on the second date."

Rosalie shouldered her purse and grinned at him. "Kill you? How would I do that, Handsome?"

His eyebrows went up, and Rosalie's anxiety jumped with it. "Handsome?"

"Before I knew your name," she said. "That's what I called you in my head." She shrugged, thinking of last week when he'd come by acting like he'd sat in a pile of burrs and it was all her fault. "And maybe after for a minute or two."

Lee simply stood there, staring. Rosalie didn't want to

spend her afternoon doing this. She needed an escape from the walls of this place, where she spent so much of her time.

She rolled her eyes in an exaggerated way. "Come on, Handsome. I'm playing hooky and you're off your farm. Let's see what this afternoon has for us outside these walls." She moved into him and deliberately laced her hands through his. "You do have a plan, right?"

"Yes," he said, his voice almost a croak. "There happens to be something going on at The Southern Bakery this afternoon."

"Something?" Rosalie teased, gently turning Lee toward the exit. "Like, us sitting down with pastries and coffee something? Or a dance party something? Or what's this 'something' exactly?"

Lee moved on wooden legs for a couple of steps, and then he seemed to melt. "Do I look like the type of man to attend a dance party?"

"Not on a Monday afternoon," Rosalie teased. They stepped outside, and she turned back to lock the door behind her. When she turned, Lee stood right there. He reached up, following his fingers with his eyes, and moved his hand down the side of her face.

"I can dance," he said. "My mama taught me. She said all women in Texas expect a man who can dance." He gave her a soft, gentle smile as he spoke of his mama. That alone made Rosalie forgive his tardiness and all of his silence from last week. "I can show you at the wedding."

"Promise?" she whispered, leaning into his touch when he neared her jaw.

"Yes," he said.

She nodded and held herself upright. "All right then. What's going on at The Southern Bakery this afternoon?"

CHAPTER NINE

Lee reminded himself of all Rosalie had said last night. She wanted to be with him, and until he proved to her that she'd be better off alone, he was going to be cool and confident. Despite the urgency in his stomach to find a bathroom and throw up, Lee managed to help the gorgeous woman into his truck and then get behind the wheel.

"Have you been to The Southern Bakery?" he asked as he secured his seat belt.

"Several times," she said.

"Are you from here?" He glanced over at her as he backed out of the parking stall. No one ever seemed to be at her office, and he wondered how she could stand being between walls all day long—alone—every day.

"No," she said. "I grew up in Dallas." She looked over to him, and Lee held the weight of her gaze just fine thanks to his internal self-talk on the way to her office. "You're from here."

"Generationally," he said. "My great-granddad started the dairy farm, oh, at least a hundred years ago." He chuckled. "That used to be a joke, but it's actually true now."

"It's pretty amazing," she said.

"My sister applied for the plaque and everything, and we got it up earlier this year. We're officially a Century Farm in Texas." His chest swelled with pride, because he could still see Daddy's face when Clarissa had presented him with the plaque. Daddy didn't cry very often—Lee had seen it only two or three times in his life—but he'd definitely had tears in his eyes when he'd gazed at the gold plaque that now rested on a stand near the highway turnoff to Sweet Water Falls Farm.

"Do you love it?" Rosalie asked. "It sure seems like you love it. The farm, I mean."

"I do," Lee said, flicking a quick glance in her direction. "It's all I've ever known, and it's all I've ever wanted to know." He swallowed, suddenly unsure about spilling such a thing. "What about you? Why'd you come to Sweet Water Falls?"

"James—my ex-husband—got stationed just down the coast. He was in the Navy. Is." She reached up and scratched at something on her face. "He is in the Navy. He just lives in California now." She turned away from Lee, and he'd seen this tactic before. Something stormed mightily in his chest, and he knew he'd go home kissless tonight unless he said something.

He didn't want to ruin anything with Rosalie, because the whole relationship felt so delicate already. He shifted in his seat, his mind spinning and screaming at the same time.

"Rosalie," he said, practically strangling the steering wheel. "I just have to ask somethin', okay?"

"Okay," she said.

"You're over your ex-husband, aren't you?" He wished he didn't have to focus on the road, so he flipped on his blinker and pulled over. He faced her fully, glad she'd turned away from the window to look at him too. "You've only talked about him twice now, which I get. *We're* still new." He gestured between the two of them. "But every time, you seem so sad. So...withdrawn. It's like you're still missing him."

Rosalie blinked, and Lee didn't like that she didn't jump to deny what he'd said.

"If you're not ready for a relationship." Lee cleared his throat, unable to volunteer a break-up. He didn't want to stop seeing Rosalie. He didn't even want to suggest it. Maybe he could just wait until she was ready. He didn't need to get married right away or anything. Between the two of them, they had two kids already.

So he let the words hang there, knotted as they were. Rosalie finally opened her mouth and said, "I can admit I didn't want the divorce."

Lee just nodded, his heart sinking all the way into his liver. "All right," he said.

"James got injured on a ship," Rosalie said. "There was an explosion and he lost part of one leg and feeling in the other. He's in a wheelchair, and he couldn't do what he used to do on the ship. So he came home, and I don't know. He wasn't the same."

Lee had never been through anything like that, so he just sat and listened. He looked down to give her a chance to breathe, and he picked at a thread on the seat cover.

"I still loved him," Rosalie said. "He didn't want to 'saddle me' with his care for the rest of our lives." She took a deep breath in, and Lee lifted his head enough to watch her do it. She seemed to strengthen right there in front of his eyes, and he'd never found anything or anyone so attractive in his whole life.

"He was here for a while," she said. "He's a great dad, and he took Autumn all the time so I could build Curious Kids."

"That's great," Lee said, the frog he'd apparently swallowed on the drive into town still in his throat. He'd been ribbiting everything he'd said for the past twenty minutes.

"He got a good opportunity in Navy Intelligence in California," she said. "He moved a few months ago." She moved her hand closer to his and covered his fingers with hers. "I'm over him, Lee. You're the first man I've dated since the divorce, and yes, maybe the idea of kissing someone else hadn't occurred to me until Thursday night."

Their eyes met, and Lee offered her a small smile.

"Maybe I panicked," she said. "But I'm over him. I want there to continue being an us."

"I'm not in a hurry, Rosalie."

"Okay," she said. "But are we in a hurry to get to something at The Southern Bakery?"

Lee followed her gaze toward the clock on his dashboard and nearly swore. "Yes," he said instead. With reluctance, he slipped his hand away from hers and merged back onto the street.

"What are we doing there?" she asked.

Glad they were on safer topics, Lee pressed harder on the accelerator. "They're doing a taste-test this afternoon. Starts at four." If he hadn't been late leaving the farm, he wouldn't be in such a rush right now. Lee hated nothing more than being late, and he dang near took the next corner on two wheels. "They're rolling out a couple of new menu items this summer, and we get to help them decide."

"Wow," Rosalie said, her voice a bit too high.

He looked over to her, finding her fingers now gripping the handle above the door tightly. "Sorry," he said. "I swear I'm not always a crazy driver."

"You're zero for two," she joked, her smile radiant and kind. Lee chuckled, but he didn't let up on the gas pedal. He did not want to be late for the taste-testing, not when Mama had called in the favor specifically for him.

They arrived at The Southern Bakery, and Lee hurried the two of them inside. Thankfully, they still had at least two minutes before the clock would strike four, and he found the woman he needed to hug and say hello to only three steps inside the front door of the bakery.

"Miss Mildred," he said, moving into her instantly. Hugging her was like getting a good, hearty hug from Mama, and Lee closed his eyes and grinned for all he was worth as the older woman's arms came around him.

"Mister Leland Cooper," Miss Mildred said. "How very good to see you, young man." She laughed in her elderly tone as she stepped back. She always wore a string of pearls around her neck, and today was no exception. Her pink and yellow tank top boasted a lot of flowers, and she wore a flowing, straight white skirt with that. She was a picture-perfect summer afternoon in the South, and Lee kissed both of her cheeks.

"It's wonderful to see you, ma'am," he said, remembering all of his proper Texas manners. "Mama sends her best regards. She misses you so."

Miss Mildred cupped his face in one hand and smiled at him the way only grandmothers can do. "You tell her I'll come out this week and bring some of her favorites. Is she on lemonade, sweet tea, or that herbal stuff she likes?"

"With the weather the way it is, she and Daddy have

broken out the lemonade," Lee said, chuckling. "I'll tell her."

"Jenni-Lynn is around here," Miss Mildred said. "Are you sure you two can't go out on just one date?"

Lee shook his head. "No, ma'am." He stepped back and made room for Rosalie. He claimed her hand in his, bringing her forward. "This is Rosalie Reynolds. We just started seein' one another." He beamed out all of his shininess at Rosalie and then Miss Mildred.

"My, my." Miss Mildred dripped her gaze down the length of Rosalie. "Aren't you a pretty thing?" She looked at Lee without a trace of kidding anywhere. "A bit out of your league, Mister Cooper."

"Shh," Lee said, starting to chuckle again. "She doesn't know that yet, Miss Mildred." He nodded toward her. "Rosalie, Miss Mildred. She and my mama go way back to Georgia."

"Lee," another woman said, and he turned to find Jenni-Lynn only a couple of feet from him. The bakery held a lot of people, and she had to squeeze past someone to arrive in front of him. He laughed as he hugged her too. His mama sure had been disappointed when there had been zero spark between him and Jenni-Lynn. Her mama too, if Miss Mildred's constant reminder that her daughter was still single meant anything.

"Howdy, Jen," he said. He hugged her quick and stepped back, once again bringing Rosalie to his side. "Jen, this is Rosalie Reynolds." He glanced at Rosalie, whose smile hadn't moved a single millimeter. "Rosalie, this is Jenni-Lynn. We've known each other about five decades now."

"Please," Jenni-Lynn said, her voice one of royals and dignitaries. "I am not fifty years old yet, Lee."

"You're not fifty, are you, Lee?" Rosalie asked.

"No," he said with a scoff. "Just a joke our mamas used to say. That we knew each other before we were born." He edged closer to Rosalie so she'd know he didn't want to be with anyone but her. He released her hand and slid his along her waist, bringing her even closer. "Where do you want us, Jenni-Lynn?"

"Table six," she said. "So lovely to meet you, Rosalie. We need someone to tie Lee down again."

"It's our second date," Lee said. "And y'all are makin' me regret I brought her here."

Jenni-Lynn gave him a knowing look, and Lee definitely should've made a better decision for this afternoon's time with Rosalie. The Southern socialite missed nothing when it came to relationships, and she'd been the one to tell Cherry that Charlie Mortimer simply wasn't into her and would never ask her to be his wife.

"Mother, we need to begin." She turned in her sleeveless sundress, and Lee nodded Rosalie toward table six, which sat in the back corner of the bakery.

"See you at the wedding, Jenni-Lynn."

"Wouldn't miss it," she drawled out. Her mama followed her toward the front of the bakery, where the refrigerated cases sat, and soon after, all the chatter in the room quieted.

"Welcome to The Southern Bakery," Jenni-Lynn said. "Thank you for coming to be part of our journey today."

Rosalie looked at him, and Lee ducked his head closer to her so she could whisper in his ear. "Not that I care, but how old are you?"

Lee tilted his head and looked at her out of the corner of his eye. He'd had this question for weeks now, after he'd read her bio on her company website. "Forty-two," he said under his breath. He didn't want to cause a problem during the taste-test, that was for sure. Mama would never forgive him if he made a scene. "I'll admit I've wondered about you," he whispered. "I read your bio on the Curious Kids site."

She leaned closer to him, and Lee couldn't help bending his back to get nearer to her too. "I'm a decade younger than you," she whispered, her breath warm on the side of his neck. "Is that a problem?"

Relief rushed through him. "Not for me. You?"

"Not a problem," she whispered.

"Isn't that right, table six?" Jenni-Lynn's voice cut through the soft moment between Lee and Rosalie.

He jerked his head up and met his friend's eyes. "That's right, ma'am," he said without missing a beat. "The peach preserves here are second-to-none." He gave her a mini-smirk, because he knew Jenni-Lynn's spiel frontward and backward. After all, she'd been born and bred in Georgia, and she'd only lived in Texas for her whole life. But her blood was made of peaches and Southern manners. Which was why she didn't cause a scene with him but smoothly went on with the rest of the treats they'd be tasting that afternoon.

"Once we finish the focus group," Jenni-Lynn said. "We'll split you into three groups, and you'll each get to make one of the desserts to take home with you tonight."

"We get to bake?" Rosalie hissed, just loud enough for Lee to hear.

He nodded, and his date laced her arm through his and squeezed as she laid her head against his bicep. "I love baking," she whispered. "This is the best date ever, Lee."

He wanted to ask her if it would end with a kiss, but their first item to taste arrived at that exact moment. "A double-chocolate fruit tart," the woman said. She wore a black apron and slid a small plate onto the table.

Lee pulled it toward himself and then past to put it in front of Rosalie. "I won't like that," he said. "You taste it and tell 'em what you think."

"You're not even going to try it?" she asked, reaching for one of the tiny tasting forks. It only had three tines, and not even a baby would find it big enough.

"It's fruit and chocolate," he said, shaking his head. That was explanation enough, but Rosalie continued to gape at him. "I don't like fruit and chocolate."

"You could try it."

"Pass," he said.

"Did you know what they were testing?" Rosalie forked off a tiny bite of the tart. The crust was dark and rich, and Lee would probably like that. A layer of lighter chocolate mousse rode in the crust, but it was the strawberry, raspberry, and blackberry atop the pudding that he couldn't stomach.

"Yes," he said. "Jenni-Lynn mentioned them."

"You came anyway?" She put the dessert in her mouth, Lee watching every moment. He'd probably like the double chocolate fruit tart if he could taste it on her lips. His whole body heated in the space of a breath, and he had to look away.

"Yes," he clipped out.

"Did you know I loved to bake?"

"No." He nudged the plate closer to her. "Eat it all. I'm not going to have any."

"I should've known you wouldn't like this one," Jenni-Lynn said as she arrived at his table. "Lee, you're still so surly about things."

"*Some* things," he said, giving her a sharp look he hoped would cut her vocal cords so she'd stop talking. "Like fruit with two types of chocolate."

"What would you put on it instead?" Rosalie asked, which caused Jenni-Lynn to raise her eyebrows.

"I like this one, Lee. It's a great question." She folded her arms and waited.

Lee switched his glare from Jenni-Lynn to Rosalie. She

blinked, her surprise evident in her expression. Instead of cowering from him, she stabbed the last tartlet and put the whole thing in her mouth, her eyes never leaving his.

So she could have an attitude too. She could be surly too.

"A peanut butter cup," Lee said, looking up at Jenni-Lynn, already knowing she'd hate that answer. "That's what I'd put on top of it, Jenni-Lynn."

She glared at him with all the power of the sun. "We're better than peanut butter cups, Leland." She turned and walked away, and Lee sat there with his humiliation burning a hole in his chest. He never should've brought Rosalie to this, though he had suspected she'd like it.

He couldn't think of a single thing to say while the tasting went on around him, and Rosalie filled out the feedback card by herself.

"I liked that," she said as if they hadn't been sitting in silence for the past seven minutes.

Lee looked at her, and she gave him a small smile. "I don't like fruit and chocolate."

"That's okay, surly cowboy," she said. "It takes all kinds to make the world go 'round."

In that moment, Lee knew Miss Mildred had spoken absolutely true—and he had too. Rosalie was so far out of his league, and she didn't even know it.

Yet, he thought. Once she figured out that he could go from hot to cold in less time than it took to look at a strawberry, she'd chalk him up as her first dating experience after her divorce and move on to someone more agreeable.

He couldn't let that happen, but he didn't know how to stop it. He thought of no one but her. He hadn't noticed another woman since her presentation at the elementary school. He wanted this relationship to work more than any other he'd had.

Then stop being such a beast, he told himself, and when the girls came around with the next round of desserts to taste, Lee put a smile on his face and thanked them profusely. He picked up his tasting fork and took a bite of the checkered chess pie.

For Rosalie, he could tame his inner beast—at least if there was dessert on the table between them. He could.

CHAPTER TEN

Travis Cooper shoved against the dairy cow in front of him, finally getting the Bertha into the chute. The sun beat down on his back, and the clock had barely reached seven. His phone blared as he got the last cow where she needed to be, and relief sagged through his whole body.

He needed a break, bad.

After tugging his phone from his back pocket, he read the message from his fiancée. Shayla Nelson was going to be his wife in just eight hours, and Trav's heart pulsed with love and desire in the same beat.

We're getting married today! she'd sent, and Trav couldn't help smiling at the words. He could feel her joy in them, and he hoped with all the energy of his soul that he could make her as happy as she was today every day of her life.

Some of us are working, he sent back to her.

You should be done by now, she replied. *You said you were only doing the first milking.*

He was, and he had just finished it. Well, as soon as this line of Berthas made it into the milking shed, then he'd be done. He reached to close the gate, tucking his phone away. He'd call Shay as soon as he was on the way back to his cabin.

Their cabin.

When the two of them returned from their honeymoon in the Canadian Rockies, Shay would move into the cabin Travis had previously shared with Will. His older brother was taking the next shift of milking, and then the cowboys at Sweet Water Falls Farm would do the third shift before boogying over to the tents that had gone up yesterday evening for the wedding.

That evening, their cowboys would do the last round of milking, and then Lee said he had everything handled for the week Trav would be gone. He couldn't wait to leave the Texas heat behind, because he did desperately need the break.

He rolled his shoulder, which ached slightly, and got all the gates closed as the first Berthas who'd gone in for milking had already started to come out of the shed. Some of them agreed with the morning milking, as they'd gone all night without relief, but some of the more stubborn cows always had to be pushed and prodded.

Sometimes Trav felt like one of the Berthas he had to

babysit into their milking chutes. He knew what he needed to do, and yet he had to be pushed and prodded to do it. Thankfully, he'd gotten out of his own way with Shay, and once the cows were only three deep going into the shed, he got out his phone and called her.

"Good morning," she said, carrying some of the joy he'd seen in her texts in her voice.

"Howdy," he said.

"Where are you?"

"Headed back to my cabin to shower," he said. "I'm not going to be late."

"It's just that once we arrive at the farm, we'll be separated, and I want my wedding day breakfast."

"You're going to get it," he said, smiling. "I'm fifteen minutes away from leaving. No one's going to stop me."

"Yeah, I've heard those exact words before," she said dryly. Trav chuckled, because he couldn't argue with her. The work on the family farm never ended, and he couldn't control a lot of the variables. Winds kicked up, and cows got out, and Trav had to be there to help.

Lee had hired a couple of new cowboys in the past few months, and that had helped a lot. Will wanted to see Gretchen as often as he could, and Travis had the same desire for Shay. They simply couldn't work fifteen hours every day anymore. Travis didn't want to, and he saw the exhaustion on Will's face most mornings.

Their paths crossed at the farmhouse each and every day, as they both arrived separately to see what their parents needed for the morning. Lee ate lunch with Mama and Daddy every day, and he made sure they were comfortable for the afternoon.

Rissa stayed after dinner—which the family ate together nearly every night at the white farmhouse—and that way, Mama and Daddy always had someone they could call on should they need help.

"Did you get the reservation at The Culinary Cabin?" Trav asked, his cabin coming into view. His long legs had eaten up the distance from the corral to the rolling hills pretty easily.

"I did," she said. "Ingrid said we'd be the only ones there, and it's going to be so amazing. Gretchen was right."

"I can't wait," Travis said. "Fifteen minutes, Shay."

"See you then, cowboy." She ended the call, and Trav jogged the last hundred yards to his cabin. He soaped and shaved, keeping his beard for the wedding. The day Shay had told him how "sexy" his beard was became the day he'd vowed he'd never shave it off.

He barely glanced at his wedding suit hanging in his closet as he pulled on a fresh set of clothes. He wore the same thing almost every day—blue jeans, cowboy boots, long-sleeved shirt. Sure, the Texas heat could suffocate a man inside a long-sleeved shirt, but Trav would rather be hot and sweaty than sunburned to a crisp or covered in bug bites.

He jogged back down the steps, his stomach roaring

at him to eat. As he trundled down the dirt lane that led past the other cowboy cabins to the main farm road, he adjusted the volume on his radio, setting it to the station Shay liked best.

When he pulled up to her house, he found her sitting on the front steps, a dozen or so boxes littering the ground in front of her. "What's this?" he asked as he got out. The brunette beauty looked up from her phone, her smile instant.

"My stuff," she said. "The essentials I need at your place. Our new place." She stood and came down the steps, picked her way through the boxes, and threw herself into his arms.

Travis laughed as he lifted her right up off her feet and swung her around. Shay squealed, and Trav settled her on her feet and kissed her right there for everyone to see. He didn't care at all, because he loved this woman with everything inside him.

He adored the shape of her mouth against his, and the way she always held a hint of coffee on her tongue. He could lose hours kissing Shay, but today, he pulled away before she did. "We can't be late," he said. "Ingrid is opening just for us."

"So Gretchen has told me a thousand times," Shay said.

"We don't want her to regret telling us about The Culinary Cabin." Trav looked at the boxes. "I'm assuming you want me to put these in the back of my truck right now."

"Seeing as how I'm not coming back here until after the honeymoon, yes," she said. "Get your muscles out, Trav." She grinned at him, and Travis shook his head.

"I had to shove a Bertha into the chute this morning," he said. "Several of them. This is nothing."

"I'll go get my dress."

Trav got to work hauling her boxes from the sidewalk to the truck, and she came out with a black garment bag, much to his disappointment. "Still not gonna let me see it?"

"It's bad luck," she said.

"You know," he said. "Most brides and grooms don't even see each other on the wedding day at all. Not until the ceremony."

"Yeah, so we're already tempting fate," Shay said, opening the back door of the cab. "Let's go." She helped with the last few boxes, and Trav sure liked how she hadn't worn anything different for their wedding day breakfast. She existed in leggings and a tank top most days, as she owned an outdoor outfitters store and usually ran five miles before breakfast.

"You didn't run today, did you?" he asked as he slid the last box into the bed of the truck.

"Nope," she said. "I slept in and showered." She grinned at him and headed for the passenger door. Trav beat her to it and opened it for her.

"You still gonna run with Will in the mornings?"

"If he'll let me," Shay said. "And if I can keep up." She put one palm against his chest. "You're sure it doesn't bother you?"

"It doesn't bother me," Trav said. He knew Will only had eyes for Gretchen, and that his brother would probably hate a running partner. Trav wasn't sure Shay would like it either, but he wasn't going to stand in their way. She ran every morning; Will did too. They might as well go together. "He's fast, and he's kind of a grump. He won't slow down for you."

"I'm aware of you Coopers and your attitudes," Shay said, pushing herself up and into the truck. "And just so you know, you and Will are like teddy bears now. It's Lee we need to sweeten up."

Trav closed her door, the urge to laugh gunning its way up his throat. He did let out a few chuckles as he went to get behind the wheel. "Good luck with that sweetening process. He's Daddy to a T, *and* he's been burned by women before."

"I know," Shay said, because she had been out to the farm plenty in the past several months. She knew Lee, and she'd been there for some pretty spectacular arguments between him and Will, as well as him and Rissa. Lee seemed to pick a fight with everyone who dared look his way.

"The heart has a miraculous way of healing itself," she

said, and Trav couldn't deny that. "Lee will figure things out, I'm sure of it."

Trav didn't argue, but he wasn't sure he could say the same. He wanted to, because Lee was an amazing brother, an excellent father, and a good friend. His fuse was just really, really short, and he couldn't hide how he felt.

So he's about like you, Trav thought, and when he glanced over to Shay and saw her grinning back at him, he suddenly knew Lee would figure out how to cage his inner beast and make something work with a woman.

Maybe not Rosalie, but someone.

"Tell me what we're gettin' into at The Culinary Cabin," he said.

"It's getting," Shay said. "With a G."

"This is how I talk, baby," Travis said, adding an extra drawl to the words. "We better not be *havin'* cheesy grits. I'm so over those."

Shay shook her long, dark hair over her shoulders and looked out the windshield. "She said she's making Texas Hill Country eggs Benedict."

"You told her I didn't want grits, didn't you?"

"I may have mentioned it."

Trav smiled and reached for his fiancée's hand. He pressed his lips to the back of her fingers. "I love you, Shay."

"I know."

"We're getting married today." He looked at her,

because they weren't even out of her sleepy neighborhood yet.

She met his eye, joy and love dancing through her expression. "Yes, we are."

"You love me, right?" he asked, though he knew the answer. He'd teased her like this many times over the past few months since they'd gotten engaged.

This time, she didn't roll her eyes and say, *Yes, Trav. I love you*, in a desert-like voice. She leaned toward him, her fingers in his tightening. "Yes," she whispered as he drew closer to her too. "I love you, Travis Cooper."

He kissed her, keeping this kiss chaste and simple. In moments like this, he could really experience how he felt about Shay, and when he could feel everything she held for him too.

"All right," he said, his voice husky and quiet as she settled back into her seat. "Let's go have our Hill Country eggs and then get married."

CHAPTER ELEVEN

Rosalie tried to keep from fidgeting in her seat, but she didn't succeed. She'd been out to the farm before, but only once. Her nerves had fired at her as loudly then as they were now, and she swallowed one more time.

"You okay?" Lee asked, his arm hanging loosely over the top of the steering wheel. "You seem to have ants in your pants."

Rosalie looked at him, her mind slowing. "First, I'm not eight."

Lee only kept grinning at her, so she shook her head. "Second, yes, I'm nervous. You're taking me to your brother's wedding. I'm going to have to meet your whole family, and they're going to judge me from the first look."

She glanced down at her dress, which was a lovely eggplant color. If Shayla hadn't chosen this exact shade for her wedding, Rosalie wouldn't know how to connect to the woman. Gems made the dress sparkle, and it might have been more of an evening wedding gown than an afternoon-on-the-farm-wedding dress.

Rosalie had decided she didn't care, but that was when she'd been standing in her bathroom in the dress. It hugged her curves and she had the perfect pair of black heels to wear with it. Now, she worried that her shoes would sink in the dirt out here, and that everyone would be in denim and sundresses, leaving her to stick out like the city slicker she was.

"Relax," Lee said, switching hands so he could reach across the distance between them and lace his fingers between hers. "They're not going to be judging you. They're all going to be looking at me."

"You?" Rosalie watched him, but the man was very good at shuttering off certain emotions. He claimed to be terrible at hiding how he felt, but Rosalie thought he harbored quite the talent for it. Sure, she could always tell if he was upset or angry, but other than that, the man existed behind a shroud. "Why?"

"I don't want to say," he said darkly, looking out his side window. He eased up off the accelerator in the next moment, and his trusty, rusty truck started to slow. He'd told her via text this week that he should probably buy a new one, but he liked this one so much.

When they'd gone out last night, she'd learned that he'd be picking up his son on the way back to the farm, and he'd asked about meeting Autumn. Rosalie had met him a few months ago, but they hadn't really started seeing one another until a week ago. Sort of.

She hadn't known what to say, and Lee had told her that she could introduce her daughter whenever she was ready. He wasn't going to push her on it.

"You can tell me," Rosalie said as he made the turn from asphalt highway to the dirt road that led down a gentle hill and then branched to the left and right. A white farmhouse could be seen on Rosalie's left, and she'd gone there to find out where Lee lived the day she'd delivered the video game he'd ordered.

She'd seen the cowboy cabins along the lane to the right, then another one back in a clearing slightly north of another T-junction. She hadn't gone south, so she didn't know what sat that way, because Lee's cabin went north and around another couple of bends. He lived out by no one, and she wondered if he liked that or not.

When she'd come to deliver the game, the farm looked like a farm. Grasses and dirt roads, serene cabins, big, blue, Texas sky.

Today, everything had been transformed into wedding central. On the left-hand side of the road sat four huge tents with pink, green, and purple streamers in the corners. Greenery hung from every pole Rosalie could see as Lee bumped the truck along. He hadn't answered her question, and she'd forgotten it as she took in the grandeur this farm had dressed itself with.

A cowboy stood at the fork in the road and waved at Lee to turn left, toward the farmhouse. He came to a stop and rolled down his window. "I'm headed to my cabin," he said.

"Of course, Mister Cooper," the man said.

"Milking on schedule?" Lee asked, no *thank you* in sight.

"Johnny and Gary are on it."

"Thanks, Mack." Lee eased away from the cowboy and went right. Rosalie wanted to turn and crane her neck to see the rest of the festivities, but she didn't. Questions streamed through her mind, but she didn't dare let any of them come out of her mouth.

She hadn't met anyone in his family, and that cowboy's name was Mack. She knew his brothers were Travis—the one getting married—and Will. Mama and Daddy were Chrissy and Wayne. He had bookend sisters: Clarissa who lived here on the farm with her husband, Spencer, and Cherry, who lived in San Antonio and worked at a college.

Ford was the only child in the bunch for the time being, but Clarissa was pregnant and due in six more months. Rosalie ran her hands along her curls, wishing someone had invented some sort of high-stress deodorant, because hers was failing, and she wasn't even out of the air-conditioned truck yet.

"You're makin' me nervous," he said.

"You aren't nervous?" she asked, wondering how to

delicately ask how much money he had. This farm screamed wealth, and as he rounded the last bend in the road and his cabin came into view, Rosalie saw all the dollar bills.

The two-story cabin boasted all wood with a reddish-gold tone and pristine windows. Rock made up the exterior on the fireplace, and the porch had obviously been stained recently for how brightly it shone.

A child stood from the top step of the porch, and Rosalie's heart ricocheted into her brain and back to the bottom of her stomach. "That's Ford," she whispered.

"Yep," Lee said. "That's my son." He brought the truck to a stop, and Rosalie suddenly felt frozen in her seat. He glanced over to her. "Rose."

Her nickname thawed her, and she turned her head to look at him. She couldn't tell if he was disappointed or angry or resigned. Maybe all three. "If you don't want to do this, Rosalie, it's fine. I have to go, but you can stay here. No one will bother you."

"I'm not going to stay here," she said. "I'm okay." She took a deep breath. "I really am."

"I won't leave your side," he said. "My sister is here too."

"Cherry?"

"Yeah, I wanted you to meet her apart from the others. She's not going to judge you." Lee turned as his door opened and Ford stood there. "Just a minute, son."

"Dad, you've got to see Cherry's boyfriend's dog," the boy said anyway.

"He's not her boyfriend," Lee said, his tone even darker than before. "I need one more minute, Ford. Go tell your aunt Charlie better not have a dog in our house."

"He's out back," Ford said, skipping away. "Hurry up, Dad!"

Lee reached out and pulled his door closed. He took a breath and pushed all the air out. "They're not going to be judging you, Rosalie. They're going to be wondering how in the world I got you to go out with *me*." He wouldn't look at her, and Rosalie didn't know how to process his words.

"Lee," she started.

"See, I'm the resident bear around these parts. Everyone knows it, even the neighbors. I do have a couple of friends over at Forrester, but that's about it. Even my cowboys call me *Mister Cooper*." He sounded absolutely miserable, and Rosalie hastened to unbuckle her seat belt.

"Stay there," she said, unlatching her door and toeing it all the way open so she could twist her whole body and get out without gaping her dress at the knees. She went around the truck, her heels a bit squishy in the gravel. To her surprise, Lee stayed, and she opened his door the way Ford had.

She stepped into the space, and he still sat a bit taller than she stood. "Handsome," she said, making it his noun. He brought his attention to her, and she offered him a tiny smile. "Just remember what *I* think of you, okay? Who cares what everyone else thinks?"

"What do you think?" he asked, ducking his head so his cowboy hat obscured his face.

"I think I like it when you call me Rose and not Rosalie. I think you're incredibly handsome. I think you have a heart of gold, almost all of it belonging to that child who just came skipping over to you." She looked over her shoulder, but Ford had disappeared. "He didn't call you Mister Cooper."

She turned to face Lee again, and he looked right into her eyes. "No one's going to be looking at us," she said. "Didn't you say Shayla's family has a momzilla?"

Lee finally cracked a smile. "Yeah."

"Then we're fine." She stepped back and extended her hand toward him. "Now, you promised me you wouldn't leave my side, and I'm not meeting your son or your sister without you. Come on."

Lee got out of the truck, immediately taking her hand. "Rose, you're...I don't deserve you."

"Why not?" she asked as he slammed his door.

"I don't know." He faced the cabin but didn't move toward it. "For a long time, I thought I'd be fine here. Just me and Ford on the weekends. I'm not sure when it became something I didn't want anymore, but I know I'm happier with you than I was before."

"Well, that's a good thing," Rosalie said, the warmth from the things Lee said seeping into her skin. He said a lot with only a few words, and if he knew that or not, she wasn't sure. "What do you want?"

"I want a wife," he said in a whisper. "Who loves me and who I am. Who understands I'm doing the best I can, and that I love this farm, that it flows in my blood."

Rosalie nodded, though she wasn't sure all that entailed. She didn't think anyone but Lee could understand that.

A woman appeared at the top of the steps, and she clearly belonged to the Cooper family. The dark red hair that she'd piled up on top of her head testified of that. She also wore the same apprehensive look of misery on her face that Rosalie had just seen on Lee's.

Lee moved, taking Rosalie with him. They walked side-by-side, and Rosalie told herself that was exactly what she needed to do today—stay at his side. He needed her as much as she needed him today. Like a flash of lightning could strike in less than a heartbeat, Rosalie realized that while Lee was very happy for his brother, he was also hurting over his own losses.

He hadn't said why he and his ex had broken up, but Rosalie would find out soon enough. Right now, she had to meet his sister and son.

"Hey, my sister," he said, releasing Rosalie as he went up the steps. He took them two at a time and reached his sister in only another moment. He wrapped her in a tight hug, and Cherry gripped him right on back. Rosalie stayed at the bottom of the steps and watched them, something tender and powerful about the way they loved each other manifesting itself right there in front of her.

Not only that, but she felt the anguish and unrest in both of them, and she wanted nothing more than to soothe it. She picked up her skirt and went up the steps, taking care not to trip. When she arrived, Lee and Cherry separated, and Cherry moved back, wiping her eyes.

Rosalie slipped her hand into Lee's and squeezed. He said, "Cherry, this is my date, Rosalie Reynolds." His voice only carried a slight edge to it, but Cherry continued to sniffle as she met Rosalie's eyes.

"I see why he likes you," she said, her voice the female counterpart to Lee's low one.

"It's lovely to meet you," Rosalie said, extending her hand toward Cherry. She shook it, her eyes darting over her shoulder as the door behind her opened. A tall man came out, but Cherry made no move to greet him.

He wore his Sheriff deputy dress clothes, and he had lines from shoulder to heel. He moved right into Cherry's side, a broad smile on his face despite her less-than-excited reception of him. "Howdy, Lee," he said.

"Charlie." Lee shook the man's hand. "This is Rosalie Reynolds."

"Howdy, ma'am," Charlie said, reaching to shake her hand too.

Awkwardness rained down on the porch, and Lee broke it by saying, "Ford says you brought a dog."

"Sure did," Charlie boomed like bringing a dog to a wedding was the greatest thing a man could do.

"It's a puppy," Cherry said. "I told him Travis was going to kill him with his bare hands."

"He's tied up out back," Charlie said, throwing a hard look at Cherry, who didn't react at all. Rosalie wasn't sure if they were together or not. Lee had said Cherry was single, but Charlie had his arm around her waist possessively. "That's all right, right, Lee?"

"You gonna leave 'im there?" Lee asked. "Because Cherry's right. You bring a dog to Trav's ceremony, and I can't promise you I can hold him back."

Rosalie looked at Lee to see if he was kidding. He sure didn't seem to be, and Rosalie wondered what she'd gotten herself into.

"I'm gonna leave 'im there," Charlie said. "Should we get goin', baby?" He nudged Cherry forward, and they started down the steps. Rosalie turned and watched Cherry go, noting she too wore a dark purple dress. Hers was lighter and moved more as she walked, and she looked more casual and country than Rosalie did.

"Let's go meet Ford," Lee said. "Then we best be gettin' over to the farmhouse. I don't need Trav at my throat either."

"You don't get along with your brothers?" she asked. "I thought you did."

"I do," he said. "Us getting at each other is how we tell each other that we care." He went through the front door and swept his hand in front of his body to indicate the house. "This is my place."

He had dark red wine-colored couches made of leather, with a puffy blue and white blanket thrown over the back of them. Matching couches, with matching blankets. Rosalie didn't know what to think.

Not a single thing sat out of place, and surely he had a cleaning service come out here to maintain this. A computer and desk sat in the kitchen instead of a table, and he had two barstools at the island. He moved to the sliding glass door in the back and whistled through his teeth.

A dog instantly started barking, and Lee yelled at it. To her surprise, the dog quieted as she took in the black appliances, which contrasted with his lighter wood and white countertops. The walls on the inside of the cabin matched those on the outside, as if she could see one side of the logs on the exterior and the other side on the interior.

She caught Lee looking at her, and she said, "I love your cabin."

"Do you?"

"Yes," she said, giving him a smile. "The fireplace is great, and there's so much wood."

"My granddad built it," he said. "He and Grams lived here until they passed. Then I moved in. Eventually, once my mama and daddy are gone, I'll live in the farmhouse."

"It's gorgeous too," she said, still amazed at this place.

"Your farm must do really well."

"We do pretty well," he said just as Ford came flying into the house.

"Ford, slow down," Lee said, and the boy complied.

"Did you see the pup, Dad?"

"Yeah," Lee said with plenty of weariness. "I saw 'im."

"We could get a dog like that," Ford said. "He's so smart, Dad. You should see all the stuff Charlie's taught him."

"Charlie's a cop," Lee said, then he shook his head as if trying to shake away this argument. He crouched down in front of his son. "Listen, bud. Remember I told you I was goin' on a date with a pretty lady last night? That I had to come get you late because of that?"

Ford's eyes moved from Lee's to Rosalie. She smiled at him and lifted her hand in a wave. "Yeah," he said, focusing on his father again.

Lee stood and faced Rosalie, his hand now tucked into Ford's. The very sight made Rosalie's heart melt into a gooey mess right there behind her ribs. Without her chest, it would've leaked out and all over his pristine wood floors.

"This is her," he said, grinning at Rosalie. "Rosalie, my son, Ford. Ford, this is Rosalie. She has a little girl and a rabbit at her house."

Ford's face lit up, and she guessed the child loved animals and probably only got to play with dairy cows. "What's the rabbit's name?"

"Ford," Lee said.

"I mean, it's so nice to meet you, ma'am." Ford stuck out his hand, and Rosalie was utterly charmed.

She took his hand and gave it a pump before releasing it. "The pleasure, Mister Cooper, is all mine." She could see so many pieces of Lee in his son, including his coppery hair and the shape of his chin. "And the rabbit's name is The USS Thumper. We call him Thumper for short."

"That's almost like the dog out back. You wanna come see?"

"Absolutely," Rosalie said, and Ford took her hand, practically dragging her behind him.

"His name is Thunder," Ford said, enunciating the difference.

"We have three minutes," Lee said, and Rosalie knew he meant it.

"We better hurry, Ford," she said. "The last thing we want to do is make your dad mad."

"No kidding," Ford said, to which Lee said, "Hey," in a wounded voice. His son didn't slow down, and Rosalie gave him all the right reactions to the small German shepherd tied up in the back yard. Charlie had put him in the shade, with a big bowl of water nearby, and when Rosalie saw the pretty flowery pattern on it, she wanted to hide it from Lee.

He looked at the dog from the deck off the back of the cabin, and Rosalie couldn't help gazing at the poured slab of concrete that made the perfect patio next to a stream. A couple of chairs waited there, and she could see herself sitting there, sipping something cold while she listened to the bubbling stream babble by.

The fantasy ended when she remembered that she spent forty hours a week trapped by four walls at her office, and then plenty of challenges at home too.

She wanted to remember the freedom she could taste out here, and she plucked her phone from her clutch and raised it to take a picture. Natasha would love this view, and Rosalie only hesitated for a moment before sending it to her. Her sister would ask and ask and ask to go there once she saw it, but Rosalie couldn't keep such glory from Nat.

"Time to go, son," Lee said, and he did come down the steps then. He slid his fingertips along her waist, and Rosalie looked up from her phone, the scattering of shivers and feelings moving through her too strong to comprehend.

"Ready, baby?" he murmured, and she nodded as she tucked her phone back into her clutch. They'd very nearly made it past the deck and the dog before Lee added, "If Travis doesn't punch Charlie today, I might."

"What, Dad?" Ford asked from his other side.

"Nothing," Rosalie said quickly, meeting Lee's eyes.

"That's my good china," he growled under his breath. "That dog better be from a royal bloodline." He looked like he was one breath away from bursting, and for some reason, Rosalie found it funny.

A giggle escaped her mouth, and Lee's hand in hers tightened. "You think that's funny?" he asked.

"A little," she said between her laughs. "I'm imagining a dog with a crown and a dismissive look." She laughed out loud then, and while Lee didn't join in, he also didn't look one breath away from tearing the Sheriff's deputy limb from limb.

Rosalie was going to count that as a win. As Lee held the door for Ford to get in the back and then came around to help her up and onto the front bench seat, Rosalie could see her daughter atop his powerful shoulders. She'd been right about this Lee Cooper—the man possessed a heart of gold, and Ford owned almost all of it.

She wondered if there was a place for her and Autumn inside this half-family. She wanted nothing more than to give her daughter everything she needed, and she'd adored James so very much. She would love Lee to death, and Rosalie allowed herself to fantasize about a complete family with Lee and Ford, her and Autumn, only for the time it took Lee to walk around the vehicle and get behind the wheel.

Then she shut it all down, because she and Lee weren't the ones who were only minutes away from tying the knot. They still had a long way to go before they'd be standing at the altar together, if they ever made it that far.

First, she had to survive meeting his parents and the rest of his siblings.

CHAPTER TWELVE

Cherry Cooper cringed every time that silly German shepherd made a single yip. Since Thunder was a puppy, he made plenty of noise, and Charlie seemed like a proud papa every time he did.

Disgust coated her throat, and Cherry couldn't believe she'd made such a huge mistake. She should've never invited him to be her date for this wedding. Literally anyone else would've been better. Attending alone would've been better.

"Is there a fire?" the Sheriff's Deputy asked, jogging to catch her.

"You brought your puppy to my brother's wedding," Cherry said dryly. "The last thing I need is to call more negative attention to myself." Cherry didn't come home very often, and while Lee and Will had received her with smiles and hugs and plenty of questions about her life, Travis had been somewhat distant.

She told herself it was because he was getting married today, and he was a little stressed about making sure everything went exactly right. That was what Rissa had said, and Cherry believed her. No one in the Cooper family sugar-coated much, and Cherry could count on her siblings to give things to her straight.

Charlie caught her hand on her next step, and Cherry's skin crawled. She didn't want to cause a scene with this man, but she didn't want to encourage a relationship with him. She wasn't sure if gently sliding her hand away would be worse than holding on, and she stepped a couple of times while she tried to decide.

In the end, she wasn't going to get back together with Charlie, and she tugged her hand free from his. The weight of his eyes on the side of her face landed heavily, and Cherry gave him a side-eyed glare.

"You don't want to hold my hand?" he asked.

Cherry kept walking, wondering why they'd parked at the farmhouse and walked out to Lee's. Oh, right, because Deputy Mortimer had said his dog needed a walk. Then he'd tied the puppy in the back yard at Lee's house, which was as far from the wedding tents as he could get.

At least when the German shepherd barked now, the nuptials wouldn't be interrupted.

"Not particularly," Cherry said. "I thought you understood this was just so I didn't have to attend this wedding alone." She'd told him that in explicit words. Via text, so it was in writing. She'd had a hard time breaking up with Charlie in the past, and she'd gone back to him three times already.

Not again, she vowed.

"Yeah, but..." Charlie trailed off, and Cherry didn't even want to know what he might finish that sentence with.

"Let's just get back to the farmhouse for the family gathering," Cherry said. The sun had already heated the day, and while May in Texas wasn't usually too oppressive, it felt like summer had arrived early. Or maybe that was the laser-gaze of the cop beside her.

"Are you seeing anyone in San Antonio?" he asked.

"I don't see how that's your business."

"I'm guessing not," Charlie said, his voice low and gruff. She'd probably hurt his feelings by removing her hand from his, but Cherry couldn't bring herself to care. She didn't have to make sure Charlie Mortimer felt good about himself. Not anymore. She'd spent six years of her life buoying him up, supporting him, celebrating his career promotions and throwing him parties as he moved up through the ranks. He hadn't even come to her graduation party when she'd earned her master's degree in educational counseling.

"Or he'd have come with you," Charlie said.

"Or I decided our relationship wasn't ready to deal with my family," Cherry said. She wasn't dating anyone in

San Antonio right now, nor had she for quite a few months. She owned three cats, and she worked with dozens of adults and young adults, so she talked to plenty of people every single day. In fact, by the weekend, all she wanted was peace and quiet—and someone to show up with dinner so she didn't have to cook.

In her quietest moments, she could admit she was lonely. It was then that she texted Lee or Will, Rissa or one of her friends in the city. She knew how and when to surround herself with people so she could feel connected to her roots and herself, and she didn't need Charlie Mortimer to point out that she was single and unmarried.

As if she didn't know.

"Yeah, your daddy is intense," Charlie said.

"You don't get to say anything about my daddy," Cherry said. No, Daddy didn't like Charlie, because of the way he'd treated Cherry over the years. Mama didn't either—no one in the Cooper family liked him. Cherry had lost her mind when she'd asked him to accompany her to this wedding.

They walked in front of the cowboy cabins, the farmhouse up ahead another quarter-mile. The big, white tents where the wedding and following dinner would take place entered her field of vision, and Cherry couldn't wait to disappear among the crowd who'd already started arriving.

A couple of the cowboys who worked for the farm

directed traffic, and Cherry's exhaustion pounded behind her eyes.

"He didn't seem less intense to me," Charlie said.

"He is," Cherry said. Daddy had changed a lot, especially in the past year. Charlie would have no way of knowing, and Cherry didn't have to explain it to him.

He was far less intense. He spoke quieter. He'd given control of the farm to Lee, Will, and Travis, and it was like all of the stress of that had melted away. So he could hug harder and love deeper, and Cherry had realized that over the past few months.

Her father hadn't driven her from Sweet Water Falls, but he hadn't been a reason to stay either. Lee had said Cherry had left because of Charlie, and Cherry had denied that too, saying there were other reasons.

But she wasn't sure what they were at the moment. She had wanted a fresh start away from anyone she knew, and she absolutely couldn't risk running into the man currently walking beside her.

They crossed the T-junction and walked along the side of the dirt road, the farmhouse getting closer and closer now.

"Do we have a minute?" Charlie asked, his hand clasping around hers again. Before she could answer, he towed her toward the east tent, where dinner would be served.

Everyone else streamed into the west tent, where the wedding ceremony would take place, and Cherry glanced toward them, wondering if she should call out for help. She didn't see anyone she knew, and she knew in that moment that she'd been out of town for a long time.

"Charlie," she protested.

"I just want to talk for another second," he said.

Cherry suspected he wanted something else, but she wasn't sure what. She wasn't afraid of him, but he was far bigger and stronger than she was. She did yoga three times a week and had taken a self-defense class a few years ago after the college where she worked mandated it for the employees who worked on campus.

"Charlie," she said again as he flipped back the closed flap of the tent and entered it. Round tables had been set up and clothed with beautiful cream-colored linens, deep purple napkins, and gorgeous vases of flowers that rose like pillars from the center of each one. Cherry realized she would like to get married one day, though she was too old to have children now. She'd come to terms with that, but that didn't mean she had to spend the rest of her life with only felines and friends.

She managed to get her hand away from Charlie, and she glared at him. "What?"

"I don't think you're dating anyone." He glowered at her, and Cherry folded her arms.

"I don't care what you think," she said. "This was a mistake. You should go get your dog and get on home."

"No way," Charlie said, shaking his head. "Dinner smells delicious."

Cherry rolled her eyes, and in that moment where she wasn't watching Charlie, he lunged at her. He grabbed her by the shoulders and leaned toward her, his mouth seeking hers.

"Stop it," she said just before he kissed her. She struggled against his strength, knowing her advantage existed in her legs. She brought her knee up, and that got the man to back away a single step.

"Cherry," he barked at her.

"I'll bite you if you kiss me again," she said, wiping her mouth. "And you're lucky I didn't have enough room to kick you properly." She glared at him, and Charlie's eyes—which she'd once found so dreamy—stared back at her.

"You wouldn't have asked me to this wedding if you didn't want to get back together."

"You're delusional," she said.

And perhaps he was, because he came at her again. This time, Cherry braced herself for a blow that didn't come, as someone had stepped into the tent and grabbed onto Charlie's upper arm.

"I think the lady said no," a man said. Cherry blinked at him at the same time Charlie did.

Jed Forrester, a cowboy who lived on the farm to the west of Sweet Water Falls Farm, flicked his dark navy blue eyes in Cherry's direction and then re-focused on Charlie. "I'm gonna let go of you now, and you should probably get."

"I'm not gonna get," Charlie spat. "She invited me to the wedding."

"I just uninvited you," Cherry said, reaching up to smooth down her hair. She felt shattered in pieces, and she hated that. She always made sure she had everything sitting in precisely the right place before she left her house and entered the public arena.

Her heart beat like a drum in her chest, and her adrenaline kept spiking and sending it into a frenzy again. She met Jed's eyes, and her pulse dang near exploded from her body. She wasn't sure what that meant, if anything, but she was grateful she didn't have to deal with Charlie alone.

"I have to go," she said, speaking to Jed now. Her memories flooded her mind, because he was the same age as Lee, and they'd been friends stemming all the way back to junior high. "My family is having a little meeting right before the wedding."

"Go," Jed said. "I'll save you a seat in the other tent, okay? I'm with my brother Chris and his wife. We've got an extra seat."

Cherry swallowed and nodded. She threw one last glare in Charlie's direction, and put one hand on Jed's shoulder as she started to pass him.

"Thank you," she murmured. Electricity flowed from his body and into hers, and she pulled her hand away and stepped out of the tent in the same motion.

Outside, she could breathe easier, and she quickly

crossed the road to the farmhouse, arriving on the porch as the rumble of Lee's truck met her ears.

At least she wasn't the last one to arrive, and since Lee was the golden child, Cherry wouldn't be in trouble either. She glanced across the lane and caught Jed walking from one tent to the other, no sign of Charlie anywhere.

She might be in trouble with the handsome Jed Forrester, but she couldn't know for sure yet. He'd probably felt nothing for her. He was just doing his Texas gentleman duty by rescuing her from her terrible choices and a pig-headed man.

Her fingers still tingled as she twisted the knob and entered the farmhouse. Rissa turned from the arched entryway that led into the kitchen and living room. She smiled and then turned back to everyone else Cherry could hear in the other room.

"It's Cherry," she called.

"Where the devil is Lee?" Will asked. "I swear, that man needs another watch to be where he needs to be on time."

"He's coming," Cherry said, moving to stand beside Rissa. "Calm down." It was a family wedding on their farm. Everyone would be perfectly fine if the ceremony started a few minutes late, for crying out loud.

Will glared at Cherry, and she frowned on back at him. "I'm going to check on Daddy and Trav. Send Lee this way when he decides to show up."

Cherry didn't respond and instead went in the opposite direction to go sit beside Mama for a few minutes before she'd have to be on public display again. Her mom didn't say anything, but she offered Cherry a smile, and she slipped her papery, dry fingers into Cherry's.

Peace and comfort accompanied this gesture, and Cherry exhaled out the tension and awkwardness of the exchange between her, Charlie, and Jed.

You're not going to date him, she told herself. She'd sit by him at the wedding, if only to keep Charlie at bay. She wasn't sure if the Sheriff's Deputy would leave or not, and she could let Jed be her buffer today. That didn't mean anything was going to happen between them, and Cherry vowed it wouldn't. She didn't live here, and she wasn't looking for a cowboy in any way, shape, or form.

Not even one with a heroic streak, a thrumming deep voice, and broad, sexy shoulders.

CHAPTER THIRTEEN

J ed Forrester couldn't help watching the entrance to the wedding tent, which was marked with tied-back flaps. Flowers adorned the twine, and he could see all the details that had gone into making this wedding beautiful.

He wasn't incredibly close with Travis Cooper, the man getting married today, but he knew Will and Lee better. Especially Lee, as they were the same age and had graduated from high school in the same year.

They'd been friends for decades, and the Forresters and the Coopers had neighboring farms and shared holiday customs on this lonely stretch of highway thirty minutes outside of the town of Sweet Water Falls.

He looked down the row at his brother and his wife, then his parents. He'd reserved the chair on the end of the row for Cherry, though he wasn't entirely sure she'd take it. She probably had to walk in the wedding party with that oaf who'd tried to kiss her when she hadn't wanted him to.

Jed could relate to the man, because one look at the gorgeous Cherry Cooper, and any man would start to think about kissing her. She was a flawless woman, and while Jed had never considered her as a potential date, he'd certainly reacted to her touch in a way he hadn't to anyone else. At least anyone in a while.

The cowboys who lived and worked out on these farms knew how hard it was to meet women, but Jed told himself that all of the Cooper men had done it now. Chris had found Deb, and they'd driven their twins into her mother's so they could attend the wedding without incident.

Jed should probably try a little harder to meet someone. *Get Cherry's number*, he thought, though he had no idea how to do that. He didn't know where she lived or what she did, other than he didn't think it was around here.

The light chatter quieted and ceased, and Jed whipped his attention back to the entrance. Travis Cooper ducked into the tent first, paused, and waited for his parents to join him. He linked his arm through his mother's, and anyone with eyes could see that Chrissy Cooper wasn't the healthiest human being. She'd been fighting cancer for five years at least, and Jed admired her greatly.

He got to his feet along with everyone else, and something tender and somber touched him as Travis linked his hand in his father's too.

Wayne Cooper was a tough old man, and Jed had plenty of experience with him too. He respected Wayne as well, and he swept his cowboy hat off his head as the trio started down the aisle to the altar. Travis beamed like the stars in heaven, and Chrissy stopped to say hello and kiss several women's cheeks.

Jed, as close to the aisle as he was, shook Wayne's hand on behalf of the Forrester's, and once the groom stood at the altar, his parents took the front two seats on the right-hand side of the aisle.

The rest of the family started to file in then, and to Jed's surprise, there was no wedding party procession. He shook Will's hand, then Lee's, the two of them grinning and man-hugging before Lee went to the front row with a pretty dark-haired woman Jed hadn't met yet.

Cherry Cooper stole his breath the moment she entered the tent with her younger sister and Rissa's husband. Jed had been out of town for that wedding, and he wondered if his body, mind, and hormones would've reacted to Cherry then.

She wore a flowing, pretty purple dress that fit in with what the other women in the family were wearing. Her shoes added a couple of inches to her height, but they weren't extravagant. She'd put on makeup that accented her dark eyes, and they pulled at him and pulled at him until he couldn't look anywhere but at her, even when he tried.

She nodded at him, and he barely dropped his chin to the end seat. They didn't have the front row but only sat a few back, and she'd have the aisle seat for a good view.

She let Rissa and her husband continue forward, and Cherry detoured to Jed's side. Relief punched him in the chest, and he wasn't even sure why. He wanted to take her hand in his and lean toward her, whisper in her ear that he'd make sure she didn't have to deal with a Sheriff's troll today, and ask her to dinner for tomorrow night.

He did none of the above. He wanted to sling his arm around the back of her chair and see if she'd snuggle into his chest. He didn't dare move at all. He held his cowboy hat in one hand and watched the back of the aisle, barely breathing so he wouldn't get too much of Cherry's perfume.

He'd already been intoxicated by the peach and vanilla scent as she'd passed him while leaving the other tent earlier. His shoulder burned as hotly now as it had then, and he cleared his throat for a reason he couldn't name. It wasn't like he was going to speak to her mere moments before her brother's bride appeared for the wedding.

She faced away from him too, giving him a few moments to drink in the darkness of her hair, which had threads of the fiery red that all of her siblings possessed in some form or another. Lee was the darkest of the redheads—except for Cherry. He wondered if she dyed her hair, and he leaned forward to ask her.

She glanced at him, and Jed grinned at her. "Do you dye your hair?" he asked.

She blinked at him, clearly surprised. "What?"

Before he could repeat the question, music began to play and the bride entered the tent. Jed told himself he'd have time to talk to Cherry later, and he employed the little patience he had as the bride danced—yes, danced—down the aisle.

A COUPLE OF HOURS LATER, JED TIPPED HIS HEAD BACK AND laughed. "I was just wondering," he said to Cherry. "I thought Lee had the darkest hair in your family."

"I beat Lee in a lot of things," Cherry said. The two of them had been inseparable since she'd sat beside him during the ceremony, and Jed had even sent his brother back to the farm without him. Cherry had said she could give him a ride the five miles down the road to Forrester Farms, and Jed wanted to spend as much time with her as he could.

He'd learned that she lived in San Antonio and worked as an academic advisor for a college there. She wasn't married, had no kids, and didn't have a boyfriend either.

Jed had no idea what he was thinking, but he picked

up his fork and took another bite of the wedding cake that had been cut and served twenty minutes ago.

"So," he said. "What does a man have to do to get your phone number?"

Cherry lifted her eyes from her own slice of cake, of which she'd eaten very little, and looked at him with surprise again. "My phone number?"

"Yeah," Jed said, keeping his voice even. "What if I want to call you?"

"Why would you want to call me?"

"To gossip about Lee and Rosalie," Jed said with a grin. "Tell you what Chris and Deb are going to do with those terrible twins." He shrugged like he wouldn't use her number at all. "I don't know. Feels like it might be safe to have it, that's all."

Cherry didn't immediately jump to give him her number. She pushed cake around on her plate and didn't take a bite of it. "I barely know your name."

"Not true," Jed said. "We've known each other for years."

She tilted her head and gave him a look that said, *Really, Jed?*

He chuckled again, liking the fire inside her. There was something intriguing about her, and Jed wanted to peel back every layer until he understood the woman beneath the perfect makeup, the silky hair, the peachy perfume, and the glamorous gown.

"Do you own any sweat pants?" he asked.

She opened her mouth to answer, then snapped it shut. "I have no idea what's going to come out of your mouth."

He grinned at her again. "I'm just wondering if you're normal or not."

"Of course I'm normal," she said, shaking her head with a look of disgust in her expression. "I don't wear a dress while gardening. This is a wedding."

"I once dated a woman who wore her platform heels to weed her rose garden," Jed said. "It happens."

"I think that's on you," Cherry said, not missing a beat. "Where do you even meet a woman like that?"

"Bingo night," he said instantly, liking her wit and intellect.

"Wow," Cherry said. "I thought I was older than you. Bingo night?" Her eyebrows went up, and Jed found he couldn't erase his smile.

"I went with my nana," he said. "Maisee was calling."

"Wow, Maisee," Cherry said, lifting her glass of wine to her lips. She took a delicate sip before adding, "She sounds like one of my college students."

Jed laughed, though he'd not taken a single sip of alcohol that evening. "I think she was in college, actually."

"I mean, you can't pick the name you're born with," Cherry said. "It's not like I enjoy introducing myself as Cherry."

"No?" Jed sobered slightly. "What would you name yourself if you could?"

She blinked at him again. "I don't know."

"Come on," he said. "You've obviously thought about it."

Cherry remained silent for several moments, gazing out at the dance floor, where all of her brothers danced with their significant others. Jed wondered what sat in her head and what pricked at her emotions. He could see himself so well inside Lee, and he suddenly wanted to be dancing too, the pretty Cherry Cooper in his arms and smiling at him the way Lee's date did.

He looked back at Cherry. "Do you want to dance?"

"That's a no," she said, bringing her eyes back to him. "No offense. I just don't want the spotlight on me at all."

"Weren't you the class VP?" he asked.

"Your memory is iron-clad." She swirled her wine but set the glass down without taking another drink. She got to her feet, and Jed looked up at her expectantly.

"Will you walk me back to the farmhouse?" she asked. "I'll take you home."

Jed's heart pinched against his ribs, but he didn't argue. She'd answered his other questions with quickness, though he realized as he stood that she hadn't even told him which college she worked at.

He once again wanted to take her hand in his but refrained. Outside, the sun had set a while ago, but plenty of lights illuminated the pathway to the parking area that had been roped off on the farm.

Cherry said nothing as they walked, and Jed didn't like the silence. "I like your name," he said.

"My great-grandmother was named Cherry," she said. "I don't hate it either. I was just saying that poor Maisee probably shouldn't be judged on her name."

"Of course not," Jed said quickly.

Cherry drove a black sedan, and Jed folded himself into the passenger seat. The urge to get her phone number intensified with every moment that passed, and he told himself not to ask for it again.

Cherry turned off the highway and onto his farm, and he directed her to his cabin, which was the foreman's cabin at the end of the line of houses where his cowboys lived.

"You live here alone?" she asked.

"Yes, ma'am," he said, gazing at the lit front porch. "Got a dog to keep me company, and my brother and his wife live on the other side of the homestead."

"What's your dog's name?" Cherry looked at him, and Jed turned toward her too. He forgot the question—heck, he forgot his own name—as he looked into those dark eyes.

Something haunted Cherry, and he wanted to find out what and chase it away. Far away, for good. He wanted to ask her if she was okay to drive home alone, but he didn't want to indicate she was weak. Cherry Cooper wasn't weak, but she definitely had some beams inside her that had been cracked or compromised.

Jed could fix those, he knew, because he spent a great deal of time fixing the buildings and fences around the farm where he'd lived and worked for his whole life. He could fix anything with only a few tools, and he wanted Cherry to tell him everything that hurt so he could heal it.

He wanted to ask her why she'd asked Charlie Mortimer to be her date when it was clear she couldn't stand the man.

Jed said nothing as he reached out and trailed his fingers down the side of her face. She pulled in a breath as a powerful tingle shot through his hand and up his arm.

"I don't know much about you, Cherry," he said, his voice soft and all traces of laughter and teasing gone. "But I'd like to change that." He pulled his hand back, the words out there now.

So many more questions streamed through his mind, but he kept them all stuffed down in his throat.

"So I guess you want my number," she said.

"I've already asked for it," he said.

"Get your phone out," she said.

Jed complied, his heart pounding in a strange rhythm that told him he was the luckiest man on the planet. He handed the device to Cherry, and she typed into it for several seconds.

She handed it back without speaking, and Jed took

that as his signal to get out of her car now. "Thanks for sittin' by me," he said, opening the door. "I'll call you."

"Thanks for saving me a seat," she said as he got out. He leaned back in to tell her good-night. "Thanks for your help with Charlie."

"Anytime," he said. "'Night, Cherry." He backed up and closed the door before he couldn't get himself to do so. He walked away from her car, noting that she didn't immediately back out of his driveway and leave.

He went inside, where his black lab came trotting toward him. "Heya, Fish," he said to the dog, giving him a healthy scrub. "You'll never guess what happened tonight." He grinned as he pulled his phone from his pocket and went to his contacts.

Cherry's name sat in the right spot alphabetically, and he showed it to the canine. "Lookit, Fish. I got this beautiful woman's phone number."

The dog nosed the device, snuffed, and trotted over to his empty food bowl. He looked back at Jed expectantly, not caring about Cherry Cooper at all.

Jed chuckled, pocketed his phone, which now held a great prize, and went to take care of his clearly starving dog.

CHAPTER FOURTEEN

Lee clutched Rosalie's hand too tightly, and he knew it. He tried to ease up, but the farmhouse loomed in front of him, and he knew the moment he went inside, bombs would be flying and exploding.

"I'm gonna go tell Grandma about the shepherd," Ford said, breaking into a run. Lee watched his son for a moment, plenty of single dad guilt tripping through him.

"He's a wonderful boy," Rosalie said, tugging Lee closer to her. Their hips bumped, and Lee's body burned at her intimate touch.

"Thanks," he murmured. "He needs a dog. Every boy needs a dog."

"Ah, but the surly cowboy doesn't want to get him one," Rosalie teased.

Lee's spirits soared, and he didn't even mind when

she called him surly. If Will had done it, Lee might have thrown ninja stars with his fierce glare. "I do," he said. "And I don't. Dogs are a lot of work, and he only lives here two days a week."

"What about his mom?" Rosalie asked. "What's she like?"

"She's not the dog type," Lee said, plenty of defenses in his voice. He didn't want to talk about Martha today. She wasn't here, and that was one saving grace for Lee. He could enjoy his family and wish Travis and Shayla well. He could, and he would.

It didn't matter that his own jealousy seemed lodged tightly in the back of his throat, the ball enlarging with every minute the clock ticked closer to three p.m. Today wasn't about him. It wasn't about Will. It wasn't about Mama or Rissa, though she sure had done her best to make every conversation about her back pain now that she was starting to show.

It wasn't even about Cherry and how she'd finally come home after a very long time away from the family farm. Lee's heart hurt for his older sister, and he ached to help her be happy. He simply didn't know how. Heck, he couldn't even find his own path to happiness at the moment, and he was tired of stumbling around in the dark.

"You're going to have to tell me about her sometime," Rosalie said.

"Who?" Lee looked at her, having lost the thread of their conversation.

"Your ex-wife," she said, giving him a sharp look. "I don't even know her name."

"It's Martha," he said. "I don't want to talk about her."

"I'm sure you don't." Rosalie dropped his hand and marched up the steps to the farmhouse. "But I told you about James when I didn't want to. That's what people do when they're getting to know one another. Sometimes baggage gets opened and dirty laundry needs airing." She put her hands on her hips and stared down at Lee.

He gazed up at her. "Has anyone ever told you how gorgeous you are when you're angry?"

"Stop it," she said in a voice that told him to do exactly that. "This isn't angry, Handsome. This is passionate."

He took the steps as quickly as he could to get to her side. He swept one arm around her and pulled her flush against his body. "I like passionate on you."

"We are in public," she whispered, her eyes glued to his mouth.

"With my sister peering through the window," Lee murmured. The desire to kiss her burned through him, but he wouldn't do it here. "Can I kiss you later?"

"Lee," she said in a scandalized voice. "It's your brother's wedding day, and our fourth date. I have to meet your whole family, and I can't be stressed about kissin' you later."

Lee grinned as widely as he ever had in his life. "It won't be stressful," he said. "Might actually be fun."

"You." She pressed her hand against his chest, and he dang near stumbled backward down the steps. "Might be fun." She patted her curls and turned toward the farmhouse door. "Says the man who hasn't been out with anyone in a while. He might be out of practice. It might not be fun at all."

Lee burst out laughing, but he had no argument for her. What he did know was that she'd cheered him up immensely, seemingly without even trying. "Wait," he said as she reached for the doorknob. He swung out his hand wildly and caught her arm haphazardly. "If I tell you about Martha, will you at least consider a good-night kiss?"

Rosalie studied his face, her dark eyes searching his. "All right," she said in her professional voice. "I suppose I can consider it."

Lee leaned down and pressed his lips to her cheek, closer to her eye than her mouth, which took a great amount of willpower, thank you very much. The way she leaned into him, one hand coming up to cup his shoulder, told him he could very well kiss her that night whether he said another word about Martha or not.

"Let's go in," he said. "Before someone comes—"

Will whipped open the door. "Get in here," he barked. "We've all been waitin' for you two forever."

"Too late," Lee said dryly, giving Will a piercing glare. "We're not late, Will."

"You're literally ten seconds away."

"Glad you've got a timer running." Lee took Rosalie's hand and led her into the house without introducing Will. If he only had ten seconds, he better get into the kitchen area of the house as quickly as he could.

"Trav wants us back in the bedroom," Will said, still hot on his heels.

"All right," Lee said. "We've got time, Will." He wanted to introduce Rosalie around, and he'd planned for this. Trav had plenty of time before he had to be out in the tent. *For crying out loud*, he thought.

"He's bringing her in right now," Rissa said just beyond the arched entrance to the left side of the house, where the Coopers cooked and ate dinner every night. "Everyone, be nice."

Lee scoffed as he entered the kitchen, every eye stuck on him and Rosalie. In that moment, he knew what a huge—*huge*—mistake he'd made in bringing her to this wedding. Attending alone would've been better.

He took one look at Cherry—a very unhappy, standing by herself Cherry—and recalled the thought. He did not want to be alone today.

"Everyone," he said in a clear voice. "This is Rosalie Reynolds. She's my guest today, so y'all show 'er that we Coopers know how to behave."

Mama glowed like a lit jack-o-lantern on a cold

October night, and Lee rolled his eyes. He met Mama's, silently begging her not to do what she did. She took the glow down to a beam, and Rissa stepped forward to welcome Rosalie first.

Lee did exactly as he promised he would—he stayed right by her side as she met everyone. Will's impatience floated on the air like a stink, and finally Lee couldn't take it anymore. "Trav," he said. "You ready?"

"Yep." His brother grinned at everyone and led the way out of the kitchen. Shayla wasn't here, and she was the only one they were missing. Even Daddy's brother had come from Beeville, and Uncle Denny looked about as old as Texas.

Lee placed another kiss on Rosalie's cheek and said, "I'm gonna leave you with my sisters for ten minutes, okay, baby? Cherry promised me she'd take good care of you."

"They're great," Rosalie whispered before Lee met his daddy at the arch to go with the other boys. He turned back at the sound of Cherry's voice, and she had stepped right over to Rosalie. She took her over to the couch against the far wall, where Mama had sat.

Lee smiled and ducked out of the kitchen, following his father down the hall to the bedroom he'd had as a kid. Mama and Daddy had cleaned it out years and years ago, and now, Travis was almost dressed in his deep, dark tux. His fingers fiddled with the bowtie around his neck until Will pushed his hands away and did it himself.

"What's with Will?" Lee asked Daddy, both of then stationed near the door.

"Somethin' about his beehives getting tipped over," Daddy said, his voice as equally as low. "I think he's wishin' today was his wedding day."

"Makes two of us," Lee said before he could censor himself.

Daddy put his hand on Lee's shoulder and waited. Lee knew this tactic, but he still took an extra moment to look his father in the eye. "Lee, you're a good man, with a good head on your shoulders and a good heart in your chest. If you want this." He indicated Travis in front of the full-length mirror across the room, pure joy streaming from him. "You'll get it."

"Thanks, Daddy," Lee murmured. "I know you just met her, but what's your first impression of Rosalie?"

"I think she suits you, son," Daddy said just as Will turned toward them.

"What are you two whispering about over there?" he demanded. "Get over here. Trav wants to do a family prayer."

"The girls aren't here," Lee pointed out, and he could've withered to dead under Will's glare. He could've —and should've—kept his mouth shut. "Sorry." He reached into his inside jacket pocket and pulled out a jewelry box. "Travis, I brought these for you."

His youngest brother took the box, his eyes wide. "What are they?"

"Open it."

He did, and he sucked in his breath. "Lee, these are granddad's."

"They're yours now," Lee said. "Actually, I thought maybe Will would wear them when he marries Gretchen, and if I ever get married again, I can have them back." He caught a glimpse of the cufflinks in the box as Travis tilted it for Will to see.

Both of them looked up at him simultaneously, and Lee hated this part of being in his family. Everyone looked at him like he should know more than them, that he should be the one saying all the wise and deep things, that he should have counsel for them.

"Or you can keep them if you want."

"I'd love to wear them," Will said softly, all the fight gone from him just like that.

"Of course we'll pass them around," Trav said. "Daddy, can you help me?"

Daddy's fingers only shook for the first second while he helped Travis get the cufflinks in place. With that done, there was nothing left to do or say.

"It's time, Trav," Will said, and the four of them stepped in closer to each other, the group hug happening spontaneously.

"I love you guys," Travis said. "Thank you for bein' here. I know it's not easy for anyone."

"We're fine," Lee said, desperately wishing that were true. He could pretend for Travis. He could.

"I'll get Mama," Daddy said.

"Gretchen will let Shay know when you're ready," Will said.

Lee didn't have a job, so he just followed everyone out of the room, his spirits high because of the good thing he'd done with the cufflinks. He offered his arm to Rosalie, and they went across the lane to the tent where the ceremony would take place.

Travis and Shay weren't having anyone walk down the aisle in front of her. Her daddy was escorting her, and apparently she had some sisters and sisters-in-law that could cause problems, so she'd opted to simply not have a wedding party.

Lee smiled at Miss Mildred and Jenni-Lynn as he went toward the front row behind Rissa and Spence. They went all the way to the end of the first row, and he was glad he wouldn't be front and center.

Will and Gretchen sat next to him, and Cherry had disappeared somewhere. Mama and Daddy sat on the other side of the aisle, right on the edge, and Trav stood at the altar. Everything dripped flowers and ribbons, from the pillars in this tent to the tables and chairs in the two adjoining tents. The catering company had set up in the fourth and final tent, and Lee hadn't checked in there to see if everything had been covered in dusky rose and forest green. Travis wore the colors on his lapel, as did Lee. Rosalie and every other woman had pink and purple flowers on their wrist. Hers actually matched her dress perfectly, and Lee took a moment to soak in the curves of her legs as she crossed them under that sexy dress.

He'd barely started to feel like everyone had stopped staring at him when country music came blasting through the speakers someone had rigged in the corners of the tent. Travis started to laugh, and Lee wasn't sure if he should watch his brother or turn to ogle the bride as she waltzed down the aisle.

It was more of a line dance, besides.

Everyone stood and started to clap, as if they were all at a weekend dance. Lee had no idea what to do, because he didn't *clap* at a wedding. He stood there, straight-faced, while Shay danced down the aisle—alone—toward Travis.

He received her into his arms, the two of them laughing together. Lee could tell that they'd shut everyone else out. This was their day, and they could only see one another. He glanced at Rosalie, who had both hands pressed over her heart, her face radiating emotions Lee couldn't even fathom.

"They're so wonderful together," she said as the crowd started to settle down. Lee took his seat along with most everyone else. She smoothed her skirt and leaned closer to him. "I have to admit, I feel better seeing you stand there, still and silent, at your own brother's wedding."

Lee jerked his head toward her. "I..." He had no excuse, that was what he had.

Rosalie looped her arm through his again and leaned against his bicep. "I'm teasing, Lee."

The ceremony started, and Lee did his best to focus on Trav and Shay. It was hard with Rosalie so close, the scent of her skin, her hair, and her perfume filling the air around him. When the pastor announced Trav and Shay husband and wife, Lee was the first to whistle through his teeth and bring his hands together in a single, loud, booming clap.

He looked at Rosalie, his eyebrows raised as if to say, *Good enough?*

She blinked and then burst into laughter, all while clapping appropriately with the rest of the wedding guests.

HOURS LATER, LEE WAS READY TO SHUT HIMSELF IN A DARK, padded room for the next two weeks. He didn't people very well, and certainly not for so long. Night had fallen hours ago, and he'd left Ford at Mama's so he could take Rosalie home.

The closer he got to her house, the more nervous he became. "Is Autumn home?" he asked.

"Yes," she said in the darkness, only the glow from the dashboard lighting her features. "My nanny came today. They'll probably both be asleep on the couch." The hint of a smile came his way, and Lee nodded.

He couldn't think of anything else to say that wasn't about Martha, so when he only had a couple more turns before they'd arrive at Rosalie's house, he took a breath and steeled himself to speak. "My wife and I broke up after she cheated on me," he said. "Turned out she didn't like the farm life as much as she'd claimed to, and she found someone else more exciting."

"No," Rosalie said, her voice made mostly of shocked air. "Lee, I'm so sorry." Her hand covered his, and Lee turned his over so their palms pressed together.

"We're actually better apart," he said. "We get along great. Co-parent and all of that."

"That's good, I suppose," Rosalie said. "Still. That leaves a wound."

She had no idea, so Lee said nothing. He made the last turn, and her house came into view. The porch lights illuminated the front door, and he'd feel like he was on a stage, under a spotlight, if he kissed her there.

Don't do it, his mind screamed at him. All of the pork tenderloin and smoked salmon he'd eaten at Travis's ritzy wedding dinner threatened to make a reappearance as he parked in the driveway. He didn't want to open the door and let the rest of the world in, but Rosalie had to get out.

"I'll come get the door," he said, hastening to do just that. When he opened the door, he stayed back only far enough for Rosalie to turn and slide to the ground. Then he took her into his arms right there in the driveway, the only light coming from the weak overhead bulb inside the cab of his truck.

"Thank you," he whispered. "For coming with me today. For giving me so much time. For putting up with the completely insane family I belong to."

Rosalie swayed with him in the semi-darkness, and Lee understood what it felt like to block out the rest of the world. He suddenly knew how Trav and Shay could look at one another the way they did. He told himself he wasn't falling in love with Rosalie already, but the truth was, he was definitely sliding in that direction.

"I had a wonderful time," she murmured, her lips right against his collar. "Sure, your family might be a little crazy, but whose isn't?"

Lee pulled back a little and looked into her eyes. He wanted to ask her about that kiss, but he didn't need to. They definitely seemed to be on the same page tonight, and when he leaned down this time, Rosalie rose up to meet him.

He hadn't kissed a woman in a while—she'd spoken true about that. He prayed with the fierceness of a mama bear that he'd do a good enough job to warrant another date and that this kiss would indeed be fun for both of them.

When his lips touched hers, *fun* wasn't the right word. Explosive, maybe. Hot, definitely.

He finally settled on *passionate* as he kneaded her closer and kissed her deeper. Lee had been dreaming about this kiss for days and weeks, and he'd lost his head once over it.

Tonight, he stayed very much in the moment, because he didn't want to miss a single, feather-light touch of her fingertips along his hairline, or the way she breathed in with him, moved with him, kissed him back like she'd been fantasizing about kissing him too.

He finally pulled away, his lips feeling swollen and hot. He had no idea what to say, because Lee didn't talk just to hear his own voice. He tucked one of Rosalie's curls behind her ear, where it promptly popped back out, smiled at her, and kissed her again.

CHAPTER FIFTEEN

osalie wasn't sure if she was kissing Lee Cooper or fighting with him for control to be able to kiss him. She experienced a flurry of fireworks up and down her spine, and she finally let him maintain the speed at which he kissed her.

He held her right where he wanted her, and Rosalie didn't fight that. She felt stronger from leaning into his broad chest, and he made her feel like a cherished queen with the way he deepened their kiss and then slowed it almost to a crawl.

She couldn't quite think clearly, and the only indication she had of where she stood was a brief breeze that skimmed her skin. She could only feel Lee. Taste Lee. Smell Lee. Hear Lee.

He pulled away again, and Rosalie wondered where

her capability had gone. It had all melted to nothing inside this cowboy's arms, and she didn't even mind it.

"You're incredible," he whispered, touching his mouth to her jawline and then her neck. "Thank you again." He straightened and took her hand in his, stepping back and allowing her to move away from his truck. He stooped and picked up her clutch, which she hadn't even realized she'd dropped.

Right. He hadn't even walked her up to the door yet. Rosalie took her tiny purse and gained strength with every step she took, and she cast a glance to Tess's house next door once she reached the porch. The light bulbs she'd put in her outdoor sockets flooded the whole porch as if the person standing there were an actor on the stage.

"You don't need to thank me," she finally said. "I enjoyed the wedding." She wanted to tell him she enjoyed being with him, which was distinctly different than liking an event. He'd been able to open his mouth and say what he thought, but Rosalie honestly didn't know how.

His phone chimed, and Lee flinched slightly. "I'll call you tomorrow?" He lifted his eyebrows and waited for Rosalie to nod. Then he dipped closer and kissed her again, this time keeping it short and somewhat chaste. The man had no idea what power he held over her, nor how weak his mouth against hers made her, because he stepped back quickly and adjusted his cowboy hat. "Good night, Rose."

"'Night, Lee," she said, placing both hands on her

clutch. She watched him saunter back to his truck, noting how slowly he went tonight. That gait was nothing like the horrible stride she'd seen the first time he'd dropped her off. He looked back when he reached his truck, and when he caught her staring, he lifted his hand, smiled, and got behind the wheel.

Rosalie turned and opened the front door before she made a bigger fool of herself. She'd already taken a couple of steps before she remembered the gate keeping Thumper from sprint-hopping out, and she couldn't lift her leg at the last minute.

She toppled forward, crying out and tossing her clutch so she could use both hands to catch herself. The gate wasn't meant to hold the weight of a grown woman, and the two of them crashed to the floor, her legs still out on the porch and the rest of her inside the house.

"My goodness," Charity said. A flurry of activity happened, but Rosalie wasn't sure what it was. All she could see was darkness, and pain fired up her legs as she realized what had happened.

"Momma?" Autumn said sleepily.

"Rosalie," Charity hurried toward her now, and together, they got her disentangled from the fallen gate. A single stomp made Rosalie's blood turn cold.

"Get him, Autumn," she said, her voice still a bit breathless from all the kissing and then the falling. She pulled her legs into the house, and Charity kicked the gate out onto the porch. She slammed the front door just as Thumper went flying past Autumn.

He came to a stand-still, and how he knew the front door was open and could be used as an escape, Rosalie didn't know. The house sat in silence, and then Rosalie started laughing. Her feet hurt, and her knees smarted, but at least she didn't have to go running around the neighborhood at midnight, wearing her dazzling, bejeweled gown, to chase down a white rabbit who didn't seem to like being indoors.

She accepted Charity's help to get to her feet, but she left her heels on the floor in the corner. "Come here, baby," she said to Autumn, and the little girl flew into her arms. She drew in a deep, lemony breath of her daughter and pushed her hair back off her face. "Were you a good girl tonight?"

"She was an angel," Charity said. "As usual."

"We did fingerpaints," Autumn said, squishing Rosalie's face with her hands. "Momma, your face is funny."

Rosalie giggled and shook her head to get Autumn's hands away. "Come on," she said, bending to put the child back on the floor. "I'll help you into bed." She glanced over to Charity, who'd just reached for her purse.

Charity met her eye and very clearly wiped her hand along her mouth. Horror struck Rosalie right behind her breastbone, and her first instinct was to touch her own mouth and figure out what sat out of place. She did, but she couldn't tell just by feel.

"Tell Miss Charity good-bye," she said, releasing Autumn's hand.

Autumn ran over to her nanny, and Charity's love for the girl filled the house as she hugged her. "Monday?" she said to Rosalie, who nodded.

"I'll have her at the office. You can come whenever." Rosalie would pay Charity through an app, and she'd add on a big tip for staying so late tonight. *And last night,* her mind whispered at her as Charity opened the front door and stepped out in quick succession.

"Come on, baby."

Autumn came back to Rosalie and put her hand in hers. "I'm not tired, Momma."

"Then you can come lay in my bed until you are," she said, smiling at her daughter. Autumn would be out in less than ten minutes, but Rosalie didn't care if she slept in the same bed as her tonight. "I'll change my clothes and come lay by you."

Autumn skipped down the hall at Rosalie's side, and she lifted her daughter into the bed on the side where James had once slept. She'd washed everything many times since the divorce, and now that she'd moved her clothes onto his side of the closet, there wasn't much of him remaining in the house at all.

Rosalie leaned down and kissed her daughter's forehead as she snuggled into the thick comforter. "Don't go to sleep, baby," she said. "I want to hear about the painting. I just need to go change and wash my face." She walked away, knowing full-well that Autumn would be asleep by the time she returned.

She shed her dress and hung it in the closet. As the hot water ran over a washcloth, she slipped out of her gown underclothes and into regular ones before putting on a comfortable pair of pajamas the color of banana skins. She could sleep as late as she wanted in the morning, which was a good thing considering how much exhaustion tugged at her eyelids.

She stepped out of the closet and in front of the sink, finally allowing herself to look into her own eyes. She felt different than she had an hour ago. She wasn't sure what the difference was, only that she'd finally been kissed by Lee, and that had definitely sent her world skittering off its regular axis.

Her gaze drifted down to her lips, and she saw what Charity had. *Your face is funny, Momma.* Even Autumn had seen the stain.

Her lipstick had been smeared off her bottom lip, and Rosalie reached up to touch the spot on her face where it didn't belong. Lee had kissed her so thoroughly and completely that Rosalie couldn't help the flush as it worked its way up through her stomach, chest, and throat. He'd practically drank her right up, and Rosalie wanted him to do it again, right now.

Instead, she went through her nightly skincare

routine, and fifteen minutes later, she returned to her bedroom, her mind still stuck in some sort of revolving thought pattern which could only feature Lee.

Autumn snoozed on her side of the bed, and Rosalie smiled fondly at her. She picked up her phone to make sure her daily alarm was off, and she found texts from Lee. A grin burst onto her face as she swiped to read them fully.

What time is too early to call? he'd asked. *I'll be up to do the morning milking about five, and I'm assuming that's too early.*

The timestamp told her he hadn't even waited to leave her driveway before he'd sent this message.

Her fingers flew across the screen. *Five is too early, Handsome. Aren't you tired?* It wasn't even her family wedding, and she was exhausted.

Her phone vibrated, and her pulse jumped into the back of her throat. She glanced at Autumn and then tiptoed in a hurry out of her bedroom, swiping on Lee's call once she made it to the hallway. "Hey," she whispered. The blue light from the clock displays in the kitchen beckoned to her, and she kept moving. She suddenly felt sixteen again, sneaking away from her parents' bedroom to take a midnight phone call from her boyfriend.

With a jolt, she realized that was exactly what she was doing.

"Hey," Lee said in a normal tone. "Is six too early?"

Rosalie giggled and shook her head, finally arriving in her kitchen. "I only saw these texts because I was turning off my alarm."

"So six is too early."

"Mm hm."

"Do y'all go to church?"

"Sometimes," Rosalie said. "I wasn't planning on it tomorrow."

"All right," he said. "Well, I'll call you tomorrow, sometime after...seven."

"Lee."

"Eight."

She laughed under her breath again, and he said, "Fine, nine," with plenty of happiness in his voice too.

"'Bye, Handsome," she said, sobering. "Drive safe."

"I'm already home," he said. "Sitting outside my cabin, talkin' to you."

"Go in and go to bed," she said. "You like to pretend like you're super-human, but I know you're tired."

"Yes, ma'am," he said, and just like that, he made her feel like the one in control of this relationship. Rosalie hadn't realized that she needed a measure of power in her romantic relationships until that moment, and she pulled the phone away from her ear.

The seconds continued to click up, and when she put the device back in place, Lee still wasn't speaking. "I mean it, Lee," she said. "I don't want to deal with you when you're all surly and sour. And I know that comes when a man like you doesn't get the proper amount of rest."

"I'm goin' in right now," he said. "Night, my rose." He hung up this time, and Rosalie let her arm fall back to her side.

My rose.

Oh, how she wanted to be his. At the same time, he gave her permission to be herself too, and Rosalie had never really had that until James had left. Even then, he hadn't listened to her. She hadn't wanted the divorce, and just like everything in their relationship, James decided for her.

Lee hadn't been willing to give up control of their kiss, but he hadn't seemed like that dominance would bleed into other parts of their relationship. A sigh came from her mouth as she started back toward her bedroom. All she could think about was what life would be like if he'd come inside with her instead of driving back to his cabin.

If they were married, and they didn't have to part at the strike of midnight, how different would her life be? How different would Autumn's life be?

Rosalie climbed between the sheets of her bed, which had always been a luxury to her. Now, it felt cold and somber as she reached to switch off the lamp and then closed her eyes. A fantasy played behind her eyelids, and it wasn't of Lee coming inside this house with her. It was of her and Autumn following him inside that pretty log cabin out on the edge of the woods. Her final thought before she drifted away was of how Thumper could possibly survive out there with the threat of coyotes and dogs.

"Say thank you," Rosalie prompted as Tess handed the flowered dish of butter to Autumn.

"Thank you, Tess," Autumn said dutifully, and Rosalie went back to spreading the raspberry jam on her scone.

"You're welcome, sweetie," Tess said, smiling at the little girl. Her attention switched to Rosalie, who quickly took a bite of her pastry. "How was the wedding?"

Rosalie nodded in an over-emphasized way, glancing at Tess's husband, Frank. He didn't seem to care about the conversation, and he helped their son with his quiche and looked back at his phone.

She lifted one hand to hide the food in her mouth. "Good," she said, hoping that would be the end of it.

"The Coopers know how to throw a party," Tess said. "Or so I've heard." She seemed to be fishing for something, but Rosalie didn't know what.

"How was the movie?" she asked, trying to get the conversation onto something else. Yes, the wedding had been wonderful. The kiss with the cowboy phenomenal. The dreams vivid. He'd called her that morning too, not one minute past nine o'clock, and Rosalie could still feel the vibrations of his laughter over the phone.

He'd wanted to see her that day, but Rosalie didn't want to try to find someone to babysit Autumn. Running her business and being a single mother had been hard enough for Rosalie from Day One, and adding a boyfriend to the mix sure hadn't made anything easier.

Lee hadn't suggested that he could meet Autumn, but Rosalie knew he wouldn't mind if the girl tagged along while they strolled around his ranch, hand-in-hand, talking the afternoon hours away. Instead, Rosalie had gotten a text from Tess about this brunch, and she'd opted for that.

Now, she was second-guessing everything in her life. Autumn was young; she wouldn't even know what a boyfriend was. Rosalie was allowed to date. For some reason, Rosalie didn't feel ready to take Lee to that level yet.

"It was great," Tess said, her voice doing that high-pitched raising thing it did when she was trying to be cool and casual. Really, she had something to say—something that Rosalie wouldn't like. "We missed you and Autumn, but it was okay."

Rosalie understood this code, but she wasn't going to let Tess guilt her into going to the movies with her instead of out with Handsome on a Friday night. "We'll have to go see it again," she said, reaching over to tap Baylor, Tess's boy, on the head. "Right, Bay? You'll come with us to see *Left Right* again, won't you?"

"Can I, Dad?" Baylor asked, and Rosalie grinned at

him. When she looked back at Tess, she didn't miss the knowing glint in her eyes.

Rosalie calmly took a bite of her quiche and said, "Tess, this is *so* good. You have to give me the recipe."

"Good luck," Frank said, finally looking up from his phone. "She doesn't give it to anyone."

"I would," Tess said slowly. She locked eyes with Rosalie again. "For the right payment." Her eyebrows went up, but Rosalie shook her head. "Fine," Tess said into her next bite of brunch.

Rosalie was finally left alone to enjoy her perfectly baked broccoli cheese quiche, but her insecurities about why she needed more time before she introduced Autumn to Lee wouldn't stop needling her.

CHAPTER SIXTEEN

Lee grunted as he lifted the hay bale from the field to the trailer, immediately moving to get to the next one. He followed behind Mack and Gary, who both worked on his side of the tractor towing the trailer. Will and Trav and Chris worked the other side. Lee rarely worked the agricultural side of the farm, but when the hay needed to be brought in, they pulled over everyone they could find, including him.

He'd worked the farm for the past thirty-five years, and most days, he thought he was completely immune to the heat and humidity in the Coastal Bend of Texas. Today, he'd been wrong about that. Today, he felt like his skin had turned to wax and was slowly melting off his bones.

He told himself to keep moving. Pick up a bale, throw

it up on the trailer. Two more cowboys worked up there, arranging the bales into neat stacks they'd then have to unload and put on the conveyor up to the hay loft.

Lee would have to get back to the administration office before that happened, but he knew the rest of his men would keep working until this field was cleared and put away. He didn't dare look up and around to estimate how many hours that would take. He'd done every job there was to do at Sweet Water Falls Farm, something Daddy had made sure all of the boys had done. That way, they could appreciate what they were asking their cowboys and cowgirls to do.

They didn't currently employ any cowgirls, which made housing a lot easier for Lee. They'd reached their maximum of clients for their milk and cream too, and Lee, Clarissa, and Will worked the morning shift to get their daily orders satisfied. Travis oversaw the entire milking operation, and Lee had missed his brother's presence and administration help while he'd been on his honeymoon.

Trav and Shay had certainly entertained the family for the past two Sunday afternoons with stories of all their fun in the Canadian Rockies. Lee could admit he'd like to travel more, especially to a climate with mountains and snow. He'd only seen such things once, when he'd gone to Salt Lake City for their new milking system training.

"Ho, there," someone yelled, and the steady growling of the tractor waned. Everyone looked up and toward the sound of the voice, and Lee found Floyd riding a horse toward them. Lee needed more time in the saddle, out under the evening sky, nothing but stars and constellations between him and the Lord.

That was where he did his best thinking, and that was where he'd remembered who he was and what he wanted out of life. Years ago, it was where he'd felt strongly that he needed to cut Martha loose from this life she hadn't liked, and Lee had always found solutions to his parenting troubles while on the back of his horse.

Rosalie wasn't really a trouble, nor a problem. Lee drove to town more often now than he had in six years, even when he'd been dating other women. He sure liked seeing her, and the way he'd jogged over to her in the grocery parking lot a couple of nights ago, swept her off her feet while she giggled, and then kissed her in broad daylight spoke of that.

He tossed his bale of hay onto the wagon and started to go around it. The difference in motion—he was now walking against its movement instead of with it—made a powerful wave of vertigo hit him, and Lee threw his hand out to catch himself. On what, he had no idea.

Lee knew he was going to fall before it happened, but he couldn't stop himself. His gloved fingers scrambled along the edge of the trailer, but they couldn't catch it. He stumbled to his knees, and then went all the way to the ground as the world spun and spun and spun.

Voices called out, and he wasn't sure if one of them was his or not. He pressed his eyes closed, the strangest feelings zipping through him. The way Ford's rice crispy cereal popped and crackled in his milk in the morning was how bright spots of light seemed on the backs of his eyelids.

Everything twirled, and Lee felt the astronomically fast rotation of the Earth as he lay on it, unable to move. Someone touched his arm, and he jerked away from the pressure. Somewhere in the back of his mind, his name came through in Will's voice, but he couldn't answer.

More shouting, and Lee just wanted them to all be quiet. He was fine. He just needed a minute to breathe.

He tried to pull in the air he needed, and slowly the spinning stopped. So had the tractor and all the yelling. He opened his eyes and found boots nearby. Several pairs, almost like everyone had lined up to protect him from something.

He groaned as he tried to sit up, and Travis appeared in his vision. "Stay down," he said firmly, even pushing Lee back with his palm against his shoulder.

"Don't push me," Lee growled as he tried to resist Trav's force. He couldn't, and he fell back onto the ground. His chest heaved, and he looked up into the cloudless sky, wondering how he'd come to be in this position.

"He's awake," Trav yelled, and boots came crunching through the dry hayfield. Will crouched down, and Lee tilted his head to look at his other brother. He held a phone to his ear.

"Yes, he's awake," he said.

"I'm fine," Lee said. "Just a little dizzy."

"He says he's dizzy." Will pulled the phone away from his ear. "When did you eat last?"

"I...don't know."

Will frowned at him, stood, and walked a couple of paces away. Lee couldn't change the fact that his brain wasn't working all the way at the moment, and he did feel better down on the ground. His mouth felt like it had been stuffed full of cotton and bandages, all chemically and dry and gross. He gagged, and Trav hurried to roll him onto his side.

"Will!" he yelled, and Will came trotting back. "He's gonna throw up."

"Did he hit his head?"

"No," Lee groaned, trying to curl into himself. "I didn't hit my head."

"He didn't," another cowboy confirmed.

"Then why is he nauseous?" Will demanded.

"It could be the heat," Trav said. "A head injury isn't the only reason someone throws up out here."

"You're sure he didn't hit his head?"

"I didn't hit my blasted head," Lee yelled into the argument. "I just need to eat. Something to drink."

"Here, Boss." Gary crouched down in front of him, a dripping bottle of water in his hand. He wore a look of concern and compassion, and Lee thought Trav and Will could take a leaf from the foreman's book.

Lee took the bottle and lifted it to Gary. The cool plastic soothed him, and he pressed the bottle to his forehead before taking a long drink. Some of the life he normally had returned, and Lee handed the empty bottle back to Gary.

"Thanks," Travis said, and Lee realized too late that he should've thanked Gary for the water. He reached out, and Gary offered him his hand. He pulled Lee to his feet, and Lee met the man's eyes. They were about the same age, but Gary had a wife and two teen boys. They all lived here on the farm, and Lee had been so consumed in his own family he hadn't taken much time to get to know the foreman.

Gary worked the agriculture side of the ranch, so Will knew him better. Still, Lee could be gracious and kind. "Thank you," he said, hearing how lame and late the words were as they left his mouth.

"'Course," Gary said. "You're probably dehydrated." He signaled to someone, and Floyd came over. "I'm gonna have Floyd take you to your truck." The dark-haired cowboy took off his hat and wiped his black hair back before reseating the Stetson. "All you boys best be goin'." He looked at Travis and Will, nodding each time.

Will was still on the phone with the emergency operator, but he nodded back.

"Why?" Lee asked. "We have work to do."

"You just fainted," Travis said.

"I did not," Lee shot back. "I started to go the wrong way to see what Floyd needed, and I got dizzy. That's all."

No one said anything in the expanse of silence after his sentence, and Lee looked around at all of them. He took one big breath after another. "Did I pass out?" he asked the closest man to him, who was Gary.

"I think so, Boss," he said.

"You definitely did," Mack said. "I said your name and shook your shoulder, and nothing."

Humiliation burned through Lee. He never lost control. He never showed weakness outside the walls of his own cabin. The frown lines between his eyes deepened, and he lowered his head. "I just got a little vertigo."

"You can't be out here if you didn't eat," Gary said. "And we have strict drinking rules."

"I've been drinkin'," Lee said. "I ate breakfast."

"Probably six or seven hours ago," Gary said, nodding to Floyd. "He didn't hear what you said."

Lee switched his gaze to the man who'd arrived on horseback, and he knew instantly that the news was not good. Floyd only added to the stress and anxiety already floating in the air by swallowing and exchanging a glance with Mack, then Gary.

"It's your mama," he said. "She wasn't doing well, and your daddy loaded her up and took her to the hospital."

Panic spiked inside Lee's chest, and he spun toward Travis. "Let's go." He took a couple of long strides to his brother, suddenly wanting to grab onto someone and hold them as tightly as possible. He did that to Travis, who stood still and straight, so much like a statue, and gripped him back.

Lee didn't know what to say. He didn't know what to do. He shouldn't be the one breaking down right now. Everyone looked to him to be the strongest, the toughest, the very best. He shouldn't need comfort from Travis or Will or Gary or anyone.

As Lee stood there in the near-June Texas heat, afraid to let go of his younger brother just in case he broke, he realized how very fragile he'd become.

"We've known she wouldn't make it forever," Will finally said, and Lee opened his eyes to find him standing only a pace away. He wore shutters over everything he must be feeling, and Lee found the courage to step away from his brother.

"We don't even know what's going on," Travis said, his voice slightly higher than normal. "We have to go find out."

"The emergency operator wouldn't tell me anything," Will said. "Said it's a different system."

"We'll call the hospital on the way in," Lee said, reaching up to brush at his eyes just in case he'd teared up. He hadn't, and relief flowed through him. He turned back to Gary and the other cowboys. "Gary, I'm sorry."

"Go," Gary said. "No need to apologize. We've got things here."

Lee nodded once, put on his own stone mask, and faced his brothers again. He said nothing as he started for the corner of the field where he'd parked his truck. Will had come with him, but Trav had driven himself and a couple of other cowboys out to the harvest. The jangling of keys met his ears, and Trav said, "I'll come get it later."

He jogged to catch up to Will and Lee, and none of them spoke. Lee had no idea what they were thinking, but he couldn't accept the fact that he couldn't eat lunch with Mama and Daddy every day. That he couldn't find the relief he'd always found with the two of them.

Yes, Mama had been sick for a long time. She'd fought really hard. He'd known. They'd all known, but that didn't make anything going on around him any easier.

The storm in his chest grew and grew until he couldn't contain it. He broke into a run, ignoring Will as he called after him. He reached the truck first and banged against the hood like he could pound out his frustration and horror at what might happen that day.

Boom, boom, boom!

He got in the truck and started it, anxious to be going. His brothers walked still, and Lee didn't know how they could be so calm. He knew they weren't. They just dealt with things differently. Trav would need to yell at some point, and Will would box it all away until he put on his running shorts tomorrow morning.

His phone rang, and Rosalie's name sat there. Lee didn't have a spare inch in his mind for her right now, but he swiped on the call. "Hey." Even he could admit his voice barked at her instead of greeted her.

"Oh, uh, hey," she said. "What's going on?"

Lee didn't know how to adequately explain. Will and Trav neared, and he maybe had ten seconds to talk to Rosalie alone. "I can't talk right now," he said, his voice gruff.

"You sound upset."

"Do I, Rose? I suppose that's because I am upset." He shook his head. "I can't talk." He'd already said this.

Will reached the passenger door and opened it.

"I have to go." Lee hung up and tossed his phone up on the dashboard. Will looked at it and slid all the way over so Travis could get in up front too. Lee strangled the steering wheel, wishing they lived closer to town.

"In?" he asked.

"Almost," Trav said. Finally the door slammed shut, and Lee stomped on the accelerator.

"Lee," Will said.

"What?" he barked. "We have to go. You two were walkin' in the park, for crying out loud!"

"We were not," Travis said. "Pull yourself together."

"I am pulled together," Lee yelled. "Don't tell me to pull myself to together. *I'm* the one who holds *everything* together! All the time!"

Trav started to argue, but Will held up his hand. Silence poured into the cab, and they all knew Lee wasn't really mad at Will or Trav. He wasn't mad at himself. He wasn't mad at Mama. He was just mad.

They also all knew that it wasn't Lee who held everything together at Sweet Water Falls Farm.

It was Mama, and without her, they were in very real danger of splintering.

CHAPTER SEVENTEEN

Rosalie couldn't wait to get out of her heels. She'd been on her feet all day at a warehouse about an hour from Sweet Water Falls. Her newest game was set to hit shelves at the end of July, and she'd wanted to be present to go over the final details. She simply hadn't been able to tell the cardboard quality, nor the true colors, via email or video.

She'd stopped at the small, organic grocer on the outskirts of Sweet Water Falls on her way home, because they had aluminum foil trays of ready-made meals that only needed heating. She normally didn't mind her time in the kitchen, as she used it as a form of detoxing from the day. There was just something about following a recipe and putting together a bunch of isolated ingredients to make something delicious and satisfying.

She supposed it gave her hope that she wouldn't have to be isolated for her whole life either. That she could mix and blend with another human being and make the relationship stick this time in a delicious and satisfying way.

Of course she thought of Lee as she perused the fresh lasagnas, chicken burritos, and mini meatloaves. She'd called him yesterday to see if he could possibly get off the farm a little early and take her to dinner, but he'd clearly been upset and beyond busy. He'd been barky and short with her, and Rosalie had stared at her dark phone screen for a solid twenty seconds after he'd hung up.

She hadn't attempted to call him back, and she'd put together a chicken pot pie last night that any chef would've been envious of. She'd eaten it with Charity and Autumn, wondering if she should ask the twenty-something for more dating advice.

In the end, she hadn't, and Rosalie fully expected to hear from Lee tonight. *Or maybe he'll go silent again*, she thought as she finally selected a tray of Southwest stuffed peppers. She'd always loved food like this, and Autumn didn't balk at anything either. She wouldn't have to make a vegetable, and Rosalie pushed her cart toward the dairy section to get another gallon of milk.

As she went, she asked herself what she would do if Lee decided not to call her back. Would she call him? Drive out there? Let him retreat while he dealt with whatever had made him upset?

She honestly didn't know, because her head and her

heart seemed to be in a constant battle with each other. She didn't want to be too needy. She didn't want to be too casual. Nothing about her month-long relationship with the handsome cowboy was casual for her. He didn't kiss her like he thought of her casually either, and Rosalie clung to that as she got her milk, butter, and cheese and turned toward the checkstands.

She hadn't even taken a step before she saw Ford Cooper standing in front of her. A smile sprang onto her face. "Ford," she said pleasantly, wondering if Lee was in this grocer right now. She knew Cooper & Co produced a high standard of organic milk, so he could definitely shop here.

Something nagged at her mind, but she couldn't quite place it yet. "Are you here alone?" she asked, moving her scanning eyes back to him.

"With my mom," he said, indicating a dark-haired woman leaning over a refrigerated case to get something out of it. Rosalie stared at her, trying to drink in all the details of the woman in only a couple of breaths.

The woman straightened and turned to find Ford, seeing him standing with Rosalie. "Ford," she said, gesturing him over to her. "Let's go, baby. We got the ground beef." Her eyes traveled up to Rosalie's, and she stuck the professional game designer smile to her face.

She stepped past her cart and put her hand on Ford's back. "Will you introduce me, Ford?"

"Yes, ma'am," he said in his dutiful voice. They walked

the few steps over to Martha, and Ford waved at Rosalie. "Mama, this is Daddy's girlfriend. Rosalie."

Martha's mouth opened slightly. Shock traveled across her face. She looked from Rosalie to Ford and back. She snapped her mouth shut and steered her son back to her side in a somewhat possessive move. "Hello," she said.

"So nice to meet you," Rosalie said, laying on the gush a little thick. "I see where Ford gets his dark lashes."

"Lee's lashes are plenty dark," Martha said. She wasn't exactly cold, but she certainly wasn't warm. Rosalie wasn't sure why. Lee had said Martha had been dating for years and years. In fact, she had a fairly serious boyfriend according to her ex-husband. "How long have you and Lee been seeing each other?"

She wanted to stretch the time all of a sudden. "Oh, a little over—about a month," Rosalie said, unable to tell a lie. He still hadn't met Autumn, but Rosalie was getting closer and closer to that.

Martha kept her mouth shut and nodded. She kept her arm around her son's shoulders, though Ford didn't stand that much shorter than her. "It was nice to meet you," she said, starting to turn.

"Are you here gettin' my dad dinner?" Ford asked.

"Ford," Martha said sharply.

"What?" the boy asked. "You said Daddy wouldn't eat at the hospital. Maybe Rosalie is gettin' him and the uncles something to eat."

Confusion ran through Rosalie. "The hospital?" she asked, hating being on the outside of this information. Both Martha and Ford clearly knew already.

Martha could've shot fire from her eyes, first at her son and then Rosalie. She was a Texas mama bear through and through. Rosalie had some experience with women like her, and she backed up a step. "Good to see you, Ford," she said. "Nice to meet you, ma'am." She nodded at Lee's ex-wife and turned back to her cart.

She could call Lee and get the information from him. Back behind her cart, she realized Martha hadn't moved. She now wore a look of compassion on her face that didn't fit the earlier interaction.

"Lee hasn't told you, has he?" she asked as Rosalie approached.

"No," Rosalie said. "I suppose he hasn't."

"His mama is in the hospital," Martha said. "He told me this afternoon when he called to say he couldn't come get Ford tonight for the weekend."

"He doesn't eat in the hospital," Ford said.

"He didn't ask for food, Ford," Martha said, clearly stressed too.

"That doesn't mean we can't take him something," her son said, and Rosalie smiled at the child. He did love his father, that much was evident. Ford glared at his mother, and Rosalie definitely recognized that fire. She'd seen the same look on Lee's face when he spoke to his brothers.

She couldn't help smiling at him. "I'll call him and see if he's eaten."

Martha took a breath and blew it out. "Ford's right. They won't eat in the hospital. The Cooper brothers know how to worry like little old ladies. They'll pace, and they'll argue, but they won't eat."

"I'll take them something," Rosalie said, her mind firing options at her now. One of them was marching straight over to the hospital and verifying what Martha had said. If Lee's mother was so ill she had to be in the hospital, why hadn't he told her?

"Lee worries for the world," Martha said softly, and all Rosalie could do was nod. She had never experienced such humiliation in her life, not even when James had come into their bedroom one morning and said he as moving out.

"I'll get pizza," she said as cheerfully as she could. That would feed all three men, and their daddy too, and Rosalie could get an extra cheese pie for Autumn. The task-master inside her quickly made a list that needed to be accomplished, and she wanted to get started right away.

"Good luck," Martha said, and Rosalie wasn't sure how to take that. She walked away, keen to be out of this grocery store and on her way. She put her items on the short belt leading to the cashier, and she pulled out her phone to call Lee.

He didn't answer, and Rosalie's irritation with the

surly cowboy grew. She paid for her few groceries and headed outside. She called for pizza, then called Charity to let her know the situation. With the fifteen-minute drive home, she'd arrive close to the same time as the pizza, and she could make sure her family was fed before heading over to the hospital.

As she drove back to her house, she called the hospital. "Information," a woman said.

"Yes, hello," she said in as positive of a voice as she could. "I'm wondering if you can tell me what room Chrissy Cooper is in."

"Chrissy Cooper..." the woman repeated. Rosalie made a left turn on Main and wanted to stomp on the accelerator. That wouldn't get the pizza to her house any faster, and she couldn't leave before the food arrived. "She's in room three-twelve."

"Thank you," Rosalie said, barely pushing the words out of her mouth. Anguish and worry snaked through her, barely dampened by her fury with the auburn-haired cowboy who hadn't called her when it was really important.

She wasn't sure if she should slap him across the face as she delivered his dinner or ask the driver to take it to room three-twelve so she didn't have to see him. He obviously didn't want to see her. He didn't want to find comfort in her arms, and the humiliation sliced through her, flooded her, choked her.

She pulled into her driveway and carried the few

groceries into the house, taking care to step over the new gate she'd installed. "I'm home," she called, her own exhaustion starting to make her muscles like marshmallows. She wanted nothing more than to change her clothes and fall onto the couch while her stuffed peppers baked.

Autumn came running toward her, and she'd barely set the groceries on the counter before her daughter clung to her legs. "Momma, you're home."

"I'm home." She bent and lifted her daughter into her arms. "How was the preschool party?" As it was almost summer, the preschool had done a summer kick-off party on a rare Friday. She wouldn't have classes for a couple of weeks, and then the summer programs would start up.

"Good," Autumn said, playing with Rosalie's collar. "I'm hungry, Momma."

"Yes, I am too." She set Autumn on the floor. "I ordered pizza. It should be here soon." She glanced over as Charity started unpacking the groceries. "Thank you, Charity."

"No problem." The blonde college student had been the only person keeping Rosalie sane for the past few months, and she suddenly couldn't hold back her tears. She turned away from everyone and started walking down the hall, the horrible heat in her nose, mouth, and eyes simply awful.

"Momma," Autumn said, but Charity said, "Leave her for a minute, honey."

Rosalie didn't want to break down, but she absolutely couldn't stand to break-up with Lee. *Then don't* rang through her mind. She drew in a breath and wiped the tears from her eyes. She wasn't going to let him walk out of her life the way James had.

She was going to take him and his brothers a pizza, and then she was going to let Lee know that his behavior was unacceptable. She reminded herself that his mama was sick, and she could perhaps give him a pass for the rude phone call. But no matter what, he should've at least communicated with her about what was going on. She should've never had had to find out from his son and ex-wife in the grocery store.

She returned to the kitchen and crouched down despite the pinching in her toes and the ache in her feet. She hugged Autumn and said, "I have to go visit a friend in the hospital tonight," she said. "I ordered pizza for us, and Charity is going to stay with you while I'm gone."

"Who's at the hops..sital?" Autumn asked.

Rosalie grinned at her and booped their noses together. "It's actually my boyfriend, honey. His name is Lee."

"Is he nice?"

"Sometimes," Rosalie said. "He just needs a pizza too, and then I'll come right back, okay?"

"Okay."

Thankfully, the doorbell rang, and Rosalie got to her feet to go get the food. She signed the receipt and handed one box to Charity. She'd have to pay the young woman extra for tonight, and Rosalie knew it was absolutely worth it.

She wanted to start crying again when she met her nanny's eyes, but Charity shook her head with a smile. "We're fine here, Rosalie," she said. "Go figure out what's going on."

"Thank you," Rosalie managed to say, all of her emotions storming through her chest. She wasn't sure she could maintain her composure once she came face-to-face with the man who'd been starring in her daydreams since the math night at the elementary school, and she wasn't sure if it mattered if she did or not.

What she knew was she suddenly understood Lee's hatred of driving and how long it took.

She arrived at the hospital, reached for the two pizzas she'd bought for the Coopers, her own stomach clawing at her and reminding her that she hadn't eaten anything in a while. Her legs shook as she entered the hospital, and she felt only moments away from passing out.

Every step took her closer to the elevator bank, and then down the hall to the block of patient rooms where Lee's mother was. She hadn't fainted and she wasn't going to quit.

If Lee didn't want to be with her, he was going to have to say it right to her face while she held the dinner she'd brought for him. The only thing she regretted as room three-twelve came into view was that she hadn't changed out of her heels.

CHAPTER EIGHTEEN

Lee snapped to attention as the door to Mama's hospital room opened. He'd dozed for a moment there, but the truth was, it could've been an hour. He really had no way of knowing. Time didn't pass correctly in the hospital.

A woman stood framed in the doorway, and Lee decided his eyes didn't work either. "Rosalie?" He glanced over to Mama's bed, where she slept. She'd been doing that a lot over the past two days as her frail physical body tried desperately to fight the virus she'd caught. She had plenty of antibiotics going into her system, and the doctors had been pleased with her progress from last night to this morning.

Lee honestly had no idea what time it was, but Rosalie wore a pair of black slacks, a plaid blouse in dark green and black, and she carried two pizza boxes. His mouth watered instantly, but he wasn't sure if that was because of the woman or the food.

"Lee Cooper," she said, using both of his names in a way only Texas women could do when they were spitting fire, disappointed, or in Rosalie's case, both.

Lee swallowed and ran his hands down his thighs. "What are you doin' here?"

She glanced over to Mama and back to him. "What am I *doin'* here?" She stomped into the room, and that had to hurt in her heels, even as low as they were. She shoved the pizza into his hands, and Lee was so glad he'd sent Will, Trav, and Daddy home for a couple of hours. Of course, Lee had no idea how long they'd been gone, and they could walk in at any moment.

Rosalie's eyes fired at him, but most of all, they shone with...hurt.

Lee turned and set the pizza on the rolling tray where the nurses brought in Mama's meals. She'd been able to eat quite a bit that day, and Lee felt confident they'd be able to go home by Sunday. That was still two more days, but he was determined to get her home by then.

How he could do that, he didn't know, but he'd been praying mighty hard over the past day and a half.

"Your mother is in the hospital," Rosalie said, gesturing to Mama with a fist. "And you didn't tell me?"

"I—"

"No," she said, drawing out the word as she tilted her

head. "You don't get to talk until I'm done. Isn't that what you want, Lee? To remain silent? To do everything yourself? To find comfort in yourself instead of with me? With anyone?"

She threw all the questions at him, one after the other, and Lee could only blink at her. He certainly couldn't argue with her.

"Instead of sending me a text with a sentence or two, I'm shopping after a long, tiring week, *and* a trip down to my manufacturer, and who do I run into? Your son...and your ex-wife. They told me you were here and needed food." She parked her hands on her hips and glared with all the power of gravity. "How do you think that makes me feel?"

Lee hung his head, because he couldn't hide from her. He wore no cowboy hat, and he had no excuse. None besides the fact that he hadn't wanted to worry her. He hadn't wanted to admit to her that he needed anyone to comfort him. "I'm sorry," he mumbled.

"Do you want to break-up with me?" she demanded.

"What?" He looked up and into her eyes. "No."

Her shoulders rose as she took in a long breath. She ran both hands over her hair and let her arms fall to her sides again. "I do not understand you, Lee Cooper." She sounded resigned and defeated, and Lee hated that.

"I didn't want you to worry."

"Not good enough," she said. "All you had to do was say, 'Rose, I'm at the hospital with my family, but things are okay.' Or maybe they're not. I don't know, because *you didn't tell me.*"

Lee didn't dare speak in case she wasn't finished. As he watched the anger and fight drain out of her, he reached for her hand. She resisted him for a moment, then two, and Lee said, "I'm sorry, Rose."

"I'm not sure you get to call me that," she said even as she laced her fingers through his.

"I'm really sorry," he said. "I...I don't want to make any excuses. I wasn't in a good place yesterday."

"Or today," she said.

"Or today," he admitted.

"And your mama?" She looked at Mama with compassion in her eyes, and Lee wondered how Rosalie could let people into her life so easily. "What's going on with her?"

"She has the flu," Lee said, stepping closer to Mama. "With her compromised immune system, she couldn't fight it off. She had another infection, and they're treating that with antibiotics. She's been responding well to those, as well as recovering pretty fast with all the fluids."

Rosalie joined him at the side of Mama's bed. "That's great," she said. Her stomach growled loudly, and Lee looked at her out of the corner of his eye.

"You wanna eat with me?"

She looped her arm through his and leaned into him, making him feel strong and necessary. "If I must," she whispered.

"Rose." He turned and took her in his arms. "I'm

sorry, okay? I've been thinking about you, and I knew you were going to your manufacturer today, and I really just didn't want to bother you or disrupt your life."

She clung to him, and Lee sure did like that. She stepped back and took his face in her hands. "Lee," she said, her eyes searching his. "You should've told me and let me make my own decision."

"I know what you'd have done," he said. "Then you'd be super stressed about your game."

"You have no idea what I'd have done," she said. "You could've explained to me what was going on and how your mom was doing, and I might not have decided to come sit with you today."

"Yes, ma'am," he said. "I should've done that."

She lowered her hands but didn't stop looking at him. "What happened yesterday?"

"I was workin' in the fields," he said. "It was hot, and someone came riding up to tell us about Mama, and I went against the movement of the hay wagon and got a little vertigo."

"He fell down."

Lee and Rosalie both looked toward the door, where Will stood with Daddy.

"You fell down?"

"I stumbled," Lee said.

"You finally called her," Daddy said as he entered the room and came closer, and that wasn't going to help Lee's case. "There's pizza here," he added, his eyebrows going up as he looked at Lee again.

"I brought it," Rosalie said. "For all of you."

"Howdy, Rosalie," Will said, stepping over to give her a kiss on the cheek. "Thanks for the pizza."

"Sure," she said, holding Lee's eyes for an extra moment. He regretted several things in his life, but none more than not texting or calling Rosalie last night. Or this morning.

He watched in wonder as she tugged a few paper plates out of her purse and handed them to Will. Mama started to stir with the increased chatter, and Daddy shifted to attend to her. "Rosalie brought pizza, Chrissy. You want some?"

"She can't eat pizza, Daddy," Will said.

"Why not?" Daddy threw him a dirty look. "The doctors said she could eat what she wanted."

"I'll get her some," Lee said, his own stomach cramping at the sight of the food. He hadn't eaten in a while, because he refused to leave Mama alone. "Looks like Hawaiian, Mama. You love that."

"Yes, please," she whispered, and Lee put a single slice on one of Rosalie's paper plates. He gave her a shy smile as they danced around each other in the microscopic hospital room. Will picked up the boxes of pizza and moved them to the narrow counter in front of the even slimmer window in the back corner of the room.

Lee put Mama's pizza on the rolling tray and moved it so it sat in front of her. "Lift the bed, Daddy."

His dad fumbled with the controls, and Lee's impatience started to crowd into the back of his throat. He told himself not to say anything, because he was already on thin ice with Rosalie. He didn't need to be showing any more surliness in front of her.

He was honestly surprised she'd forgiven him already. One glance at her as Daddy finally remembered how to raise the bed so Mama could sit up and eat, and Lee knew he wasn't out of the doghouse with Rosalie.

"Can I talk to you for a sec?" he asked.

"Trav is on his way," Will said, a piece of supreme pizza in his hand. "You should go home, Lee."

"I'm okay." He moved toward the door, hoping Rosalie would come.

"You haven't been home yet," Daddy said. "You need to go, Lee."

"I'm okay, son," Mama said, and Lee looked between the two of them. He didn't want to leave Mama here. Daddy hadn't stayed over last night, because there was nowhere to sleep, and Lee had caught a couple of hours in the recliner he'd been sitting in when Rosalie had arrived.

Lee took a step back toward them, slipping his hand into Rosalie's. "I'm just gonna talk to Rose for a minute, and then I'll come say good-bye."

Daddy nodded, and Mama took a bite of her pizza. Lee

tugged on Rosalie's hand, and they went out into the hall together.

"You haven't been home?" she asked.

"Daddy couldn't stay last night." He kept walking down the hall, no real destination in mind. "Trav is going to stay tonight. She'll be home soon."

"Lee, I'm so sorry," Rosalie said. "I can *feel* your stress."

He wanted to tell her that was just another reason he hadn't called her. He didn't. "Are we okay, Rose?"

"I suppose," she said. "But Lee, either you want to include me in your life, or you don't."

"I do," he insisted.

"You told Martha."

"Because of Ford."

Rosalie didn't say anything, and she wouldn't look in Lee's direction. "Listen," he said. "I don't know what she said to you, and I really am sorry. I was going to call you tonight. I really was."

They reached the corner, and he turned right to lead them further from the patient rooms. He'd been all over this floor in the past day and a half. A lobby where he'd never seen anyone waited ahead, and he figured he could sit there awhile with his girlfriend.

"She said you worry for the world," Rosalie said.

Lee didn't know how to respond to that. They arrived in the sitting area with a couple of couches and a lot of single chairs. He sat on the couch, glad when Rosalie crowded in beside him. "I don't worry for the world, Rose. Just my family."

"And who worries about you?" she asked.

Lee looked at her, finding her expression open and unassuming. "I don't need anyone to worry for me."

"Yes, you do," she said, giving him an arched eyebrow. "Everyone needs one person to worry for them. You can't let your pride get in the way of letting someone care for *you*, Lee."

Lee gave her another shy smile. "Maybe you could worry for me."

"Maybe I could," she said. They breathed in and out together. "You'll tell me about things in the future? I can't imagine this is the last time your mama is going to be ill."

Lee couldn't hold the weight of her eyes, and he dropped his to study the floor. "I want you to be involved in my life," he said. "I want to be involved in yours." He squared his shoulders, trying to find another well of strength inside. He couldn't, not really. "I'm so tired, Rose." Maybe he could do as she said. Maybe he didn't have to carry everything. Maybe he could let her worry about things for him for a while. Just five minutes would be beneficial.

"Let me take you home," she whispered.

"I don't see how that's possible," he said, lifting his eyes to look at her. "My truck is here."

"You can't borrow a farm truck or something?"

Lee could, absolutely. "I don't want to make you drive

me home, and then drive back to your daughter." He shook his head. "No, I'm fine."

"You're not fine."

"But I will be," he said, smiling at her. "As soon as you kiss me."

Rosalie blinked, her gorgeous eyes broadcasting her surprise. "You think you're so smooth," she said.

"I miss you," he whispered, his smile faltering.

"You'll call me and tell me what's going on from now on," she said, not asking as she let her eyes drift closed as she leaned toward him.

"Yes, ma'am." Lee kissed her, keeping the union slow and sweet. He'd told the truth in all aspects. He *had* missed her the past couple of days, and he *was* going to call her that night. Now, he could only hope that he didn't mess up like this again.

ANOTHER COUPLE OF WEEKS PASSED, AND LEE STOOD AT THE kitchen sink in the farmhouse, washing his hands when the front door opened.

"Hey-ho!" Will yelled. "We're here." His boots clomped on the floor, and he entered the kitchen a couple of moments later, laden with tray upon tray of chocolates.

Lee stepped away from the sink and took a towel from the handle of the oven. "Wow," he said, eyeing the sweets. "What have we got here?"

"These are the truffle choices," Gretchen said, following her fiancé into the back big room of the house with a single tray in her hands. "I made eight flavors, but I really only want to serve four at the wedding."

Will slid his trays onto the counter, and as they were stacked perpendicularly, they didn't smash the candies below them. "Trav said he was almost here."

"Yep." Lee re-hung the towel. "He went to get Shay, and he picked up Rose at her office too." Things with Rosalie had been better over the past dozen days. Lee had kept all of his promises, and when he went to town to pick up Ford, he saw her. When he dropped Ford back at his mother's, he then swung by Rosalie's.

He still hadn't met her daughter, but Lee hadn't brought it up again. He was all-in with Rose, and if she needed extra time to be sure about him, he'd let her have it. He probably wouldn't have introduced her to Ford so early in the relationship had it not been for Travis's wedding, and he didn't worry about meeting Autumn. He had supreme confidence that he would when the time was right.

"How are things with you and Rose?" Gretchen asked. She didn't look at him as she started moving chocolates around according to some pattern Lee couldn't follow.

"Great," he said. He and Will exchanged a glance, wherein his brother smiled at him. Lee wasn't sure what to do with a conversation where he wasn't growling at someone about some problem around the farm, so he didn't say anything else.

"Where's Mama?" Will said into the silence.

"She and Daddy went for a walk," Lee said. "They said they'd be back in time for the tasting."

The door that led into the garage opened, and Daddy came up the last step and into the house. He held the door with his foot and reached back to help Mama. She'd been doing well since her time in the hospital. The doctors had released her on Sunday morning as Lee had predicted. He, Rissa, Will, and Trav had taken an around-the-clock vigil for the first three or four days, just to make sure their parents had someone here should they need anything at all.

"Mama," Rissa said, and Lee's attention swung back to the arched entrance from the front door. "Daddy, where's her oxygen?"

"We were just out in the oxygen," he said, frowning at his youngest daughter.

"The tank is too cumbersome," Mama said, though she did look a bit pale. With the way the sun beat down these days, that shouldn't be the case.

"Rissa," he said, moving around the island. "It's right here." He latched onto Mama and steadied her over to the couch, where her oxygen tank waited. "Sit down, Mama." He whispered those words as Rissa and Will started to argue behind him. He blocked them with his body and helped his mother onto the couch.

He handed her the tubes, and she fitted them into her nose and around her ears. "Thank you, dear." She patted Lee's hand, but he didn't straighten.

"You're okay? Thirsty?"

"Daddy's getting me a drink," she said. "The pond is lovely." She gave him a smile, and Lee couldn't help his soft, loving smile in return.

"Ford said the same thing over the weekend," he said.

"Dad!"

Lee twisted to see his son as he heard his voice. He got to his feet as Ford came running around his uncle Will, and the joy on Ford's face brought whole new life to Lee's chest. "Heya, buddy." He scooped him up into a hug. "I didn't think you were comin' until tomorrow. Your mom said you had a practice tonight." Piano or swimming or something. Lee couldn't keep up with all the things Martha enrolled Ford in during the summer months. She still had to work as a dental hygienist, and Ford often spent the whole summer at the farm.

This week, he'd been at Martha's for a swim meet. That was right. Swimming.

"The meet got canceled." Ford's whole face was one big sunbeam. "The pool had to close because of some chemical issue."

"Too much chlorine," Travis offered from across the kitchen island. "People were goin' home with burns."

"Wow," Lee said, looking back at his son. "But you're okay?"

"Yep." Ford squirmed, and Lee put the child down. "Uncle Trav said there was gonna be a lot of chocolate." He catapulted himself onto a barstool while Lee looked for Rosalie.

She stood back by the arch, neither in the conversation but not out of it either. She wore a smile as she watched Ford, and when she lifted her eyes to meet Lee's, she seemed angelic to him too.

"Hey, baby." He went past everyone else to take her into his arms. She smelled like cardboard and vanilla, and Lee loved it. "Travis didn't kill you on the way in. That's good."

"I'm a good driver," Travis said.

"You did block that driveway that one time," Shay said.

"Stop it," he said, grinning at her. Lee could hardly stand to be around them. Travis grabbed his wife and tickled her, which was just too intimate in a crowd. Lee released Rosalie and took her hand in his. He could stand out of the way and still participate. Trav and Shay were far too public about just how crazy they were for each other, which he supposed wasn't a bad thing.

"Knock it off," Will growled, and Lee kept his smile to himself though he secretly wanted to high-five his brother and glare at the younger one. "Gretchen spent the last two days makin' these for you animals."

Travis lowed like a cow, and Lee had to admit that was funny. He chuckled, cutting off the sound the moment Will's piercing green eyes flew toward him. "Sorry."

"Where's Spence?" Gretchen asked, tucking her arm into Will's, which did calm him down.

"He said he was on his way in," Rissa said, frowning at her phone. "He should be here in a minute." She looked up. "We can start without him. I can catch him up."

"All right," Gretchen said, looking up at Will.

He looked down at her. "What?"

"Did you want to say something?" she asked him.

"No," he said. "Why would I want to say something? They're your chocolates." He seemed so confused, and Lee shook his head.

"I'll say something," he said, and that brought every eye to him. "Gretchen and Will are gettin' married in five weeks. Or so. Six weeks? Somewhere in there. She's made us eight different flavors of truffles to sample, but she only wants to serve four at the wedding."

"Thank you, Lee." She shot a glance at her fiancé. "We're not doing a big dinner like Trav and Shay," Gretchen said. "But a candy bar. Truffles are only part of that, so the menu can't be overwhelmed by them."

She pointed to the first plate, but it was Will who jumped in with, "These are the mint truffles." He looked at Gretchen. "Right, sweetheart?"

She smiled and nodded, and Lee felt a flash of victory for his brother. That was so much different than the sparks of irritation that usually flew through the Cooper homestead.

"These are raspberry," he continued while Gretchen pointed out the next platter. "Then we have hazelnut, caramel, coconut, peanut butter..."

CHAPTER NINETEEN

Rosalie opened a snack-size bag of pretzel sticks and watched her daughter through the glass. Autumn sat on the top step of the back deck, her phone pressed to her ear. Somewhere out in the yard, Thumper roamed. Charity had the long, holiday weekend off, and Rosalie couldn't help feeling nervous about James talking to Autumn.

She hadn't asked about Lee ever, and Rosalie wasn't sure why she would. She'd mentioned him once, almost three weeks ago, while there was pizza in the room. Autumn hadn't been upset by the time Rosalie returned home from the hospital, and she didn't have to disclose to James that she'd started dating someone else. They weren't together anymore, and all she was required to do was let him talk to Autumn.

He hadn't returned to Texas, citing his new job was simply too busy. Rosalie believed it was, and she hadn't questioned him on it. She did bite along her thumbnail now as Autumn got to her feet. She skipped across the deck and Rosalie turned from the kitchen window as she pulled open the sliding glass door.

"Momma," she said. "Daddy wants to talk to you now."

"Okay, sweetie." Rosalie took the phone from her daughter and started to lift it slowly to her ear while the girl returned to the deck. She didn't close the door behind her, and Rosalie went to stand in the opening of it. "Hello, James."

"Rose," he said. His voice used to tickle the inside of her ears and hum all the way down into her chest. Now, it just sounded like the supplier she spoke to on Tuesdays about the manufacturing of her new board game.

"How are you?" she asked, though he'd called her. "How's California?"

"It's great," he said. "Listen, I'm wondering if Autumn can come here for her birthday."

Rosalie straightened from the doorway and began to slide the door closed. "Did you tell her she could?"

"Of course not." He sighed. "I'm asking you first."

Her mind spun. Of course she knew when her daughter's birthday was, but it still took her several moments to get the date into her head. "How is she going to get there?"

"My mom is coming about then," he said, almost under his breath. "She said she had a layover in San Antonio if you could drive her up to the airport. She won't have to fly alone."

Rosalie couldn't see why she should say no. "I have my new game releasing three days before her birthday." She hadn't told James that either. "When is your mom coming through?"

"Three days before."

Rosalie sighed and reached up to run her free hand through her hair. "Uh, I need to think. I need to be in front of my calendar."

"Maybe someone else could take her."

"Maybe your mother should come here and get her," Rosalie said, her tone somewhat snappy. James's family lived in New Orleans, and honestly, they could drive through here, get Autumn, and then fly out of San Antonio. Or Dallas for that matter.

"She already has her flights."

"Well, I already have my game release."

James let out another long sigh, but Rosalie found she didn't care. She didn't know what to do with this void inside her, because she'd always wanted to make everything so easy for him. For everyone.

"Listen," she said, her voice strong. She didn't need to make things difficult on purpose. James had left several months ago, and she was sure he missed Autumn. "Let me look at my calendar and task list on Monday morning, okay?"

"Can you look now?"

"No," she said, not willing to give him a holiday weekend. "We're headed out to...my boyfriend's farm for the holidays."

She could see his thick eyebrows shoot for the sky. "Your boyfriend's?"

"Yes," Rosalie said. She didn't elaborate, and she could practically hear the steam accumulating on the other end of the line.

"Rose," he said, with obvious effort to stay calm. "You're not putting our daughter in...anything she shouldn't be involved in, are you?"

Rosalie blinked and then burst out laughing. That really was the only reasonable reaction to what he'd said. "Like what?" she said between her giggles. "Come on, James. You made it sound like I was involved in a drug ring."

"No," he said.

"Yes," she argued back, not laughing anymore. "He's a nice man. A cowboy. Owns a big dairy farm north of town. There aren't any...*situations* she shouldn't be involved in. I don't even know what you're talking about."

James said nothing, and she wanted to remind him— again—that she and Autumn weren't in the Navy. "We live in a sleepy town of ten thousand," she said. "Autumn's biggest concern for this afternoon is a sunburn. And maybe getting licked by the family golden retriever." Queenie had certainly licked Rosalie's hand several times when she'd been out to the farmhouse. "It's fine."

"Who is it?" James asked.

Rosalie heaved a sigh. "I don't see how this is any of your business, but his name is Lee Cooper." She'd fall down dead if James knew Lee.

He didn't say he did, because of course he wouldn't. For the three years he'd lived in Sweet Water Falls, he'd been deployed on his ship or recovering in the hospital. Then he'd moved out, and then away.

"I'll look on Monday morning," she said. "Okay? There's still plenty of time from July sixth to July twenty-sixth to make plans."

"Fine," James said, less bark in his voice than she anticipated. "You're doing okay?"

"Yes," she said, surprised by the change in conversation. "You?"

"The games are going well?"

"Yes." She hadn't told him about her new board game at all. He hadn't asked. James had never made it a big point to ask her about her own endeavors, even when they'd been married. Anything he knew was because she told him, not because he asked.

"Good," he said. "I'm glad."

"Me too," she said. "I'll talk to you later, James."

"'Bye, Rose."

The call ended, and Rosalie looked at the phone as it darkened, her ex-husband's face disappearing from her immediate view. She sighed, because she'd harbored some tension in her shoulders and back she didn't need.

She slid open the door and called, "Autumn, baby, come get in the tub. We need to start getting ready to go out to the farm."

Butterflies danced through her stomach as her raven-haired girl came running toward her, the humongous white rabbit keeping pace at her side. She was taking Autumn out to Sweet Water Falls Farm today to meet Lee and the rest of the Coopers. He'd said he could come get her and make it a smaller affair, but she didn't see the point of that.

She'd planned to go to Lee's cabin first, and they could have the meeting there. Then, there was, according to Lee, a massive picnic planned for the whole family and everyone who lived and worked on the farm. When she'd asked him for an approximate number, he'd seemed confused.

Thirty? he'd guessed. *Maybe forty. And then the Forrester's are coming from next door. So maybe more like fifty or sixty…*

Sixty people. It wasn't as many as the wedding, but Rosalie's stomach didn't seem to care about a missing zero on the end of the number. It felt like a lot of eyes would be on her and Autumn, and it took a lot of strength and willpower to remind herself that she'd met Lee's whole family before. Several times.

She'd already dressed in a pair of navy blue shorts that went halfway down her thigh, and she'd paired them with a bright red shirt with white stars. Completely patriotic and Texan at the same time.

"Should we braid your hair?" she asked Autumn as the tub filled with hot water.

"Can you, Momma?" Her daughter's eyes filled with hope.

"Yep." Rosalie helped her step out of her pajamas. "And you can wear that cute dress we got the other day."

Autumn ran her fingers along a star on Rosalie's shoulder. "The one like your shirt."

"Yep. Get in now, baby. It's warm enough." She steadied Autumn while the spindly girl stepped over the tub, and then she squeezed some bubble bath into the stream of water still filling the tub.

Rosalie couldn't help herself. As Autumn splashed and played with her ponies in the bubbles, she checked her schedule. She had planned to go live the day of her game launch, but her major appointments with schools and retailers were all the week before Autumn's birthday.

She didn't have plans specifically for her daughter's birthday, but that didn't mean she wanted Autumn to be out of the state on the day she turned five. Only two weeks after that would be the open house for her kindergarten classroom, and Rosalie would need to get supplies and clothes and all the things Autumn needed to start school.

Three days before her daughter's birthday, Rosalie had an online meeting with a major distributor of games. Play Now sold educational games and jigsaw puzzles all over the Midwest and western half of the United States, and she'd already pitched Paul her board game. He'd liked it, and they would be finalizing their order that day.

The meeting was set for ten o'clock, and she supposed as long as she didn't have to leave for San Antonio until noon, she could accommodate James's request.

She wasn't going to tell him that right now. She'd text him on Monday morning, as they'd agreed. Right now, she helped Autumn wash her hair and rinse all the conditioner out. She braided her silky strands into a single French braid and helped her daughter into the red-and-white starred sundress. With a pair of white sandals on her feet, Autumn was ready for the picnic.

Rosalie grinned down at her. "Ready?" She extended her hand toward her, and Autumn slipped her palm against Rosalie's.

"Ready, Momma."

Rosalie was too, at least on the outside. She'd put on her makeup and paired a pair of gold cowboy boot earrings to her clothes. On the way out the door, she grabbed a white sunhat for herself and the small backpack she'd put together the night before. It held Autumn's refillable water bottle and two spray cans of sunscreen, Rosalie's lip gloss, and a phone charger.

They had plans to be at the farm until at least eleven o'clock tonight, as Sweet Water Falls Farm was hosting fireworks on their land tonight once darkness fell. Rosalie stayed calm and strong for the entire drive out to the farm, but the moment she made the turn, her nerves rioted.

She could easily see herself driving out here every single day after work. That turn had been easy and natural. This place felt so homey and down-to-Earth. *She* felt safe here, and tears pricked her eyes.

She made all of the turns to get to Lee's pretty little cabin against the woods, wanting the size of her family to suddenly double—and for the handsome cowboy setting his guitar aside and rising to his feet to be her daughter's everyday father figure.

She could *see* it. Hear it. Feel the joy such a thing would bring into her life.

Lee smiled and waved, coming toward her stopped sedan slowly to give her a second to breathe. Rosalie appreciated him so much, and she quickly undid her belt and said, "Autumn, get unbuckled and get out."

She did that and smiled at Lee, only the farm fresh air between them. "Howdy, Handsome."

He chuckled and whistled as he dragged his eyes down toward her shoes and back. "Look at you, Miss Patriotic."

"It's the Fourth of July," she said, giving his yellow shirt a cursory glance.

"Not until Saturday," he said, stepping closer.

Rosalie opened the back door and helped Autumn with the last latch. Her daughter stood on the lip of the car and then jumped to the ground, where Rosalie took her hand. "Autumn," she said. "This is Mommy's boyfriend, Lee Cooper. Lee, this is my daughter Autumn."

Lee dropped into a crouch, his smile as wide as the ocean. She felt his happiness and adoration of her daughter, because Lee Cooper didn't fake anything. Rosalie was sure he didn't even know how.

"Howdy, Little Miss," he said. "You look as cute as your momma."

Autumn looked at him and twisted back and forth, making the skirt of her dress swing.

"Say hello, baby," Rosalie said.

"Hello," she said.

"So," Lee said, reaching into his back pocket. "I heard somethin' about you." He brought his hand forward again. "Someone told me that you like rabbits and things that glitter and sparkle." He opened his palm, and Rosalie herself gasped.

Autumn shrieked and ran at him. "It's a rabbicorn!" She grabbed the sparkly, pink stuffed rabbit with a single unicorn horn poking out of its forehead, right between its long ears. Autumn danced around in a circle and held it up. "Momma, look! The rabbicorn! A rabbicorn!"

Lee laughed and straightened, so pleased with himself. Rosalie couldn't help grinning too, and she picked up her daughter. "Baby, what do you tell the cowboy?"

"Thank you," Autumn said dutifully. "Thank you, thank you." She lunged out of Rosalie's arms and toward Lee, who had the reflexes of a ninja, for he caught her.

Rosalie stumbled forward with the shift in weight, but Lee held everyone up as he took Autumn from Rosalie and didn't let her fall forward either.

"Thank you," Autumn said, wrapping her skinny arms around Lee's neck and squeezing him tight.

"Sure thing, sweetie," he said. "What are you gonna name 'im?"

"It's a girl," Autumn said, pulling back. She'd spoken in her little-girl-duh voice, and Lee nodded along.

"Of course, sure," he said. "A girl." He set Autumn on the ground, and she stroked the rabbicorn's multi-colored fur back.

Rosalie watched her for a moment, then lifted her eyes to Lee's. "Thank you," she whispered, stepping into her handsome cowboy's arms. There was no sign of the surly side of Lee, and Rosalie didn't care if he argued with his brothers later or not.

He'd presented her daughter with the perfect gift, and she wanted him to know how much that meant to her. She touched her lips to his, intending to only kiss him for a moment. As the kiss lengthened, Rosalie's blood turned warmer and warmer until finally Lee pulled back.

"Come on," he said, taking Rosalie's hand and falling back a step. "Let's go see if Ford can help Autumn name the rabbicorn."

Rosalie glanced at the guitar leaning against the railing. "Will you play for me someday?"

"Count on it, sweetheart," he said, leading her up the steps.

CHAPTER TWENTY

Lee recognized how much help he'd gotten over the past couple of months. First from Cherry, who'd helped him get the reservation at Montague's. Then from Mama and Jenni-Lynn for telling him about the baking class at The Southern Bakery and letting him and Rose come last minute. Gretchen had helped him with sweets from her shop, and Karyn Harlow had helped him with cabbage and carrots for Thumper.

He had no idea what he'd done to get Rosalie to look at him with the same stars in her eyes that she wore on her shirt, but she did. He surely would wake up in the morning and find that he'd dreamed all of May and June. She didn't really want to be with him. She hadn't shown up at the hospital with pizza because of *him*. She hadn't kissed him just now like she was falling in love with him.

He felt like he was living a dream, and he really didn't want to wake up at all.

"Ford," he said as he went inside his cabin, one hand still in Rose's and the other holding his guitar by the neck. His son looked up, a spatula in his hand. "Did the cookies come out?"

"Yes, sir," Ford said, going back to the task of getting the treats off the pan and onto the wire cooling rack.

Lee stepped over to the instrument holder and positioned his guitar in place. "Come meet Rosalie's daughter, Autumn."

Ford slid the spatula under one more cookie. "I just have two left," he said. Autumn skipped into the house behind her mother, and Rosalie smiled at her as she went by. Rose closed the door and glanced over to Lee, and he wasn't quite sure what she was thinking.

She wore that professional grin, the one she'd had plastered to her face on math night. The one that didn't tell him what she was really thinking or feeling. He had a similar mask, and even if his was much surlier, it accomplished the same thing.

"Did you make these yourself?" Rose asked Ford as he scooped up the last cookie.

"No," he said. "My dad helped."

Lee thought it was the other way around—Ford had helped him make the cookies—but he didn't correct his son. He simply tried on a smiling mask too, hoping his was as convincing as Rose's. He couldn't control his thoughts in that moment, and all he could envision was Rose and Autumn living here with him and Ford in this cabin at the farm.

He and Rose hadn't really advanced their relationship much further than it had already gone. They weren't talking about serious things yet, and Lee had been waiting for her to introduce her daughter into his life. Now that she'd done that, perhaps it was time to talk about more serious things.

"You two are so domestic," Rose said, shooting Lee a flirty smile.

"I told you I could cook," he said.

"Yes, every Wednesday," she said, reaching for his hand. He gladly slipped his fingers between hers.

"Yeah," he said. "You and Autumn can come out any Wednesday you want."

"He doesn't always cook," Ford said, turning to put the spatula in the sink.

As the utensil clattered, Lee said, "I do too. Every Wednesday."

"No," Ford said with plenty of attitude. The boy would be nine soon, but Lee wasn't anticipating him being eight-going-on-sixteen.

"Yes," Lee said dangerously, his pleasant attitude already starting to slip.

"Who grilled the hamburgers and hot dogs last

night?" Ford put his hands on his hips, his dark eyes throwing fire at Lee. "Oh, that's right, *I* did."

Lee scoffed, his smile reappearing in a genuine way. "Grilling isn't cooking, Ford."

Rose started to giggle, but quickly covered it. "I don't know, Lee," she said. "He has a point." She even stepped around the island to stand next to his son. "What did you make to contribute to the dinner last night?" She blinked her long lashes at him, clearly teasing him.

"Well," he said, rapidly blinking his eyes too, though he was sure they didn't have the same effect behind his glasses. "I cut up a couple of tomatoes."

Rose looked down at Ford, who looked up at her. "Chopping?" Rose asked.

"Slicing," Lee said. "That's some serious kitchen skills."

She shook her head. "There was no actual heat. I'm with Ford on this one."

Lee chuckled as he held up his hands. "Fine, all right. You two win. Ford or I or the two of us *together* make dinner every Wednesday night out here. The offer stands. Y'all can come join us anytime you want."

"Yeah," Ford said, his perfectly agreeable third-grade persona back in place. "Next week, Dad says he's gonna show me how to make pronto pups."

"What's a pronto pup?" Autumn asked, stretching to try to see more of what was up on the counter.

Lee scooped her up and lifted her onto a barstool. "It's a corndog," he said. "We make the batter from scratch and fry 'em up fresh."

"Oh, my gramma does that sometimes," Autumn said. "She calls 'em hush puppies."

"That's something else, honey," Rose said, smiling at her daughter.

"Can I have a cookie?" Autumn asked, and Ford reached out to get her one.

"Sure," he said. "Wait." He pulled the cookie back. "You're not...lergic?" He looked up at Lee. "Lartic? What's the word, Dad?"

"Allergic," Lee said.

"Allergic to peanuts or anything?" Ford asked.

Autumn looked at Rose, and so did Lee and Ford. She shook her head, and Ford handed over the cookie. "We can't eat 'em all. Dad says they're for the picnic."

"They are," Lee said. "Aunt Rissa will fillet us and fry us up for dinner if we show up without any cookies." He took in the dozens of them spread around every flat surface in the kitchen. "Although, we seem to have plenty." He didn't want to be on Rissa's bad side today, he knew that.

She'd been working for two weeks to get this picnic and fireworks party put together. Spence had been put in charge of getting all the explosives, and Gary had invited everyone at the farm next door.

Jed Forrester was a friend of Lee's, if he had any time for friends. Right now, he sure didn't, because he spent all of his spare time with Rose. If she wasn't available, Lee tried to make sure he talked to Trav and Will one-on-one often. They were all going to live here and work the farm, and Lee wanted them involved in as much as possible at Sweet Water Falls Farm.

Lee picked up a cookie and took a bite, the peanut butter and semi-sweet chocolate a match made in heaven for him. His eyes rolled back in his head, and a groan came out of his mouth. Rose giggled, and Lee smiled at her while he chewed. Maybe not the best option, as the cookies were a bit crumbly, and some spilled out of his mouth.

He started to laugh, and that wasn't good either. He turned away from the island full of cookies before he sprayed crumbs everywhere, embarrassment shooting through him. He couldn't stop laughing though, and when Ford joined in, Lee didn't care.

"Sorry," he said, still laughing with half a cookie in his hand.

"That's why we take a smaller bite," Rose said. "Okay, Autumn? Learn from Mister Cooper there." She'd picked up a cookie too, and Lee watched as her pink-painted lips parted and she took a delicate bite. Mm, he wanted to do that too, but he contained his hormones for later, because he got to spend the rest of the day with Rose and Autumn.

"Come see the stream," Rose said, extending her hand

toward Autumn. "Can I take her back there? I've told her all about the fish."

"I'll go too," Ford said, and Lee wondered if his son knew he would miss packing up all of the cookies if he went into the back yard with Rose and Autumn. Probably. He was eight, not stupid.

"I'll pack these up," Lee said loudly, thinking maybe someone would stay to help him. He got a swing and a miss on that one, and Ford led Rose and Autumn into the back yard. Lee sighed, still so dang happy, and started packing up the cookies to take to the homestead. In the end, he filled eight Tupperware containers before the back door opened again.

"Mister Lee," Autumn said, a sniffle in her voice. "I falled and got bleeding."

Lee abandoned his clean-up of the cookie mess he and Ford had created that morning and swept the tiny girl into his arms. His powerful protective instincts pressed in on him, and he took her down the hall as he shushed her. "It's fine," he said. "It's just a scrape."

He cleaned it all up and put a Band-Aid on it. "There." He looked at the robots on the bandage. "Well, Ford likes these ones. I'm afraid I don't have any princess stuff."

Autumn simply looked at him with the deepest, darkest eyes he'd ever seen on a person. Her father must've been dark-haired and eyed too, because she didn't have an ounce of anything else in her. Lee had plenty of red, and his beard—when he let it grow out, which wasn't often—definitely held gray.

"Say thank you," Rose said, and Lee dang near jumped out of his skin.

"You scared me," he said.

Rose rolled her eyes at him and said, "I don't see how that's possible."

"It is," he said, not daring to tell her what he was thinking about.

"Will's here," Rose said, reaching for Autumn. She balanced her on her hip as she turned to leave the tiny hallway bathroom. "He says we get him for five minutes if we have anything we want to haul out to the and I quote, 'back forty.'" She continued down the hall. "I wasn't sure what that meant or how far it is, but I figured we better take him up on it."

"Yeah," Lee said, following her and admiring her feminine shape. "We better." He emerged into the front of the house, where Will stood with Gary and Mack. "Howdy, boys." He smiled at them and gestured right back the way they'd come in. "I've got lawn chairs and blankets out by the garage."

"You couldn't get them in your truck?" Will grumped at him, already turning to leave.

"No," Lee called after him. "I was afraid Ford was going to burn down the whole farm while we baked these *fifteen billion cookies.*"

"I'm not gonna eat your cookies anyway," Will yelled

back. "Shoulda gone to the store like everyone else."

Mack grinned at Lee. "I'll have some cookies, Boss."

Lee wasn't sure if he should scowl or smile, and he landed somewhere in the middle. "What's with Will?"

"I guess someone forgot to turn off the sprinklers, and the spot he'd staked out for the fireworks is now soaking wet." Mack shrugged one shoulder and turned to go help load things too. "Why he needed a spot for a family fireworks show, I don't know."

Lee knew, but he kept his mouth shut. Mack left the cabin, and Rose came to his side. Lee looked at her while she watched the exit. "Why did Will want a separate spot?" she finally asked, turning her attention to Lee.

"He's engaged," Lee said simply. "My guess is as good as yours."

Rose linked her arm through his, a smile blooming on her face. "So you're saying he wanted to sneak away with Gretchen."

"I'm not saying anything," Lee said, chuckling. "Certainly not that I've stowed some of these cookies somewhere only I know, away from everyone else." He leaned toward her, glad when she reacted physically to him too. "Because I'm surely going to kiss you good-night later."

"You think so?" Rose asked.

"Mm."

"Dad," Ford said. "Should I get my hat?"

Lee turned away from Rose and focused on his son as he and Autumn entered the kitchen. "Absolutely," he said.

"And then Uncle Will and Mack need help loading up the chairs and blankets and cookies."

"All righty," Ford said, dashing past Lee and Rose on his way down the hall to his bedroom. He came back in a gallop, his child-sized cowboy hat on his head. "Ready."

"Get some cookies then," Lee said, reaching to hand his son one of the containers. He collected most of them, and Rose picked up the rest.

They went outside to find the truck loaded and Will getting into the farm truck he and Mack had driven over. "See you there," Lee called, and Will just waved, no smile in sight.

Lee had a very distinct feeling that if a man as crotchety as Will could get a woman to fall in love with him, he should be able to as well. A flush worked its way up his throat and into his face, but he kept silent as he went down the steps and sidewalk to his truck.

The four of them loaded into it, with Rose bending to swing Autumn up onto her hip and then into the back seat. "Slide over by Ford," she said before climbing into the front.

Lee drove them all over to the white farmhouse where he'd grown up, the number of trucks parked out front making his heart leap into the back of his throat. He nearly choked but managed to turn it into a cough instead. As he came to a stop, he said, "Here we are." He decided to lead by example, and he got out of the truck without hesitation.

Rose followed with Autumn, and Ford could get out by himself. "I'll take the cookies inside," Rose said.

"Ford and I will get the blankets and chairs set up," Lee said, already dreading the afternoon in the heat. He swapped out his glasses for his prescription pair of sunglasses and got to work doing just that.

Several more people had gathered out in the back yard behind the farmhouse, each of them claiming a patch of grass for their blankets and chairs. They'd eat on the back deck and in the farmhouse, and then the fireworks would happen over the corn fields directly behind the house. The lawn sloped downward slightly, so setting up at the top of the rise was the best seat in the house.

"Just right there, bud," he told Ford, because he didn't want to be right in the middle of the crowd. He didn't need Will counting how many hamburgers he ate tonight, nor did he want to admit he hadn't eaten much today in anticipation of Daddy's famous Fourth of July bean dip.

He and Ford set up the chairs, and Will spread his blanket beside him, wordless. Lee wanted to say something, but he didn't know what. He didn't want to tease Will for wanting to have a romantic evening with his fiancé under all of the sparking and festive lights. Heck, Lee wanted that for himself too.

"Cherry's here," Will said without looking up, and Lee glanced over to the east side of the house where everyone had been walking.

Sure enough, Cherry came around the corner, and she

wasn't alone. It took Lee a moment to recognize who she was with, and his heart played yo-yo in his chest. His only thought was, *At least it's not Charlie.*

The man she walked with was Jed Forrester, the second son who lived and worked on the farm next-door to the Coopers. Jed had clearly just said something that Cherry didn't find amusing, but which he did. He laughed with his head tipped back, and Cherry rolled her eyes.

Lee pretended to continue to set up his chairs while he watched Cherry put her chair along the back of the hill too, out of the way on the other side of the deck. She'd positioned herself for a quick getaway should she need it, and Lee recognized her strategy.

She must've felt him staring, because she looked straight at him. He lifted his hand in a wave, and Cherry smiled. She said something to Jed, who was setting up his chair beside hers, and came Lee's way.

"You made it," he said, taking his older sister into a hug. "How was the drive?"

"Busy," she said. "Everyone seems to be going to the beach for the fireworks."

"We might be able to see them too," Lee said, looking south, though he couldn't see the ocean or hear the waves from here. They might see the popping lights in the distance, set against the pitch-black sky that existed over the vast Gulf of Mexico.

The annual fireworks show for Sweet Water Falls took

place on the beach, but Lee couldn't stomach the crowds this year. Any year, really.

Cherry stepped back and kept smiling at him. "Where's Rose?"

"She took the cookies inside," Lee said. "She brought her daughter."

"That was going to be my next question," Cherry said, her hazel eyes lighting up as if she'd set the brightest white fireworks inside her expression. "You met Autumn. How was it?"

Lee couldn't help the smile that brought joy to his soul. He wondered if Cherry could feel it the way he could. "She loved the rabbicorn."

"So my assistant was right."

"Tell her thank you for me," Lee said, even as the ribbon of worry wafted through him. "Cherry, do you think...?" He didn't know how to finish his question. He disliked this doubt inside him, but it had been festering for a while.

"Do I think what?"

"Cherry," Rissa called, and she came jogging across the deck. "You're here." She thumped down the steps and engulfed Cherry in a sisterly hug, complete with squeals and immediate talk about pregnancy and babies.

Lee grinned at his sisters, but he stayed out of the way when the two of them were together. A man had to stay sane, after all. He ducked his head, gathered his son, and headed for the steps that led up to the deck. "Come on, son," he said. "Let's go see what Grandma needs."

"I just talked to her," Rissa said. "She's not giving up control of the potato salad."

Lee waved over his shoulder, because his specialty wasn't potato salad. It was worrying about whether he'd be able to come up with the right thing to do for Rose and Autumn by himself. He'd had *so much* help planning the right dates, and taking Rose to the right restaurants, and getting the exact right gifts.

What if what he'd been doing all this time to get Rose to like him was making her fall in love with someone he wasn't? Had he done that with Martha? Was that why farm life was so hard for her? Had he not prepared her enough for it?

Perhaps he needed to make sure Rose knew what it was like to live on a very busy dairy farm, and it wasn't always family picnics, fireworks shows, and peanut butter chocolate chip cookies.

"Mister Lee," Autumn said, and Lee tore himself from his thoughts.

"Yeah, baby doll?" He bent and picked her up, ignoring the protest in his old back.

"I can't see you," she said, giggling as she reached to take off his sunglasses.

He grinned at her and blinked. He couldn't see distance without his glasses, but he could make out Autumn's features just fine close-up. "I can see you." He took off the sunglasses and tucked them up on top of his head.

"Momma said I have to ask you if I can have a baby cow for a pet."

Lee burst out laughing, because the Berthas definitely weren't pets. He met Rose's eye, and it was clear he was supposed to be the heavy in this situation. He looked back at Autumn and booped his nose against hers. "Sure you can, baby. You can have all the baby cows you want."

CHAPTER TWENTY-ONE

Rosalie could not believe Lee Cooper. Now she'd have Autumn begging for a pygmy cow every single day until she turned eighteen. Maybe even after that.

She also couldn't believe how quickly the four-year-old had twisted the surly cowboy around her pinkie finger. She should've been more prepared for that. She'd seen Lee with Ford, and even if the boy did almost everything his father said, the moment he said it, didn't mean Lee wasn't compassionate and caring with his child.

He was, and Rosalie cocked one hip and folded her arms as Lee continued to chuckle with Autumn. She wanted to believe this could be her reality, so when Gretchen said, "Rosalie, will you come grab these buns?" as if they were already both married to a Cooper brother, Rosalie went to do it.

Gretchen was as nice as peach pie on a summer afternoon, and Rosalie had grown quite fond of her over the past couple of months. "Sure," she said. "What else needs to go out?" Out of all the women in the Cooper family, Gretchen was the easiest to approach. Rissa had as loud of a bark as her brothers, and Shayla seemed even busier than Rosalie was.

"Everything on the counter," Gretchen said, already carrying a huge tray of hamburger toppings. "I'm going to yell at everyone on the lawn."

Better her than Rosalie, but she did pick up several bags of buns and follow the blonde past the huge dining room table—and Lee and Autumn still making plans for a miniature cow. Rosalie hadn't even known such a breed existed, and she shot Lee a dirty look as she passed.

His eyes sparkled like dark emeralds, and Rosalie wouldn't be able to stay mad at him for long. Not if he entertained and took care of Autumn the way he currently was.

"Come on," Spencer called from the kitchen. "Lee, come get something. Trav has the grill going, and we've got to get people fed."

Rosalie went out onto the deck, where several folding tables had been set up. Blue and white checkered cloths covered them, which were perfect for the holiday. Rosalie put the buns on the end of the food table and turned to go get more. Several more people joined the fray, and Rosalie hadn't met them all. She knew the Coopers, but there were more cowboys than ever.

She recognized a couple from Travis's wedding, and soon enough, Lee appeared at her side, easily slipping his hand into hers. "I set Autumn with Mama on the swing," he said. "Okay?"

"Sure," Rosalie said. "That'll keep her out of the way for a bit."

Once they emerged out onto the deck again, the scent of grilling meat lifted into the air, and plenty of smoke rose from the largest grill Rosalie had ever seen. She shouldn't have been surprised. The Coopers didn't seem to do anything small—or quietly.

The back deck held no less than two dozen people, with more arriving all the time. Lee took her around as he shook his cowboy's hands. She met or re-met Mack, Gary, Chris, Floyd, and Cole.

When he started introducing the Forrester family, Rosalie decided she didn't have to memorize all the names or know who was who right this minute. She smiled and shook hands, made small talk, and watched Lee's older sister flirt openly with one of the Forresters.

Jed, she thought, but her memory continued to develop holes with every new face she looked at.

"And these are the boys from Hope Eternal Ranch," Lee said, indicating yet another group of cowboys Rosalie hadn't met. Lee laughed and shook hands with a tall, dark-haired cowboy holding a baby with shocking red hair.

"Nate Mulbury, and his wife Ginger." Lee hugged the redhead. "She actually owns the ranch. Nate's just infested it with all of his friends."

That got a laugh from everyone, and Rosalie kept smiling and shaking hands with Ted, Dallas, Luke, Jill, Emma, Jess, Hannah, and finally Slate.

"I used to work over there," Spence said, grinning as he joined the group.

"Somehow we lost him to Sweet Water Falls," Ted said, his voice loud and boisterous.

"It's the fireworks," Lee said.

"Or your sister," Nate said, and another round of laughter went up. In that moment, Rosalie realized how they were all connected—through friendship—and a powerful sense of belonging accompanied her smile now.

"Daddy, let me," Lee said, releasing Rosalie's hand as his father went by with a huge platter of desserts in his arms. "Go sit in the swing with Mama. Have you met Autumn?"

"He did," Rosalie said, giving Wayne Cooper a smile. "He even had her favorite treat, mysteriously." She watched Lee and his father exchange a glance, and Rosalie knew there was something going on there.

"Everyone loves a moon pie," Wayne said. "It wasn't anything special."

"It meant a lot to her," Rosalie said sincerely. Cherry

let out another peal of laughter, and a couple of people turned in her direction. She clung to Jed's arm now, and Rosalie quickly turned her attention back to Lee to judge his reaction.

He wore a frown from here to the Mississippi, his eyes locked onto his sister.

"Is she okay?" Rosalie asked.

"I'm not sure," Lee said. "She doesn't like coming home much. I've never seen her take a shine to Jed, though."

The two sure seemed to like one another now, and Rosalie and Lee weren't the only ones to have noticed. Rissa stepped over to Cherry and said something to her. The laughter and joviality slid off Cherry's face, and she snapped at Rissa.

So the men in this family weren't the only ones with a stubborn streak or a bark that could echo for miles.

"Rosalie," a weathered voice said, and she blinked away from the drama on the other side of the deck.

"Miss Mildred." Rosalie's spirits soared as she hugged the elderly woman. "Tell me you brought brownies."

"Mint and walnut," the woman said as she stepped back. She wore the sun in her smile, and it only died slightly when she turned to Lee. "I see the Forresters are causing plenty of trouble again this year."

"I don't know what you mean," he said diplomatically. "They're our guests."

"Well," she said, stepping to Lee's side so she faced

the rest of the deck too. "Easton over there sure has got his sights on Jenni-Lynn again."

"What?" Lee practically roared. "Where?"

Rosalie saw Jenni-Lynn with her arm through a tall cowboy's, and the two of them seemed like they were chatting with the press at a red-carpet event, not standing on the back deck of a farmhouse while hamburgers and hot dogs roasted.

"I'll talk to her," Lee said, already starting in that direction. "There's no way she's getting back together with him."

"Hmm." Miss Mildred stayed with Rosalie as Lee marched across the deck, practically shoving people out of his way to get to Jenni-Lynn. She looked scandalized when he touched her and she turned toward him. She spoke, shaking her head, and Lee made a gesture for her to come with him.

Unfortunately, someone was walking behind him at that precise time, and he hit them—and the plate of rice crispy squares they were carrying.

A commotion ensued, and Rosalie started toward Lee. Will entered the fray, yelling something about being more careful with so many people nearby, and Lee fired back at him with, "I'm not an idiot, Will. It was a mistake. It's not like you've never made a single mistake!"

"It's fine," someone said. "They're rice crispy squares. There's more inside."

Jenni-Lynn didn't bend to help clean up the fallen

treats, and she pressed one palm to her heartbeat as the argument continued.

"Lee," Rosalie said, and she bent to help pick up a square that she'd just stepped up to. Their eyes met, and while he looked about as pleasant as a raging whitewater river, he didn't throw another word in Will's direction.

They got the dessert cleaned up, and Rosalie noticed the plate and started stacking the deck-dirty squares on it. "Can I talk to you for a sec?" she asked Lee. She didn't wait for him to answer before she went into the house. He followed, and it was much quieter inside the farmhouse.

"What?" he barked at her.

"You've got to go talk to Will," she said.

"Wh—at?" Lee's question didn't seem to have an identity. "Why?"

"Because there's obviously a problem between the two of you," she said. "Go, now." She took the treats to the trashcan and tossed them in. She turned back to Lee, who stood there, staring.

"Well?"

"Well, Will usually comes to me when he's ready to talk."

"Oh, you and your Cooper pride," she said.

"It's not pride," he argued back. "It's just the way we do things."

"Break the mold then."

"Rose," he said.

"Lee," Daddy said. "We're prayin'."

"Okay," Lee said, but he didn't turn away from Rosalie. The noise from outside came in, and Lee visibly flinched with it. "I can't talk to Will right now. We're prayin'."

"I heard," Rosalie said, folding her arms and cocking her hip so he'd know her first motion wasn't to send up a plea to the Lord for good food and good company.

Lee turned around and stood still while someone out on the deck prayed. When the "Amen," chorused into the air, he stepped outside, leaving the sliding glass door open for her. Rosalie sighed, shook her head, and sent up her own prayer that Lee would recognize his pride before the entire picnic got ruined.

HOURS LATER, HE HADN'T SNUCK AWAY TO SPEAK TO WILL, AT least not according to Rosalie's knowledge. The food had been delicious, even the store-bought items, and Rosalie could admit that everything the Coopers touched seemed to turn to gold. Even watermelon and definitely potato salad.

"Fireworks starting in five minutes!" Spencer yelled. "Everyone find a seat and let's get this show on the road." He swung into the back of a pick-up truck, along with a couple of other cowboys, and they rumbled into the corn field.

Rosalie sank into the chair Lee had set up for her.

She'd eaten two cupcakes there, and she wanted another one. She watched Autumn and Ford on the blanket in front of her, and they seemed to get along well enough for a four-year-old and an eight-year-old. He showed her something on his tablet, and Rosalie wasn't going to argue about screen-time today.

Lee reached over and took Rosalie's hand in his, his fingers tightening. "You ready for our second dessert?"

Rosalie turned toward him, no explosions in the sky yet. Someone turned on some patriotic music, and it blared out over the yard.

Lee got to his feet and bent down to say something to Ford. His son nodded, and Lee tugged Rosalie away from the rest of the people all set up on the hill, waiting for the fireworks to start.

"Lee," she half-whispered with a giggle. "Where are we going?"

"I hid some cookies over here," he whispered back. "Come on, we have time." He ducked behind the shed and reached to lift the lid on his mama's garden box. He'd tucked a zipper bag of cookies on the top, and he lifted them out triumphantly.

Rosalie looked at the handsome cowboy, the light shining from the house going out. The crowd she couldn't see made some noise, and she giggled. "Lee."

"Rose," he whispered, pulling her closer and dropping the cookies on the top of the garden box. "I'm falling in love with you." He didn't give her time to respond properly. He simply kissed her, and Rosalie could feel herself falling in love with him too. She could feel the truthfulness in his words in the slow, deliberate way he moved, the way he kneaded her closer, and the way he let his actions speak louder than anything he'd ever said.

He was still kissing her when the first big boom filled the sky. Rosalie jerked, and Lee pulled away. He breathed in deeply, and Rosalie did too, finally opening her eyes and looking up between the buildings.

She couldn't explicitly see the multi-colored sparks, but the sky definitely held more light than before.

"Come on," he said, his voice lodged in his throat. He picked up the cookies and tucked her hand in his again. "We don't want to miss the fireworks."

Rosalie felt like the real fireworks show had started the moment he'd murmured the word *love*, and the pops, bangs, and spectacular light display of the Fourth of July bounced through her bloodstream.

Back in their chairs, he opened the saved bag of cookies and let her take one first. He then took one, and then he offered them to the children. Beside him, Will asked in a hushed voice, "Lee, can Gretchen and I have one?"

Lee handed over the bag without a word, and Rosalie knew the two brothers had made up. She didn't know how, and she didn't even know what the problem had been. Perhaps the Coopers did have their own way of communicating and working through problems, and perhaps she should just let Will and Lee do what they'd always done.

She took a bite of her cookie, the salty peanut butter mixing perfectly with the semi-sweet chocolate. She leaned further back in her chair and smiled up into the bright white splay of fire in the sky as it began to drift downward, leaving a trail in the sky.

She'd had no idea she wanted a country life, but the thought of putting on a skirt and heels come Monday morning made a pit in her stomach open which had nothing to do with the cupcakes and cookies she'd eaten that day.

During the show, with the Stars and Stripes playing in the background, she started to fantasize about what being a farm wife would be like. Blue jeans, sunscreen, and freshly baked cookies every day.

It sounded like heaven to Rosalie, and during the grand finale, with the sky full of sound and smoke and shockingly red lights, she kissed Lee again, hoping that her unspoken words of *I'm falling in love with you too* went through loud and clear.

CHAPTER TWENTY-TWO

Travis Cooper dismounted from his red mare before Pockets really stopped. "Stay," he told the equine as if she were a canine. He bolted toward the house, sure his mare would find plenty to snack on to keep her occupied while he went inside.

All he could hear as he ran up the steps was the pinched, high-pitched sound of his wife's voice when she'd called. *I need you to come home.*

He'd just finished the first milking of the day, and the sun had already started to reheat the Texas air. He'd been out in the stables working through a couple of their dirty stalls, and he'd saddled Pockets for a walk through the corrals later.

Since she was ready, and Travis's truck was on the other side of the stable, he'd swung onto the horse's back and come.

His heart pounded in the back of his throat as he twisted the doorknob and entered the house. "Shay?"

She wasn't in the small living room or the kitchen at the back of the house. He flew toward the hallway that sat between the two and led down to two small bedrooms with a bathroom between them.

The cabin was nowhere near the mansion a queen like Shay required, but Travis had met with Lee, Will, and Daddy last week about building something bigger and more family-oriented for him and Shay.

Lee's cabin was already two stories and probably plenty big for the family he'd have. Not only that, but he'd move into the farmhouse soon. Probably when Mama passed away.

Travis's boots hit the floor hard as he rounded the corner and he spotted Shay in the bathroom at the end of the hall. "Baby," he said. "What's goin' on?"

She'd been out running with Will when Travis had gotten up and dragged himself over to the corrals where they kept their dairy cows. He and the cowboys he worked with were in a rotation right now, where they were switching out their cows, as a cow couldn't give good milk forever. Or even for longer than six or eight months.

Shay sat on the tiny vanity in the bathroom, and Travis caught sight of the blood on her leg as he neared. "I fell," she said, her voice much calmer now.

Travis crowded into the bathroom too and took the

wet washcloth from her. It wasn't warm, and he twisted the hot water handle on the sink and rewetted it. "How?" he asked. "I saw Will going into the admin office during the milking." He looked at her, wrung out the rag, and reached to start wiping the blood from her shin.

"He cut out about halfway through," she said. "Said he had to shower and get over to the office for a call."

"Yeah, the Albertsons," Travis said needlessly. Shay winced as he touched the warm cloth to her leg. There wasn't a wound there, but her body trembled. Probably from shock.

"I went up into the hills on the other side of the highway," she said. "And back. I stumbled over this stupid rut literally a hundred yards from here." She sniffled and wiped her face. "Went right down."

"It's all right," Travis said, steadily moving closer to her knee, where the actual injury lay. "This isn't going to feel great."

"I've fallen before," she said, her voice going super-high again. "I don't know why I couldn't clean it up. I just...couldn't."

Travis looked up, questions running through his mind. "What do you mean?"

"I couldn't look at my own blood," she said. "It's making me queasy. So I called you."

Travis didn't know there was anything that shook Shay, but as he searched her face, he could clearly see that his strong, capable, brilliant wife *needed* him.

"It's not making me queasy," he said. "I can do it." He went back to tending to her wound, and Shay's teeth actually chattered while she pressed through the cleaning and bandaging of the wound. She cried quietly during the whole thing, and then Travis lifted her into his arms to take her back to bed.

"I'm sorry," she said, wrapping her arms around his neck and letting her head rest against his shoulder. "I swear I've taken care of myself before. I just don't feel well."

"Maybe you should set your alarm for six instead of five," he said. "Or take a few weeks off running." She'd have to anyway, as that knee wasn't going to support the hill hiking she did on a daily basis.

"I love running," she whispered.

He bent and laid her in the bed they shared. "I know, sweetheart." He helped her get her legs under the blankets and tucked her in, the comforter all the way up under her chin. "But not tomorrow, okay? And I'll call Jade and Elaine and tell them you're not coming in today."

Shay looked at him with wide eyes, but she didn't argue. Surprisingly, as Shay owned her outdoor outfitters company, and she worked about as much as Travis did around the farm.

He smiled softly at her and leaned down to kiss her. "All right. You're all right."

"Will you come home for lunch?"

Travis usually came home for lunch, unless he was

driving to town to eat with his wife. "Yes," he said. "I'll make something amazing."

"I'll cook."

His eyebrows went up. "Is that so?" He wasn't sure he wanted boxed macaroni and cheese. They'd finally gotten through all of the leftovers from the huge Independence Day celebration at the farmhouse, and Trav was secretly glad. He couldn't eat another bite of potato salad, even if his mama's had won a Texas State Fair blue ribbon seven times.

"Okay," he said anyway, straightening and heading for the door.

He turned back and watched Shay snuggle in deeper into her pillow and closed her eyes. He envied her with a powerful jolt, but he couldn't join her. The farm never slept. It didn't rest. The cows had to be milked, and Travis turned and walked out before he lost a battle to his desire to go back to bed with his wife.

HOURS LATER, TRAVIS ARRIVED BACK AT HIS HOUSE, THIS TIME IN his pick-up truck. Shay's SUV still sat in front of the cabin, and he reached over to the passenger seat to get the folder of floorplans that had arrived at the farmhouse today.

His excitement shot off the charts, and he hurried toward the house in much the same manner as he had that morning. He'd texted everyone for Shay that he'd said he would, and he'd talked to Lee and Will just before the second milking had gotten started.

Will had said he'd go check on Shay, as he was going to be out this way to check on some leaking sprinklers in the fields behind the two cabins out here.

"Travis," someone called, and Travis looked right, finding Rissa coming down the front steps of the cabin next door.

"Heya, sissy." He detoured toward her, smiling at the way she held tightly to the railing, her front-heavy belly making her more unstable the closer her due date came.

"How's baby Trav?" he asked, his favorite joke for Rissa.

"He's great," Rissa said. "We're not naming him Travis."

"Come on," Travis said, embracing his sister in a hug. "Maybe just a middle name."

"We're using Spencer as a middle name." She smiled at him as she stepped back.

"So what's his first name?"

"We haven't decided," Rissa said, but Travis didn't believe her any more now than he had the first time she'd said that.

"Come on," he said. "I'm so good at keeping a secret."

Rissa laughed and slapped at his chest. "You're literally the worst secret-keeper there is."

"Worse than Lee?" Travis grinned and danced away from his sister's reach.

"Fine, I'll give you Lee."

Travis looked over his shoulder to his cabin. It was still standing, with no smoke rising from the corner where the kitchen sat. Shay wasn't the best cook in the world, but Travis didn't really think she'd burn the place down.

"Did you need me?" he asked his sister.

"I was hoping to do something fun for Ford's birthday," she said. "Will and Gretchen are going to help. Mama and Daddy are on-board. I've even talked to Rosalie. You and Shay are the only ones I haven't talked to yet."

"Thanks for coming right next door and running things by us first," he said dryly. Travis already hated being the last son in the Cooper family, and he strongly disliked being left out in any way.

"You and Shay work so much," Rissa said, frowning. "I didn't leave you out on purpose. I just talked to Rosalie on the phone this morning."

Travis swallowed back his hurt feelings. "All right," he said. "What's the plan?"

"Is Shay home?" She nodded toward the SUV in front of Travis's cabin.

"Yeah, she fell on her run this morning."

Alarm passed through Rissa's expression. "Why didn't you tell me?" She whapped his bicep. "I could've taken her some lunch."

He flinched away from her. "Ow. Will checked on her, and *she* said she was makin' lunch for us today."

"You're making your *injured* wife cook lunch for you?"

"I'm not making her," Travis said crossly. "She volunteered. Come on." He turned and started back toward his house. "She probably went to town and picked something up."

He waited for Rissa to come to his side, and he matched his pace to hers. It seemed to take forever for his sister to make it up the steps. She was six months along now and growing a lot every single day. Since she was so short, the baby had nowhere to go but out.

Travis and Shay had talked about having a baby, but not in great detail, and they'd made no plans to definitely start trying to expand their family.

He opened the door and called, "Hey," as he entered. The balloons distracted him, and his step slowed to a stop.

"Trav," Rissa said from behind him, her voice none too happy. "Keep moving."

He couldn't, because Shay stood in the kitchen, a brilliant smile on her face. The living room furniture and the island in the kitchen separated them, but Travis could clearly see the huge "Congratulations" banner she'd strung along the hanging pot rack above the island.

"Shay?" he asked.

The counter in front of her didn't hold any food,

unless a giant cake counted as food. Travis supposed it did, but not the kind he'd expected.

He got his feet to move, and as he got closer, he saw the pinks, blues, yellows, and greens in the frosting. All pastels. All soft and fluffy and very much like something Shay would serve at a...baby shower.

"Surprise," she said, her voice somewhat rusty in her throat. It seemed to scratch, and Travis's eyes read the same word on the cake before he looked up at his wife.

"We're going to have a baby," she whispered, and that simple sentence blew up Travis's whole world.

Joy streamed through him in a way he'd never experienced before, and he reacted to it by laughing and darting around the island to get to his wife.

"Are you serious?"

"There are balloons, a cake, and a banner," Shay said, her eyes filled with tears and her smile stuck to her face. "What do you think?"

Travis whooped and lifted her off her feet as he hugged her. She giggled too, clutching his shoulders as he spun her around.

He set her down and gazed into her eyes. "I love you so much."

"I love you too." Shay tipped up to kiss him, and Travis could carry that on for a while.

But Rissa said, "Ohhh, I probably shouldn't be here."

He'd forgotten about her completely, and he pulled away and looked at his sister. He wouldn't let go of Shay, and he grinned at Rissa. "All right, Clarissa," he said. "You get to show us how amazing of a secret-keeper you are."

Shock covered her face, and she held up both hands. "I'm leaving," she said. "I saw nothing." With that, she turned and walked out of the cabin, closing the door behind her decisively.

Travis chuckled and looked back at his wife. Then he kissed her again, because she'd made all of his dreams come true, and he loved her with his entire body, mind, and soul.

CHAPTER TWENTY-THREE

William Cooper opened his front door, expecting to find Travis or Lee standing there. He got both of his brothers, each of them holding something Will would wear in just a few minutes. "Morning," he said, suddenly overwhelmed with love and gratitude for the two men in front of him. The three of them had been through so much in their lives, and while Will got the angriest with them the easiest, he also loved them deeply. He turned away and cleared his throat before he could start weeping.

He'd been so emotional this week, and he knew why. Everything he'd waited for and wanted for so long was happening. Today.

In two hours, he'd be married, and in four, he and Gretchen would be on their way to Galveston. He'd planned a couple of days there on the beach, and then he and Gretchen would set sail on a ten-night cruise that would take them down to South America and back.

Will absolutely could not wait. He loved his farm life, and Gretchen swore up one side of their conversations and down the other that she couldn't wait to live in this cabin, on this land, with him. He'd told her countless times that he'd move in with her after they got married, because she had a cute little house with all those wreaths for the front door.

They'd also talked about moving to Short Tail, where her father lived. Reggie, her dad, had been alone for a few years now, and he had a big, beautiful piece of land that Will could help him care for. In all honesty, Will believed he and Gretchen would end up there eventually. Probably sooner rather than later, as Reggie's health wasn't great, and he and Gretchen spent two or three evenings with her dad already.

"You ready?" Lee asked.

"Yes," Will said without elaboration.

"Gretchen's at the farmhouse," Travis said, closing the door behind him. "Shay's there with her and Mama. Her dad's currently being educated on all the finer points of running a dairy farm by Daddy."

Will turned and looked at Travis, sure he was joking. He grinned like the Cheshire Cat, which meant he wasn't.

"Daddy," Will said, shaking his head.

Lee smiled too. "They're fine,' he said. "Reggie likes Daddy."

"The aisle is set," Travis added, draping the garment bag he carried over the back of Will's couch. "Reggie said he was going to practice before the wedding."

"It's smooth?" Will asked. He'd been out to the new barn that morning too, and the flooring hadn't been done yet. What had been done certainly wasn't level or without things that could trip up the older gentleman, and he'd left it with his trust that the ceremonial suppliers knew what they were doing.

"Not a single seam," Lee said. "It's going to be amazing." He gave Will an encouraging smile, his happiness beaming from him in a way Will hadn't seen before. Rosalie Reynolds had such a big part to play in Lee's transformation, and Will's heart expanded once again, this time to make room for her because of her influence on his older brother.

"You've got to relax," Travis said, his smile slipping. "Why is it that Lee and I are happier than you are?"

"I'm happy," Will said, switching his gaze from Lee to Travis. "Just worried."

"About what?" Travis asked, moving into the kitchen. "The truffles are done. Your bride is here. Her dad is going to be able to walk her down the aisle, which is beautiful and utterly smooth. You don't have to work for the next eleven days." He opened the fridge and took out the milk Will had there. He uncapped it and met Will's eyes. "Seriously, Will, cheer up."

"I'm happy," Will said again, this time the words

almost a growl, especially when Travis tipped the glass bottle back and drank right from it.

"Will." Lee approached and put both hands on his shoulders. "There is nothing for you to worry about today. Nothing."

Will looked into his brother's eyes, feeling his own courage and faith strengthen. Lee had always been able to reassure Will, and since he'd been so busy on the farm, with Gretchen, or with his parents or her dad, Will had grown a bit distant these past few months.

He nodded now and said, "Okay." He drew in a breath, and finally, the anticipation and excitement he'd felt previously about this wedding—his wedding—could flow through him.

He smiled, and Lee's mouth curved up too. "There you are. I see you now, brother."

Lee had always been able to *see* him, and Will drew him into a hug. "Thank you, Lee."

"Hey, I want in on this," Travis said, spreading his arms around both Lee and Will. The three of them laughed, with Travis always the loudest of them.

"All right," Lee said as the huddle broke up. "Let's get you dressed and over to the barn. You don't want to be late to your own wedding."

~

GRETCHEN BELLOWS REACHED UP TO RE-SECURE HER VEIL IN HER hair. She hardly felt like herself amidst all the fabric currently wrapped around her body and flowing in stiff waves that looked like silky layers. She felt exotic and beautiful—and ready.

Shayla Cooper had been nothing but helpful today, providing the sister Gretchen had never had. Her brother's wife, Missy, had been in town for two days, and she'd been an absolute Godsend to Gretchen. She'd brought Daddy to the Coopers, and she'd gone back to Sweet Water Taffy to get the truffles after that.

Then, she'd helped Chrissy come into the brides' room so she could participate in helping Gretchen get dressed and ready to marry her son. Gretchen loved Will's mother with the same fierceness with which she'd loved her own mother. They were so much alike, at least in Gretchen's mind, and there was nothing she liked more than hugging Chrissy.

Well, maybe hugging Will. Her heart beat out a nervous rhythm as the door behind her got opened. She turned that way and accepted the bouquet Missy gave her. The flowers would make a gorgeous wreath for her and Will's front door, and Gretchen couldn't wait to make it.

The brides' room started to empty, and Gretchen felt like Cinderella heading to the ball up at the castle. Her castle came in the shape of a big, red barn, and she didn't want anything else.

Will said he'd be dressed in a midnight black tuxedo, and she couldn't wait to meet her dark, grumpy cowboy at the altar and become his wife. He'd changed a lot in the past several months, and even if he didn't show everyone his softer side, he always gave his best to her, and Gretchen loved him for that. She loved him for his good heart, and his hardworking spirit. She loved him for his devotion to his family and his farm, and she loved him for his ability to look at her and anticipate what she needed, and then do his best to give it to her.

She exited the room before Clarissa, who gave her a glowing grin, followed and closed the door behind her. Gretchen loaded up in her carriage—a luxury pick-up truck that had vinyl lettering on the side that said "Just Married." Not yet, but Will and Gretchen would drive this new truck to Galveston in just a few hours.

The drive from the farmhouse to the new barn Will had overseen the construction of in the past few months took only a few minutes, and Gretchen let all the women crowd around her to hide her from any cowboy eyes who might be trying to get a peek of her before the wedding.

They bustled her into a room on the north end of the barn. She'd walk through the barn to the doors on the other end, where Daddy would be waiting for her.

Will should be standing at the altar outside, another hundred feet beyond the south doors of the barn. There should be matching lilies and roses on that side of the barn, as well as down the aisle, which he'd had custom-constructed so her dad could walk her toward her groom.

Her back-up plan had included Max, her other brother, walking her down the aisle, but she hadn't had to call on that yet. Daddy had been at the farmhouse until ten minutes before Gretchen had left, and he claimed to be ready.

"Let's go," Shay said, leading the way down the center aisle of the barn. No animals lived here, as this barn was only for hay storage. Gretchen loved the smell of it, as it often accompanied Will home in his clothes and hair. He did some administration work in the morning with their milk deliveries, and in meeting with Lee and their daddy. Then he spent most of his time managing the cowboys who worked the agricultural side of the farm, and he worked right alongside them out in the fields, barns, and stables.

He'd been her biggest champion the past few months as she got her candy shop open and running again. He'd taken her father to several appointments when she had things come up that prevented her from being there. Tears sprang to her eyes that such a good man wanted her, but she sniffed and pulled them back. She wouldn't cry today, not even happy tears. She'd already let her sadness that her mother couldn't see her get married move through her. Daddy was here. Cory and Max. Their families, and her whole new family in the Coopers. She had all of her employees and plenty of customers from around town who'd come to celebrate with her. They hadn't come for the truffles; they'd come because they loved her or they loved Will.

It was such a blessing to be surrounded by people who loved her, and Gretchen would not cry that only one person wasn't there. Or that she had so many people who'd made space inside their lives for her or Will.

Her eyes found her father, and they burned once again. "Daddy," she breathed, her feet moving faster. He wore such an elegant suit, and he'd taken out his oxygen tube. She didn't mind it or the tank at all, but she wasn't surprised.

He smiled at her, and she hugged him with every ounce of strength she possessed. "My, you are wonderful," he whispered.

"Thank you," she whispered back, hoping he knew it meant for everything, not just this. "All right," Aunt Patty said. "Missy, get her train right. Shay, can you fix her veil? It looks a bit crooked. Then we'll go take our seats, and when you're ready, I'll signal to have the doors open."

Gretchen did what her aunt said, because Aunt Patty had been an excellent wedding planner today. She sounded bossy, but kind, and everyone had responded to her requests that afternoon.

With her train and veil fixed, and all of the ladies who'd helped her gone, Gretchen linked her arm through her father's and faced the closed barn doors. They opened outward, and her feet fidgeted for that to happen quickly.

Another minute passed, and Daddy asked, "Do you think they don't know we're ready?"

"Aunt Patty is slow," Gretchen reminded him. "It's almost time."

Only a few more seconds passed before the doors opened and a trumpeted fanfare filled the air. The scene opened up before Gretchen's eyes, and it was like walking into the most beautiful country wedding in the world.

The aisle lay before them, a deep golden wood that didn't hold a single thing for Daddy to trip over. Posts sat every three rows, wrapped in fresh flowers, the stems interwoven with hay, signaling the union of Will—a farmer—and Gretchen, the softer side of the pair.

The posts held up a glorious white tent that blocked the evening sunshine, and Will waited down at the end of it, the light coming in from behind him, making him a sexy silhouette.

Somehow, she could still see his smile, and hers popped onto her face as she and her father took the first step out of the barn and onto the aisle. Fresh, green hay bales sat at the end of every aisle, and the sides of the tent were open to the farm beyond.

Beautiful music played—not the wedding anthem, as Gretchen disliked that song—and she smiled at their guests with every slow, delicate step she took. She felt more like she was walking Daddy down the aisle than the other way around, especially with the strong grip he maintained on her arm.

She didn't mind at all, because she'd dreamed of this day all her life. The closer she got to Will, the bigger her heart grew. The wider her smile stretched. The more she couldn't look at anyone but him.

The last few steps narrowed the world to only William Cooper, and she had to force herself to lean over and press her lips to her daddy's cheek. She whispered that she loved him, and then he passed her to Will.

He kissed her cheek too, and Gretchen pressed into his touch unable to straighten her lips as they faced the pastor together.

Their relationship had been full of learning, passion, and fire—literal fire—but Gretchen had zero reservations about marrying him. So when it was her turn to say, "I do," she did in a loud, clear voice.

He repeated the same words at the right time, and the pastor pronounced them husband and wife.

Will turned toward her at the same time she faced him. He wore joy on his face, his smile the biggest she'd ever seen. "I love you," he said, and he gave her no time to repeat the sentiment before he dipped her and kissed her with all the passion with which he always had.

She giggled against his mouth, and he raised her back up a moment later, also laughing.

They faced the crowd and lifted their joined hands into the air, which only increased the volume of the applause and whistles in the crowd.

She suddenly wanted to run away to the Just Married

truck with only her new husband, and she was so glad she and Will had forgone a big dinner. They'd opted for a heavy appetizer and candy bar, and it was only slated to last for ninety minutes.

Then they could slip away amidst more cheering and clapping, and finally, Gretchen would have her cowboy in shining armor all to herself.

CHAPTER TWENTY-FOUR

Lee spun in the rolling chair and opened one of the filing drawers behind the big desk in the office where he ran all the dairy operations. He put the newly signed contract for one of their decade-old customers in the right file and turned back to the desk. He didn't love the indoor work that Cooper & Co required, but Daddy had systems in place, and Lee hadn't messed with them.

If it wasn't broken, Lee didn't have time to fix it. Today alone, he'd already worked in the office to get the day's orders printed on time. Clarissa usually did her orders by the week, but she'd been slowing down more and more lately. Lee had taken over the prepping of the paperwork for the day, and he did it the morning of the delivery.

Then Will and Rissa showed up, and together, the

three of them pulled the product for all those coming to pick up their deliveries. On Wednesdays, Lee had to oversee the loading of a huge commercial shipment that went to six grocery stores from here to Arkansas, and that took a couple of hours.

He usually then ran over to the farmhouse to start something for dinner if he was using the slow cooker, and no one wanted the oven on in the thick of the summer months. School was about to start in another week, and Lee already mourned the loss of having Ford with him full-time.

Rose, Rissa, Gretchen, and Shay had put together an amazing birthday party for Ford that had dang near brought Lee to tears. Seeing how many people loved his son brought a dose of gratitude to Lee's heart every time he thought about it. Seeing Rose interact with Ford was a special kind of magic, and while Martha was obviously very active and present in Ford's life, Lee knew it would make a difference to have a mother and a father in the home full-time.

Martha hadn't remarried yet, and Lee just wanted what was best for his son. He co-parented really well with her, and that hadn't changed since introducing Rose into their lives. He'd always tried to be supportive of Martha's dating adventures too, and he was glad they currently existed on a two-way street.

"Dad," Ford said, a hint of frustration in his voice.

Lee looked up from the ledger on the desk. "Hey, son."

He held up his hand, and Lee caught sight of a pick. "You missed our lesson."

Panic pounded through his veins. His shoulders slumped. "Shoot, I'm sorry, bud. I just got going on some paperwork here." He didn't see a guitar. "Did you bring your instrument?"

"No." Ford walked further into the office and slouched onto the couch. "I rode my bike over."

"Let's go do it," Lee said, laying down his pencil. The ledger would wait. "You see if you can beat me back to the house on your bike." He gave his son a bright smile and dashed for the door, Ford calling out behind him, "Da-ad! No fair!"

Lee laughed as he burst from the administration building, Ford right behind him. He pretended to hurry to get out his keys while Ford fumbled with his bike. Lee would let the boy win, something he'd literally never done for Will or Travis. His brothers were his best friends and closest confidantes, but Ford was his son, and Lee would do anything to make and keep him happy.

If that meant he "accidentally" dropped his keys and yelped like the world was about to end because of it, that was what he did.

Ford cackled as he biked away, standing up and pumping hard. "I'm gonna catch up!" Lee called after him. He yanked open the door and reached in to start the truck. The engine roared, but Ford didn't look back. Thankfully.

He wanted his son to win, but he didn't want to be caught losing on purpose. He did get behind the wheel and take a moment to buckle his seat belt. Accidents could happen, even in only a half-mile or less, and Lee took off down the road after his son.

Ford moved fast, but Lee caught up to him quickly on the straight parts of the road. He had to slow way down for the corners, and he let Ford pull ahead. Then he'd rev his engine and come up behind him again.

His son weaved out onto the dirt road, making it impossible for Lee to get by without hitting him, and Lee laid on the horn and laughed. He rolled down his window and yelled, "That's cheating!"

"Is not!" Ford yelled back to him.

They pulled up to the cabin with Ford only a foot or two ahead of Lee, and he jumped off his bike with both hands in the air. "I won!" His chest heaved, and Lee should probably make sure the boy ate an extra-large lunch to make up for the energy he'd just exerted.

"Fine," Lee said good-naturedly. "You won." He laughed with his son and they went in the house together. Ford wiped his face with a towel and got a big glass of water from the filtered spout in the fridge door. Then he came into the living room where his child-sized guitar rested next to Lee's full-sized one.

"All right," Lee said, pulling his phone from his pocket as it started to buzz. Rose's name sat there, and his heartbeat bobbed through his veins. He loved that the simple act of her calling him made his world brighter and his happiness soar. He swiped the call away, because he'd already missed Ford's lesson.

As he did, his other notifications came up, and Lee saw he'd missed his son's phone call four times. He frowned at the number, sure he hadn't seen it right. His glasses were a smidge dirty, but nothing bad enough to make the four unreadable.

"You called?"

"A bunch," Ford said. "You didn't answer."

"I had my phone." He looked at Ford. "Sorry, bud. I wasn't ignoring you on purpose."

"I know." He put down his water and picked up his guitar. "We were doing the G-chords."

Lee knew what they were doing. His phone rang again, this time with his mother's name on the screen. He tilted it toward Ford. "It's Grandma."

Ford nodded, his fingers moving along the strings of his guitar, and soft sounds coming from the instrument. He had a lot of talent, and Lee loved teaching him and listening to him play. In truth, he was probably better than Lee, and he hoped his son would love to play the guitar his whole life, the way Lee did.

"Hey, Mama," he said after swiping to answer the call.

"Lee, baby," she said. "We need you at the farmhouse."

"Right now?" he asked, a spark of irritation flaming inside him. "I'm doin' Ford's guitar lesson."

"We're fine," Daddy yelled from somewhere nearby.

"You're not fine," Mama snapped. "He's hurt himself, and he won't go to the doctor."

Lee stood, already ready to fly back down the lane to the farmhouse, guitar lesson or not. "Hurt himself? He was fine this morning."

"I'm fine now," Daddy said, but a pinch of pain existed in the words. "I just twisted my leg is all. I'm fine. Took some medicine, and I'm fine."

"I'll be over in a minute," Lee said, gesturing to Ford. "Don't try to do anything, Daddy. You're not a physical therapist."

"I know what I am," Daddy said crossly. "I can do the exercises they gave me last time."

"Don't," Lee barked at him. "You don't know what those were meant to do, and you could hurt yourself or something. I'm on my way." He lowered the phone and said, "Bring the guitar, Ford. We'll do the lesson at the farmhouse."

They loaded up and off they went. The farmhouse sat seven minutes down the road on a leisurely day, and Lee made it in six today, because it was a curved and dirt road. Inside the house, he called, "We're here."

"In the family room," Mama called. Lee knew right where they'd be, and he was already under the arch and entering the kitchen. A couple of couches sat in the room across from the long dining table, and Mama stood at the end of one, her hand gripping the top of it.

"Mama, why are you up?" he asked with a frown.

"I'm fine," she said, giving him a rare dirty look. "It's your father who won't see reason."

"I'm fine, Chrissy." He didn't try to get up or gesture Lee back. He went around the couch, finding his father with his leg straight out and resting on the ottoman. He had an ice pack tied to his hip and a blanket over the rest of him.

"Daddy," Lee said, pausing. "Are you sure you don't need to go to the hospital? Maybe we just call Doctor Friendly and find out what *he* wants you to do."

Daddy could've seared off Lee's face with the intensity of his glare. "I took some pain medication. I'm going to fall asleep in a few minutes. I'm icing it. I will be fine."

"You're not going to do any of the exercises," Lee said firmly. "Promise me."

"I promise."

"Mama?" Lee switched his gaze to his mother.

"I won't let him."

"Mm. You'll call me if he tries."

"I'll call you if he tries," she amended. Mama had never been able to stop Daddy from doing what he wanted to do. He did tend to think he knew better than someone who'd gone to medical school and done countless hours of residency training, and that annoyed Lee to the ends of the earth.

The situation handled, Lee put his arm around Ford's shoulders. "All right," he said. "Ford wants to play for you.

Maybe he could do a lullaby and put you to sleep faster, Daddy."

"I'm not an animal," Daddy grumped. "No one needs to put me to sleep."

Lee could only smile at him, and then he nodded at his son, who started to play quietly on his guitar.

AUGUST SLIPPED THROUGH HIS FINGERS LIKE SMOKE, AND FORD went into the fourth grade. Lee only saw him on weekends again, but he drove into Sweet Water Falls much more often than he used to. He wanted to see Rose every single day, but their schedules made it difficult. She'd launched her new game and her daughter had gone to California for a week or so to see her dad. Both had been stressful for Rose, and Lee had been at her side as much as possible.

Things for her had settled again, and Lee called her, texted her, and saw her a couple of times each week. It wasn't enough for him, and he decided he needed to do something about that. She'd been in on the planning for Ford's birthday, and a plan for their four-month anniversary started to form in his head.

They'd been to a dozen restaurants around town, and Lee wanted to do something more than take her to dinner. Lee left his cabin early one weekday morning, hoping to catch Will before his brother got started for the day. He parked in front of the cabin around a couple of bends from his and waited.

Before long, Will came running toward his house at an even gait. He slowed and then walked the last little bit, eyeing Lee's truck like it might turn into a viper and strike. Lee got out of his trusty, rusty truck then and nodded to his brother.

The sun shone low on the eastern horizon, with a patch of dawn shade here and there because of the hilly land. It was already hot, and Lee finished the last of his first cup of coffee.

"What are you doin' here?" Will asked. He wore a pair of running shorts and nothing else. The man had muscles all up and down his body, and Lee could admit maybe he needed to get up an hour earlier and join his brother on the running trails.

"I have a question," Lee asked. "A personal one."

Everything about Will relaxed. "C'mon in. You can make my coffee while I shower."

"Joy," Lee said in a deadpan.

Will grinned at him and together, they started for the front door. "What's on your mind? Things are still good with Rosalie?"

"They're good," Lee said, a bit too brightly and definitely with some falseness in there. "I'm just...I don't see her very often. I want to do more."

"You want to get serious," Will said as he opened the door and went inside.

His relationship with Rose had always been very serious to him. He found himself nodding anyway. "Yeah," he said. "Something like that."

"Have you guys talked about serious?"

"No," Lee said. Neither of them had brought up another marriage, merging their children into a single family unit, or having more kids. Lee wanted to, and he swallowed. His nerves about bringing up such serious topics had turned his throat to sand.

"What's in your head?" Will asked. He started to wash his hands, and with his back turned, Lee could think for a minute without being on the spot.

When Will faced him again, wiping between each finger with a towel, Lee said, "I want to plan something fun for our four-month anniversary next week. Something more than a restaurant and whatever."

Will nodded and tossed the towel on the stovetop. "All right."

"You had that one date that was pretty amazing."

Will's eyebrows went up. "The one where my girlfriend's shop caught on fire?"

Lee's face heated. "Yeah," he mumbled.

His brother blew out his breath. "I wouldn't recommend replicating that one, Lee." He smiled and held Lee's gaze for a few long moments. "If you want to do more than dinner and flowers and all of that—you're romantic, Lee. Don't think you're not—look on the community events board. That's what I did. Find something goin' on on the date you want, and take her to that."

"The community events board."

"Women just want to know you thought about them while planning the date."

"I don't know what that means," Lee said. "I never stop thinking about Rose." He swallowed again, because that was more emotion than Lee usually peeled back for Will, at least inside his romantic relationships.

"It means you're not going to take her to a horse auction," Will said with a smile. "Because *she* wouldn't like that. You're considering *her* when making the plans. So if she likes gardens, you take her to the wildflower festival. If she likes...I don't know. What does she like?"

Lee tilted his head. "I get it."

"Do you? You didn't answer the question."

"I don't have to tell you what Rose likes." Lee turned away from his brother's scrutiny. "Thanks, Will."

"I don't think you know what she likes," Will teased as Lee strode toward the front door. Lee rolled his eyes and left his brother's cabin while Will chuckled. He hadn't started his coffee, thank goodness, because suddenly, Lee had a lot more work to do that day.

He needed to figure out what Rose liked best, then plan a date around that where he could be romantic—and then he could bring up the subject of marriage.

He swallowed at the mere thought of getting all fancied up and dressed in his tuxedo again. Of buying another diamond ring and getting down on one knee to ask her to be his wife. Of saying "I do," and pledging himself to another woman as her husband. Rose had talked and talked about the farm and how much she liked it out here, but coming to visit for family dinners and to watch the fish in the stream for a few minutes was completely different than living here full-time.

Lee knew that, and he had to make sure Rose did too.

CHAPTER TWENTY-FIVE

Rosalie's attention tore in two when the timer on her brownies went off at the same time her phone rang. She reached to silence the timer, then twisted to pick up the phone from the counter behind her.

James.

A sigh pulled through her whole body, but she swiped on the call from her ex-husband. "Hey," she said, already opening the oven. She slid on the oven mitt and pulled the square pan out.

"Rose," James said, his voice tight and stuck somewhere in his throat.

She slid the brownies onto the stovetop and stared at the crinkly, crackly top. They were done, but she couldn't move. "What?" she finally said. She'd heard the man on the other end of the line speak in that voice before. He usually said something she wanted to believe but had learned to think through first.

"I guess I'll just say it," he said, and he sounded authoritative and nervous at the same time. "I want you and Autumn to come here."

Rosalie blinked, the words tumbling into one ear and out the other. "What?" She laughed, and she heard the incredulity in her tone.

"I'm serious," he said, none too happy with her reaction.

Rosalie cut off the laughter. "I don't—I can't just pick up and move to California." Her heart raced through her whole body at the thought.

"Why not?" James challenged.

She spun away from the stove, suddenly angry. "Why not? *Why not?* Because we're not married, for one."

"I made a mistake," he said.

"Two years ago," Rosalie said. "You made this mistake two years ago, James, after I begged you not to leave. After I said I didn't care about the injury, and that I loved you and would take care of you, no matter what." She didn't mean to hurl the words at him, but they came out rapidly, without any compassion in them. "*You're* the one who broke us, James. Not me."

He said nothing, which was fairly typical for James. Of course, Rosalie rarely stood up to him. His job had moved them around until they'd landed in Sweet Water Falls. It was supposed to be a three-year assignment, but James had been injured inside the first twelve months. He'd filed for divorce only six months after that, and Rosalie didn't have to face a future of moving every few years for her husband's job.

Lee owned his family farm, and it had been in his family for generations. He wasn't going anywhere, ever.

"I miss you," James said softly. "I miss my daughter. Having her here last month was amazing."

Rosalie wanted to once again remind him of all *he'd* chosen. He could've stayed here in Sweet Water Falls to be near Autumn. He could've found another job outside the military. He could've done so many things in his life that kept him near his daughter.

She said nothing, her heartbeat screaming through her body and her mind loud with voices, all of them clamoring at her about what she should or shouldn't do.

"Momma," Autumn said, and her eyes flew toward the sliding glass door. She was soaked from head to toe, standing there without a towel. She grinned at Rosalie, who offered a shaky smile back. "I need a towel."

"Is that her?" James asked. "Can I talk to her?"

"You can talk to her anytime," Rosalie whispered. She moved quickly toward Autumn, the phone held out in front of her. "It's your daddy. Go sit on the step, and I'll get you a towel, baby."

Autumn's face lit up when Rosalie told her her dad was on the other end of the line, and she grabbed the phone and skipped toward the back step. Rosalie's eyes filled with tears. Perhaps she should go to California so Autumn and James could be closer to one another. They'd always adored each other, and she couldn't stand the thought of making her daughter unhappy.

He chose, Rosalie thought. *He made all of his choices.*

She turned away from her daughter and her dripping, dark hair. As she went to get a towel, she reminded herself of why she was making the cookie dough brownies.

For Lee.

Her boyfriend and the man she'd steadily been falling in love with for almost four months now. He'd planned "something special" for their four-month anniversary in a couple of days, and Rosalie wasn't going to break the date so she could fly to California for a man who'd given up his wife and child because he was embarrassed of his injury.

She was not.

"James doesn't get to choose for you anymore, Rose," she told herself firmly as she pulled a towel from the linen closet.

When Lee had asked her about tonight's schedule, he'd said he wanted to talk to her about something. She hoped it was something about the two of them building a family together, and she'd called her mother to arrange a visit to Dallas. Nat's birthday was coming up, and Rosalie had asked if she could bring Lee to introduce him to her parents and sister.

She was planning to talk to him about taking that

next step in their relationship, and she didn't think the cowboy would be so surly and cruel as to plan an amazing anniversary date only to break up with her.

She'd left the date open, because Lee had a busy schedule, and Rosalie didn't pretend to understand all he did during work hours. He'd taken calls on several of their dates, as he claimed that the work on a dairy farm that grew a lot of hay and a lot of corn never really stopped.

Rosalie hadn't minded, because he always kept the calls short and brought his attention right back to her. He was attentive and caring, sweet and smart and sexy.

No, she wasn't going to ruin her chance at happily-ever-after with Handsome and a future on his farm for her selfish ex.

She took the towel out to Autumn, who happily babbled to her father about her first week of kindergarten. Rosalie had loved her stories too, and she was more than happy to co-parent with James. She wanted him to be involved in Autumn's life forever.

Rosalie simply didn't love him the same way she once had, and she wasn't going to pack up her whole life and follow him again. Instead, she went back inside and started putting together the edible cookie dough that went on top of the brownies she'd just finished. She planned to cut them, freeze them, and ship them to Lee in the morning.

He'd get the treats the same day, and she warmed at

the thought of him smiling when he opened the package and saw what it was and who it was from.

A COUPLE OF EVENINGS LATER, ROSALIE CHECKED HER PHONE for the umpteenth time. Lee had not called or texted, and he was now a half-hour late. She dialed him, because if she didn't need to pace in front of her window in her heels, she wasn't going to.

He didn't answer, which only added fire to her frustration. She didn't bother to leave a message, because he'd see she called.

Once, then twice ten minutes later, then three times ten minutes after that.

Her stomach roared at her for something to eat, and Rosalie kicked off her shoes. Her boyfriend was almost an hour late picking her up for their "special" anniversary date, and she honestly didn't want to go anymore.

She went into the kitchen and pulled out a container of leftovers. She didn't even know what was inside as she tossed it in the microwave and hit the minute button. Fuming, she ran through the reasons why Lee would be so late and not answer his phone.

His mama.

His daddy too, for that matter.

A family emergency.

Something had happened on the farm.

Perhaps he'd gotten dizzy and fallen again.

He'd lost his glasses. Or his phone. "Or his sanity," Rosalie muttered, the anger inside her still simmering.

For any of the above reasons—besides the one where he didn't have his device—he could've called her or answered her calls. He was so proud, always trying to handle everything himself. He did carry a lot of responsibility around Sweet Water Falls Farm, but some of that he chose to shoulder alone.

If he was having a family emergency, he should've called her specifically because then he wouldn't have to go through that alone. He'd *promised* he would.

While her dinner-for-one heated, she went down the hall and changed out of her carefully chosen clothes for the evening. Whatever Lee had planned was surely ruined. No one held a table at a fancy restaurant for over an hour. Events didn't simply wait for the mighty Lee Cooper and his date to decide to show up before they started.

Rosalie wished her thoughts weren't so poisoned, and as she pulled on a tie-dyed sweatshirt and a pair of loose, black pants, she released another breath, forcing all of the tension out of her muscles. She didn't want to feel negative toward Lee. He was a busy man, and he did work hard. He tried, and he cared, and she knew that.

"He's also very proud," she whispered to herself as she sank onto her bed. She studied her hands, the next question in her head too dangerous to give voice to.

Do you think he'll ever let you take care of him?

Why should he? Lee didn't need anyone, least of all her. Helplessness lashed through Rosalie, bringing stinging tears to her eyes. Somewhere outside of her consciousness, the microwave beeped, and she got to her feet to go eat.

The container held a sausage-stuffed pepper with Tex-Mex rice, and Rosalie ate half of it before the doorbell rang. She got to her feet, her pulse pounding, especially when a fist joined the party, and Lee said, "Rose, it's me."

She flew toward the door then, fueled by adrenaline and a bit of cayenne pepper. She yanked open the door to find the handsome cowboy standing there with an anxious look on his face. "Howdy."

Rosalie scoffed, spun on her heel, and marched away from him.

"Rose," he said after her.

"Don't," she said, several years of holding her tongue about to be broken. She picked up her fork as if she'd take another bite of pepper, but she couldn't. She faced him, lifted her chin, and got ready to vomit out everything.

"I'm sorry," he said, his eyes scanning down to her bare feet. "You're not dressed."

"Sure I am," she said. "For a cozy evening in, without my daughter, because the nanny I have to pay overtime tonight took her to a movie. So I can't just go pick her up and save myself a few dollars."

Lee opened his mouth, but Rosalie held up her hand.

The cowboy was smart, because he snapped his lips shut. "I called you three times," she said. "Tell me your phone is lost or broken."

He said nothing.

Rosalie folded her arms and cocked one hip. "Tell me your mama or daddy is in the hospital."

Lee dropped his chin toward his chest.

"So it's the farm."

"Yes," he said.

"Fine," she said. "I don't care about the farm, Lee. I care that you didn't call me."

"Time moves funny out there," he said.

"Then you need to figure out how to rope it and make it move right," she spat back. "Or at least look at your blasted phone when it rings."

He looked up, some fire in the forest now. "To be honest, it was the farm, and then Mama. There's a lot going on all the time. Something I think will take five minutes takes an hour. Then Mama needs help getting up. Then I get tied up in a conversation there. Then, then, then."

"One of those *thens* should be you calling your girlfriend and letting her know she doesn't need to spend an hour getting ready for a date that isn't going to happen."

"I didn't want to cancel," he said.

"No." Rosalie picked up her half-eaten dinner and took it over to the sink. "You just want me to be styled and ready for whenever you are."

"I didn't say that."

"Why did you make the drive at all?" she demanded. "You could've called when you got in the truck—a half-hour ago—and rescheduled."

"I didn't want to reschedule."

They could talk in circles forever, and Rosalie was suddenly too tired to say another word. She shook her head and said nothing.

"This is how life is on the farm," he said, throwing the words at her. "This is what I wanted to talk to you about. If you think you can live a farm life, with my sick, crazy, loud family. Be a farmer's wife, who might have to keep the time for her husband, because things get away from him sometimes."

He sucked in a long breath, and Rosalie looked over to him, finding fury and anguish on his face. She wanted to reassure him instantly that she could do what he'd just described. *Of course* she could be his timekeeper, and his secret-keeper, and the keeper of his heart too.

She wanted to tell him that she'd been dreaming of moving into that cabin with him, and leaving town behind to escape into the hills and woods with him, to live the exact life he'd described.

Autumn would have a full-time father, and Ford would complete their family on the weekends and all summer long. Heck, she was a lot younger than Lee, and she wanted more kids. Especially a child with his auburn hair.

Lee was a good man, and he tried hard. But what if trying wasn't enough? What if she'd always be disappointed by him?

Her emotions tornadoed and tangled, and nothing came out of Rosalie's mouth.

CHAPTER TWENTY-SIX

Lee sat on the edge of his bed, the world dark around him. Heck, the world was dark inside him too. He stood, a groan accompanying the twinge of pain that pulled through his lower back. He half-hobbled, half-walked into the bathroom, mentally berating himself for working himself so hard yesterday.

Not only was it not necessary, but it didn't drive away Rosalie or the silence between them. He wanted to call her and try to explain everything again. The first time had gone so poorly, and Lee couldn't get his mind to focus on all he had said, what she'd said, and what the next step should be for the two of them.

In all honesty, it felt like there was no next step for the two of them. Lee's mood worsened, and he hadn't even left the cabin yet. He curled his fingers into fists and pressed his knuckles against the granite countertops in his bathroom as he leaned forward to look into his eyes.

Exhaustion ran through him. Over him. Around him. He wanted to go back to bed and forget the past five days, but he didn't know how to do that. Dawn came every single day at Sweet Water Falls Farm, and with it came customers. Lee was responsible for making sure their commercial customers stayed up-to-date with everything, from the freshness of their products, to when the truck left with their butter, and when the delivery would happen.

He'd started talking to someone about building a Cooper & Co app, so their customers could track everything from their phones. They could make payments, see invoices, get tracking numbers, and create new orders. Anything. Everything.

The weight of the entire farm rested on Lee's shoulders, and he sagged under the burden of it. Not only did he have to carry the load of the administration office, but he had to make sure Mama and Daddy were taken care of, and he had to now avoid Will and Gretchen, the happiest newlyweds who'd ever existed. He also hadn't gone out of his way to talk to Travis, because it felt like every other word out of his mouth was, "Shay."

Shay this. Shay that. Gretchen this. Gretchen that.

Lee didn't want to hear about how blissful everyone was when he was so terribly miserable.

His phone buzzed back in the bedroom, and Lee had

the strong desire to throw it out the window in the general direction of the pond and hope with everything he had that he'd hit the water. Hard.

He ignored his device for now, because if there was a problem before five-thirty a.m., he didn't need to know about it. He really didn't.

He showered and shaved, dressed and dropped his phone in his back pocket without looking at it. In the kitchen, he started a pot of coffee and pulled out a single-serve container of oatmeal. As he held it in his hand, he felt like the most pathetic man in the entire world.

He tossed the oatmeal away from him and pulled his phone out again. He dialed Cherry while swiping away the texts from his other sister. It was her night to cook, and he hadn't seen her whole message. Only enough to know she wanted him to trade her nights.

His first inclination was to say no, but in the end, it didn't matter. He didn't have anything going on tonight. He didn't have anything going on tomorrow night either. He didn't drive to town mid-week anymore, and he'd force himself to go pick up Ford on Friday night, just like he had over the weekend.

"Leland Howard Cooper," Cherry said, her voice set on growly bear. "Why are you callin' me at five-forty-five in the morning?"

He hadn't paid much time to the time, though he knew it was early. "I—"

"Is it Mama?"

"No," he said, changing the form of his sentence.

"Daddy?"

"No."

"Is anyone we're directly related to in the hospital?"

"No."

"Then I'm hanging up, and you can call me back in two hours."

"Cherry, I need—" He stopped talking when something triggered in his brain that his sister had actually hung up on him. He stared at the phone as it darkened, and he immediately wanted to call her back. Her or Rosalie, and since he couldn't summon the courage to call his girlfriend, he set his phone on the counter and pulled open the fridge.

"She's not your girlfriend anyway," he muttered to himself. They hadn't exactly broken up. He'd never said the words. She hadn't either. Rose wouldn't change back into her nicer clothes and go to the violin concerto with him either, and Lee had left her house only twenty minutes after he'd arrived at it.

Of course, every other night since then had been low-key and drama-free. He could've driven to town any of those nights and taken Rose out for an amazing candle-light dinner with a group of musicians playing sweet, romantic songs nearby.

He should've rescheduled with her. Or called her back. Or texted. She would've been happy with a text, and since he hadn't done it, now Lee wasn't sure she'd ever be happy with him in general.

The doubts flew from one corner of his mind to the other as he made himself scrambled eggs and two slices of asiago cheese toast. He loved the nutty flavor of it, especially with a lot of butter, even if he didn't like the burnt cheese smell in the cabin. It would air out by lunchtime, and Lee wouldn't even be able to remember what he'd eaten for breakfast.

His phone rang, and Lee swiped on the call from Rissa. "Yes," he said into the phone. "I can switch you."

"You could've texted."

Lee pressed his eyes closed in a long blink. "I had a couple of things on my mind," he said, not trying to hide his annoyance. "We can't all be perfect, you know?"

"I didn't say you had to be perfect. I said you should've texted me back."

"I'm hanging up," Lee said.

"Lee," Rissa practically yelled, and he slowed the motion of his phone away from his face. He said nothing, but he didn't hang up, and Rissa seemed to take that as a sign to keep talking. "We all know you and Rosalie aren't together anymore."

He lifted the phone back to his ear, his heart pounding through his whole body. He didn't know what to say to that, so once again, he stayed quiet.

"I can help you come up with some ideas to talk to her again," Rissa said, her voice much quieter and less bossy.

"Not tonight, because Spence and I have a late doctor's appointment, but tomorrow."

"I might die today," Lee whispered. Deep down, he knew he wouldn't. He'd broken up with women before. He'd had them lie to him, cheat on him, and misunderstand him. He knew the depths of despair keenly, and that was precisely why he'd given up dating.

But this separation from Rosalie felt deeper and more personal. He completely felt like he might expire later that day if he didn't speak to her soon. He knew in that moment that he was in love with Rosalie Reynolds, and he had to do something about it.

"I'm coming over," Rissa said.

Lee's phone beeped and vibrated, and he pulled it away from his ear to see his other sister's name on the screen. "You don't need to come over today," Lee said. "I'm okay."

"You're a liar," Rissa said.

"Cherry's calling. I have to go."

"This early?" Rissa sounded suspicious, and Lee needed to get her off the phone, quick. "Tell her I want that pumpkin pancake mix!"

"'Bye," Lee said, hanging up by swiping over to get his older sister's call connected. "It hasn't been two hours."

"I have learned through the grapevine that you've broken up with Miss Rosalie."

Lee's chest caved in on itself. "No hello?"

"I'm assuming she's why you called me before six o'clock this morning."

"It's been five days," Lee said. "I'm dying, Cher. Help me." He wasn't above begging, not with Cherry. They'd been through so much together, and Lee would help her in any situation. "Please help me."

"Start at the beginning," Cherry said, with a huge sigh. "You're on speaker, and Mister Whiskers gets yowly for breakfast about seven. I can't be responsible for what you might hear."

Lee smiled to himself, because Cherry could always make him smile. "Doing your hair?"

"If I'm up this early, I might as well go into work with perfectly straight hair."

"Is Doctor Freeman going to be in the office today?"

"There may or may not be a meeting," Cherry said with plenty of self-righteousness in her voice.

"What about you and Jed?"

"What?" Cherry asked, and a loud crash came through the line. Speaker phone. Lee stirred sugar and cream into his coffee, thinking Will would never add calories to his morning caffeine. "There is no me and Jed." Cherry's voice held plenty of acid.

"Yeah, well, you flirted your face off at the picnic."

"That's called practice," Cherry said. "For Doctor Freeman."

"Flirting is what you're calling practice now?"

"Did you think we were together?"

"I thought you might be interested in him, yes."

"How are we talking about me?" Cherry asked, and Lee knew there *was* something to her and Jed. Cherry wouldn't talk about it until she was good and ready, that much he knew, and he didn't press the issue at the moment. "Tell me what happened with Rosalie. Don't leave anything out."

Lee wasn't sure if he could start at the beginning and get through everything by seven a.m. Still, he thought he better try. "I think it started when Mama went into the hospital when she had that infection..."

To his credit, he finished only twenty minutes later. Cherry remained silent, and that didn't give Lee much hope. "Cherry?"

"First off, I just want to say that I love you, because you're my brother. But Lee, seriously? The Good Lord put us on this earth in the day and age where we have cellphones. You should've called her."

"I didn't ask for a lecture," Lee said. "I need you to help me get her back."

"I'm going to need some time to think," Cherry said. "This is bigger than a fancy restaurant."

"I was going to take her to the violin concerto, but it ended over the weekend."

"Does she like classical music?"

"Yeah," Lee said with a sigh. "And sour candy, her daughter, the beach, baking, and all of her cute pencil skirts. I don't know how to take all of that and make something for her that tells her I love her." Lee only realized what he'd said after the words had come out of his mouth. He couldn't take them back, and the best he could do was hope Cherry had gone temporarily deaf.

"Lee," she whispered, all traces of her annoyance and exasperation with him gone.

"I know, okay?" He didn't want to repeat it, though the love he felt for Rosalie flowed through his bloodstream. "Help me, Cherry. Think fast, please."

Cherry didn't speak right away, and a heavy thread of guilt pulled through him. "I'm sorry, Cher. There's really no you and Jed?"

"There's really not," she said. "Or me and Doctor Freeman." *Me and anyone* echoed through the line, and Lee wished he hadn't involved his sister. She'd been in love with Charlie Mortimer for as long as Lee could remember, and she hadn't really dated since him. It had been a decade now, and Lee would like to see Cherry find someone who could love her as much as she wanted to be loved.

"I'm sorry," Lee whispered.

"You're thinking too, right, Lee?" she asked. "You know Rosalie better than I do. What can you do to get her back?"

"I'm thinking, yes," Lee said, though he had to admit he'd always known he'd call Cherry and ask for her help. He hadn't been able to do anything in his relationship with Rose by himself. Sure, he executed someone else's plans or suggestions, but his mind felt blank when it came to the educational game developer he hadn't stopped thinking about for months.

"Talk later," Cherry said.

"Talk later." Lee hung up, and he stood in his kitchen for several quiet moments, trying to piece together a plan without his glasses and with only paper clips.

It felt impossible. Utterly impossible.

Sour candy. Flowers. Pencil skirts.

Lee moved papers from files to his desk and back, his mind revolving around the things Rosalie liked.

Beef short ribs. Baking. Peach cobbler. The color purple, particularly the deeper eggplant.

He loaded up milk and cream for a customer. Oversaw the filling of bottles and the loading of them for the organic grocers out in the Hill Country.

Her games. Her daughter. Her sister.

Lee looked up from the last bit of office work he had to do that day. "Her family." Rosalie's family was extremely important to her, and she'd told Lee a couple of times that she enjoyed spending time with his as well.

She'd told him not to let his pride get in the way of being with her.

She'd told him to call her or communicate with her, to value her time, and to reschedule if he had to.

He could combine all of those things...somehow. Someone entered the administration building, and Lee logged the last payment into their accounting software as both Will and Travis appeared in the doorway of the office, one right after the other.

They exchanged a glance, and Lee knew that look well. He held up one hand and said, "I know, you guys, okay? I already know."

Will settled onto the couch and crossed one ankle over his knee. "How are you going to get her back?"

"Did Rissa send you?"

"Maybe," Travis said at the same time Will said, "No." He whipped his attention to Travis, who'd leaned against the doorjamb. "Maybe? You're the worst at keeping secrets."

"I am not, or you'd know Shay is pregnant."

Silence rained down in the office, all while Travis's face grew redder and redder.

"You weren't supposed to tell us that, were you?" Lee asked, fighting back a laugh.

Travis cleared his throat. "It would be great if you could pretend to be super excited in a couple of weeks when we make the official announcement."

"Yeah, because Will's *so* great at acting," Lee said, finally letting his laughter out.

"Hey, you're no Emmy-award winner," Will said, chuckling too. Once the two of them had quieted, Will focused on Lee again. "Seriously, brother. We know she's really important to you. What are you going to do?"

"I'm formulating a plan right now," Lee said. "A... loose plan."

"You've got nothing," Travis said.

"No," Lee protested. "I have something. I just need a little bit of help from my two favorite brothers." He grinned at them and gestured Travis toward the couch. "Sit. If I'm going to bare my soul to you, I'm not doing it while you hover over me."

CHAPTER TWENTY-SEVEN

Cherry couldn't believe she was once again in her car, driving south. Lee had insisted she come for the weekend, that he needed her help. *Desperately needed* were the words he'd used. She'd asked him several times to tell her what he planned to do to get Rose back into his life, but he'd steadfastly refused to tell her.

Just come to the farm, please, he'd said. *I only need you on Saturday afternoon. Please.*

Cherry couldn't say no to Lee, not when he asked her so nicely. Not when he was so heartbroken and when Rose was so perfect for him.

A heavy weight settled around her neck, and she wasn't sure how much longer she could hold it. Lee knew how much she wanted to find someone she could spend the rest of her life with. She'd made a huge mistake by asking Charlie Mortimer to attend Travis's wedding with her.

She wasn't getting anywhere with Dr. Freeman, that was for dang sure. No amount of hair straightening seemed to make him think of her as more than a secretary, and Cherry was tired of flirting with the man and getting nowhere.

Jed Forrester hadn't stopped texting or calling her, and a new kind of warmth moved through her as she navigated off the freeway and started to slow down. She couldn't believe she'd kept talking to him, especially as he possessed one of the saltiest personalities she'd ever encountered.

He had helped her immensely at Travis's wedding in May. He'd allowed her to show up at his cabin late at night, with glassy eyes and a blubbering explanation about Mama in June. He'd held her in his strong, warm arms for a good twenty minutes while she'd wetted his T-shirt with her tears.

In July, she'd done nothing but flirt with him at the family and friends picnic, and everyone in the family had noticed. Only Lee had said anything to her about it, and Cherry had denied everything when it came to Jed.

Right now, she couldn't deny the way her heart thumped and bumped in her chest as she pulled into the parking lot where they'd agreed to meet for a late lunch. She'd insisted on this location, because neither of them knew anyone in Casper, a smallish town halfway between San Antonio and Sweet Water Falls.

She didn't see his truck, and she came to a stop in the stall and put her sedan in park. She went over August, when she'd seen Jed at Will and Gretchen's wedding. She hadn't invited him specifically to be her escort or guest, but they'd sat beside one another, and he'd definitely held her hand when no one was looking.

Now that September had arrived, and Cherry was going to Sweet Water Falls for Lee, she'd suggested this date. She didn't think she'd be able to see Jed otherwise, and for some reason she couldn't name, she wanted to see him.

A truck pulled up beside her, and she recognized the hulking black beast. Jed Forrester sat behind the wheel, and his personality matched his vehicle. He raised his hand, a glorious smile on his face.

He was gorgeous, with dark hair and eyes, his beard salted with gray and a hint of red. She didn't think two redheads should ever get together, because she already carried enough fire in her veins for the both of them. Jed had no problem saying what was on his mind, and somehow, Cherry liked that about him.

Sometimes. When he was talking about something on his farm, or someone besides her.

She got out of her car and clicked her fob to lock it behind her. Jed laughed as he came around the front of his truck in a jog, and Cherry couldn't help smiling at him too.

"Howdy, pretty lady," he said, wrapping her in a hug right there in the parking lot. They'd been talking a lot over the past four months, and while they only saw each other once a month, Cherry hadn't minded.

She held him too, the width and strength in his shoulders evident beneath her touch. "How was the drive?" she asked.

He pulled back, a frown already between his eyes. "I don't get why we couldn't have met closer to town."

"I didn't want to run into anyone I know." Cherry didn't want to have to explain again, that was for sure.

"Are you embarrassed of me?" He stroked her hair off her face and tucked it behind her ear. She'd straightened it for him that morning, as Cherry always took great care to put herself together completely before she left her house.

"No," she said, thinking of all the jagged edges inside her. She felt like an old house on a great piece of property. People would come see the house to determine if they wanted to purchase it, and they'd say things like, "She's got great bones. She just needs a little work."

Or, "With a little elbow grease, she'll be perfect."

Or, "The land is fantastic, but the house needs a lot of work."

She knew she needed a lot of work. New plumbing and an updated roof. She had a lot of preconceived notions about men—especially cowboys like Jed—and no one she'd ever been out with had been able to convince her that she was wrong.

Jed kept his head down as his hand slid along the side of her neck to the back of it. He wore a small smile as he said, "Good. I'm not embarrassed of you either. Of us." He looked up, and Cherry found desire swimming in his eyes.

Charlie hadn't looked at her like that for a long time, not even during the wedding. Dr. Freeman hadn't either. She was faceless and nameless to him.

Not to Jed.

"Cherry Cooper," he whispered. "Am I your secret boyfriend?"

"No," she said, leaning into his arms. She grinned up at him too. "You're not my boyfriend."

His eyebrows went up. "I'm not?"

"Not until there's kissing happening."

His smile widened. "I can take care of that right now."

"You're so arrogant," she said, pressing against his chest.

He stumbled back a single step, righted himself, and moved right back into her personal space, bringing her flush against his body. "Can I kiss you, Miss Cooper?"

Cherry took a few moments as if she was really considering it. She could admit to herself that she'd thought about kissing Jed, especially since their flirt-fest over the Fourth of July. "All right, Mister Forrester."

He leaned down, taking his sweet, Texas time, his

smile oh-so-charming and his eyes oh-so-sparkly. She closed hers, the anticipation building the way category five hurricanes did out in the Gulf of Mexico.

He finally touched his lips to hers, the pressure light and sweet and utterly powerful. She reacted to him instantly, and the kiss became firmer and deeper in less time than it took to breathe.

This cowboy knew how to kiss a woman, and Cherry let him lead her down a path where she could never kiss another man and not compare him to Jed. He pulled away before she was ready to let him go, and she pressed her lips together to try to prolong the tingling sensation happening there.

He chuckled low in his throat and said nothing, which Cherry really appreciated. Instead, he backed up, took her hand, and turned to lead her into the restaurant. They got a booth, and when they had menus in front of them, Cherry finally asked, "Have you been here before?"

"Here?" Jed looked over his menu to her. "An hour from where I live and work? In a town I didn't know existed?"

She scowled at him. "You don't have to be so mouthy."

He cocked one eyebrow at her and looked back at the menu. "I haven't been here."

Neither had Cherry, obviously.

"Are you gonna tell Lee about us?" he asked without looking up.

"I don't know," Cherry said.

"How long are you gonna be in town this time?"

"A couple of nights," she said, watching him and trying to figure out where this conversation was headed.

He looked up, those dark blue eyes pulling at her the way they had in May. She'd known Jed for a long time. He and his brothers had already taken over the farm for their father, much the way Lee had for Daddy. He and Lee were the same age, and they'd been friends for a long time. Cherry had known him growing up too, though there'd never been anything romantic between them.

"You can stay at the farm," he said. "I've got a cabin open right now."

Surprise darted through Cherry. "I'm not staying at your farm."

"Where are you going to stay?" he challenged, both eyebrows up now. "I know you won't stay at your place."

Cherry couldn't argue with him about that. She hadn't told him everything about her past, obviously, as their conversations had mostly been superficial stuff, like favorite foods and tons of flirting and teasing.

"You won't stay somewhere for free," he said. "Five bucks a night. You can pay me five dollars per night for the cabin."

"Five dollars?" she asked with plenty of sarcasm.

He grinned at her. "Fine, I'll take ten."

Cherry smiled back and shook her head, though the idea of staying at Jed's farm held some appeal for her.

"It's cabin four," he said. "You can come any time, because it's not locked."

Their waiter arrived, and the conversation paused while they put in their orders. With the menus gone, Jed reached across the table and covered Cherry's hands with both of his. "I'll bring you breakfast tomorrow morning. Cabin four."

"You don't have to do that."

"I know I don't," he said. "I want to. I think you'll be busy with Lee tomorrow, and then you'll be gone on Sunday. I feel like breakfast tomorrow is all I'm gonna get."

He was probably right, but Cherry didn't confirm it. "We're having lunch today."

"Yeah, and I want to see you tomorrow too."

She liked how he just said whatever he thought, at least in instances like this. "I suppose I'll be needing breakfast tomorrow."

"I suppose so." He grinned at her and pulled his hands back. Their late lunch passed quickly, with Jed talking about the work on his farm and Cherry telling him a bit about what she did at the college in the city. Out of everyone in her family, Will knew the most about what she did, while Lee knew the most about her love life.

As she and Jed left the restaurant, he asked, "So that's a yes to cabin four? You've got twenty bucks?"

Cherry looked up into the bright blue sky, wondering

where she'd misplaced her sanity. "All right," she said. "Cabin four. I'll leave a twenty on the kitchen counter."

Jed whooped and said, "Lord," into the sky. "Just once, I want to hear this woman say *yes* to me. Just once!"

Cherry laughed, because she did fight Jed on a lot of things. He did work extraordinarily hard to have her in his life, and she leaned into him as a way of telling him *thanks for not giving up on me yet.*

She wondered if he would eventually, or if he'd keep needling at her until she gave into everything he asked of her.

He led her over to her sedan and put his hand on the door handle. "You'll tell me yes one day, right, Cherry?" He grinned at her, clearly flirting.

She placed both hands against his chest and smiled up at him. "Maybe, cowboy."

He chuckled, shook his head, and leaned down to kiss her. He left the parking lot first, and Cherry took a few minutes to check her make-up to ensure she wouldn't show up at her brother's house with smudged lipstick. There'd be way too many questions then, and Lee would know to bring up Jed's name.

Cherry wanted to keep her secret boyfriend to herself for a bit longer, and her stomach turned with every mile that took her closer to home.

"It's just a weekend," she told herself. "And Jed will bring you breakfast. It won't be all bad."

She hoped.

Her thoughts switched to the salty, mouthy cowboy, and while she couldn't put her finger on exactly what about Jed called to her, something definitely did.

"Lord," she whispered, her fingers tightening around the steering wheel. "Help me to know when to say yes to him and when to say no."

CHAPTER TWENTY-EIGHT

Rosalie rolled over when her bedroom door squeaked. "Momma?"

"Yeah, baby," she said, peeling back the covers so Autumn could climb into bed with her. Her daughter had been the only reason she'd survived the past week and a half. Without Lee, Rosalie wasn't quite sure how to function.

During the week, she got up and went to work to the best of her ability. Life had turned numb and very dull around the edges. She'd forgotten a meeting this week, and that hadn't happened once since she'd opened Curious Kids.

Autumn snuggled into her chest, and Rosalie wrapped her arms around the little girl. "Momma feeling bad still?"

"A little," Rosalie whispered. She didn't know what

time it was, but light filled the bedroom. It had to be late, but on a Saturday morning, she didn't care.

"Can we go see the giant pumpkin?" Autumn asked.

Rosalie had forgotten she'd promised to take her daughter to the Fall Festival this weekend. She seized onto it with both hands, using it to pull herself up and out of her depression. "Yes," she said. "Let me get showered, and we'll go."

Autumn cheered and climbed out of the bed. "I'll get dressed."

Rosalie didn't argue, but she'd have to kindly and gently re-dress her daughter once she finished getting ready. Autumn would likely choose her Halloween costume or a dress that wasn't right for an outdoor festival.

For now, Rosalie just let her skip out of the room while she went to shower. She'd just finished getting dressed in a pair of shorts and a pale blue tank top when her phone rang. Natasha's name sat there, and her sister had always been able to cheer her up.

She could barely smile today, but she answered the call and lifted the phone to her ear. "Hey, Nat."

"Rose," she said, her voice far too loud. "I'm sending you a picture of our garden."

Rosalie smiled fully now. "Sounds good, Nat. Are the sunflowers huge?"

"So big!" her sister yelled. "Mom said I can send pictures now, but I have to ask her first."

"That's a good idea," Rosalie said. "How's the new manager? What's his name again?"

"Scott," Nat said. "He's nice. He knows a lot of math."

Rosalie sank onto her bed. "I bet he does."

"I saw a new cheerleading routine," she said next, the topics changing like the weather in Texas sometimes. Rapidly.

Rosalie enjoyed talking to her sister, and for the next ten minutes, she felt like she might be able to recover from the silence and distance between her and Lee Cooper. Neither of them had ever said they were going to break-up, but she hadn't called or texted him, and he hadn't attempted to communicate with her either.

She regretted standing up to him so powerfully last week, but at the same time, she wanted to be happy inside her relationships. She hadn't realized how unhappy she'd been with James until he'd left and she'd had to pick up all the pieces of her life alone.

Even then, she hadn't known.

She hadn't truly understood what happiness and joy and love was until she'd met and started to date Lee.

I have to get him back, she thought, with another immediate question of, *How?*

"Oh, I have to go," Nat said. "My ride is here."

Rosalie's radar pinged at her. "Your ride?"

"Say good-bye," Mom said, and Rosalie hadn't even known she was on the line.

"Bye!" Nat said, and Rosalie knew she'd be gone.

"Mom," Rosalie said. "Why is she getting a ride? Where is she going?"

"The grocery store," her mom said, but something sounded off in her voice. "The school is doing weekend outings, and today's is for Nat to get her shopping done."

"You're not doing that with her anymore?"

"We signed her up for some classes," Mom said. "It's been really good for her. And us. We told you this last week, Rose."

Rosalie frowned, because she truly couldn't remember that.

"Anyway, we'll see you soon," Mom said. "Daddy and I are excited to come see you and Autumn for Halloween."

"Sure," Rosalie said, already tired and she hadn't left the house yet. Not only that, but Halloween sat weeks from now, and Rosalie seriously considered taking a trip home to see her parents. She could use a good, tight hug and some reassurance that she'd find someone to love her and Autumn the way they deserved to be loved.

"Are you okay, dear?" her mother asked.

Tears pricked Rosalie's eyes, and her neck tightened to the point where she couldn't speak. Her first instinct was to tell her mother that she was fine. Maybe a little tired. Maybe work wasn't going super well. Oh, and had she mentioned she'd broken up with Lee?

No, she hadn't mentioned it. She didn't want to say anything out loud for fear that it would actually be true, and she'd have to face the fact that she was completely and utterly miserable without him in her life

She felt like the future she'd started to imagine for herself had vanished in a single evening, and she needed more time to mourn the loss of it.

"I'm okay," she finally said, but the tone of her voice suggested otherwise.

"Rose," her mom said. Nothing else. The open invitation to keep talking sat there, but Rosalie didn't know how to fill in the blanks.

"They need me at the door," her mom said. "I'll call you back real soon, okay?"

Rosalie nodded, but she couldn't voice any words. The call ended, and Rosalie tossed her phone onto the bed beside her. Then Autumn came through the door, and she wore a bright pink shirt with a cheetah print on it and a pair of shorts that had once been part of a pajama set.

The little girl brightened her whole world, and Rosalie smiled at her and wiped her eyes at the same time. "Ready, baby?" she asked.

"Let's go!" Autumn thrust her rabbicorn into the air, and just the sight of that stuffed animal made Rosalie weepy all over again.

She quickly got to her feet and twisted to get her phone, hoping she could get control of her emotions before her daughter saw her crying. The Lord *had* reached down and helped her in that single moment, because she steadied herself emotionally in an instant and turned back to her daughter.

"Let's go." She wasn't going to correct her clothes. She wasn't going to criticize them. She just wanted to spend some time out in the sunshine, and she prayed that she'd find a way to think about something—anything—except Lee Cooper for just a few hours.

FOUR HOURS LATER, ROSALIE TOED OPEN THE FRONT DOOR AND found Thumper waiting on the other side of the gate. He stomped, and Rosalie wanted to do the same gesture back to him. She felt petty and small taunting a bunny rabbit, so she didn't.

"Go on, Autumn," she said with the last of her patience. She carried a very heavy pumpkin in her arms, while Autumn had a plastic sack with paints in it. Her face had been colored with pinks and purples and sparkles and glitters at the face-painting booth, and she steadied herself against the doorjamb as she lifted her leg over the gate and entered the house.

Rosalie wanted to toss the gourd on the front porch and let it rot there, but she towed it into the house amidst a few more stomps from Thumper, who clearly wasn't happy about being ignored that morning. "Just a minute," she said darkly. "You're certainly not wasting away, buddy."

Autumn sang to herself as she skipped into the kitchen and put the bag of paint on the dining room table. Rosalie made it to the island and slid the pumpkin onto it, instant relief flowing into her tired arm muscles. There were so many things that would be easier if she had a partner to help her carry the load, but she didn't.

"Momma, can I go outside?"

They'd just spent hours outside, but Rosalie nodded. "I'll order something for dinner." They'd eaten trashy festival food for lunch, and her stomach hadn't liked all the grease and carbs. She had no energy to cook, and by the time she'd cut up a few carrots and shredded a bit of cabbage for Thumper, ordering food, her pajamas, and a romantic comedy on the TV was all she wanted for the rest of her afternoon and evening.

Her phone had become a dangerous thing, because after she'd collapsed onto the couch, her fingers tapped to get to her text string with Lee when they should've been looking through the food delivery app for something to eat that night.

She read back through several inches of messages, finding them precious in a way she didn't know how to describe. She had been the last one to message him, and she could feel, see, and hear her frustration in the texts.

She'd called him too, but she hadn't left any messages. She hadn't saved any of his previous voice-mails, and she found herself wishing she had.

She tapped on the phone icon at the top of the screen,

and his number went into the calling app. All she had to do was tap the green icon, and through the miracle of technology, she could hear Lee.

Perhaps she could simply apologize and tell him she'd been thinking about him, about them, and about what to have for dinner. She could ask him what he felt like eating that night, and if he might possibly have time to drive to her house to eat with her and Autumn.

They wouldn't even have to talk. She just wanted to be in the same room as him, to breathe in the warm, musky scent of his skin and feel the shape of his jaw in her palms as she cradled his face and kissed him.

The phone rang before she could gather the courage to tap the green phone icon and make the call. James's name sat on the screen, and all she had to do is pull down the bar that had appeared at the top to connect the call.

She hadn't spoken to him since last week, when he'd called on the same day Rosalie and Lee had been slated to have their romantic four-month anniversary. She didn't want to talk to him today either, and she simply looked at the phone while it rang and rang and finally went to voicemail.

The house sat in silence, save for the very quiet munching of veggies that came from Thumper. He hippity-hopped toward her, appearing at the end of the couch, his pink nose twitching. "Did you get enough to eat?" she asked him, sure he'd scarfed it all and had come to tell her to chop up some more carrots. No *please* in sight from the long-eared mammal.

He stared into her soul, his way of wearing her down until she gave in to his silent demand for more foliage. She stared right on back, determined to win this time. Her heart simply couldn't take it when someone wasn't happy, and she'd always given in to him.

To Nat, to Autumn, to her neighbor down the street who'd insisted she'd needed help with a bake-off.

She hadn't given in to James recently, and she'd stood up for herself when it came to Lee dictating when he'd show up and how long Rosalie had to wait for him. A flash of strength and pride worked its way through her, giving her a boost of energy and a moment of clarity.

Inside that moment, she realized that she'd always worked hard to make everyone around her happy. She'd usually succeeded, and now, *she* was the unhappy one.

She needed to make sure she took care of herself and did what she needed to do to be happy. She got to her feet, a question forming and coming out of her mouth. "So what's it going to be, Rosalie? What do you need to be happy?"

The answer floated through her mind, clear as a summer sky without a cloud.

Lee Cooper.

She turned back to pick up her phone, but the door-bell rang, distracting her. Thumper hopped around the couch and headed for the gate, as if it would somehow disappear when she opened the door this time.

Rosalie pushed her curls back out of her face, wishing she'd cared enough to put on makeup that morning. She hadn't, and she'd spent the day outside getting sweaty anyway.

She didn't care, because whoever stood on the other side of the door didn't matter.

She glanced outside to make sure Autumn was still okay, and she found the girl swinging in the hammock in the shade between two trees. So Rosalie faced the door and walked the length of the couch to open it.

Just as the doorbell rang again, she twisted the knob, her irritation at the other person's impatience firing inside her.

"Just a second," she said, the door already swinging inward. "I was coming." Her voice muted after that. Her irritation turned to adrenaline and spiked through her whole body simultaneously.

Lee Cooper stood there, no smile in sight, and strangling the neck of his guitar tightly in one hand.

CHAPTER TWENTY-NINE

Lee's nerves fled at the first sight of Rose. His beautiful, talented, smart Rose. He couldn't believe he'd let his temper and his tongue get between them. Guilt and anger at himself simmered in the background, but he wasn't going to allow his pride to keep this barrier between them.

"Ford," he said, finally tilting his head to the side and tearing his eyes from Rose. His son came forward, his guitar already strapped around his shoulder. His fingers plucked through a few chords while Lee threw his strap over his shoulder and positioned his fingers on the strings.

He met his son's eye, and they nodded in tandem. Since Ford was just a beginner, and Lee would have to say everything in his heart, he hadn't planned to play a particularly romantic love song. Instead, he and Ford strummed out a harmony, and he prayed that everything they'd just practiced down the street would happen flawlessly.

"Rose," he said, clearing his throat so his voice could travel easier and farther. "You once said I'd have to come play my guitar for you, so here I am." He heard footsteps behind him, and his heartbeat dive-bombed to the toes of his boots. His fingers nearly stumbled, but he knew these chords like he knew his own face, and he steadied everything inside him.

"I asked my whole family to come with me," he said. "Because they're important to me, and I'm important to them." He swallowed and continued with, "I know how very important family is to you as well, and I can promise you that our family will be first for me. Always."

His chest caved, but he breathed in deeply as Cherry arrived at his side, and then Will stood next to Ford. They didn't have any lines. They could leave as soon as it looked remotely like Rose would forgive him.

She reached up and brushed at her eyes, and Lee's hopes soared.

"I went and met your parents," he said next, and he knew the moment she caught sight of her parents and sister. "Because I know how very much you miss them and need them and love them. They are important to you, and therefore important to me."

"Lee," she said, and she started to step over the gate

keeping Thumper in the house. He didn't see Autumn, and he had more to say anyway.

"Stay there, dear," her mother said, and Rose did what she said. Her eyes filled with tears now, and she didn't try to clear them. She looked at Lee again, and his heart squeezed with love and compassion for her.

"I gathered everyone together," he said. "So they'd all know how much I love you. I can't live another day without talking to you. I just can't. I made a stupid mistake—a lot of them, actually. I was selfish, and I was proud, and I just wanted everything to be perfect for you in a world where that's pretty impossible."

"Lee." She shook her head and said nothing else.

"My life is a bit crazy at the farm," he said. "Maybe I am selfish for wanting you out there with me. Maybe I am proud enough to think you could possibly love me and help me and work at my side out there. I will work as hard as I can to be the man you deserve, to take care of you and Autumn, and to be the husband and father you want me to be."

He looked at Ford, and they wrapped up the harmony. In the silence that suddenly arrived on the porch, Lee drew a deep breath, and said, "I'm sorry, Rose. Please forgive me. I love you." He looked over to Will, and his brother stepped forward with a bouquet of flowers. Cherry moved with him, a giant bag of sour cherry candy for Rose.

"Mama?" Lee asked, twisting to look over his shoulder. He couldn't believe she and Daddy had come, but when Lee had told them his plan, they said they wouldn't miss it. Mama hadn't left the farm for more than a doctor's appointment or to go to the hospital in over a year.

Now, she stepped through the crowd holding two pizza boxes. Daddy came right behind her with three more. Rose's mom, Carla, lifted the three bags of salad Lee had bought that morning, and her dad, Roger, carried the garlic bread.

"I brought dinner," he said. "In the hopes that you'd take me back and we could all stay and eat with you and Autumn." He met Rose's eyes again, and the next thing he knew, Travis had taken his guitar.

"Go on," his youngest brother said, plenty loud enough for everyone to hear. "She's dyin' for you to kiss her."

Lee wanted to tell him to shush and grin at Rose at the same time. He moved toward the gate and right over it, careful not to step on the white rabbit lurking nearby. "Is that true?" he whispered, taking Rose into his arms.

She positively melted into him, her hands coming up to cradle his face and push up his glasses. "I don't need flowers," she said in the intimate space between them. "Or candy or dinner, though they are nice to have. Thank you." She touched her lips to his cheek, and Lee closed his eyes in bliss.

"What do you need, my rose?"

"Just you, Handsome."

He opened his eyes, sure he'd heard her wrong. She smiled at him, the gesture wobbly and somewhat timid. "You drove to Dallas and got my family?"

"They're so great," he whispered. "Just like you. I wanted everyone to know that you're my priority."

She searched his eyes for a breath, and said, "I love you too."

Lee dipped his head then and kissed her, his heartbeat finally settling into a rhythm he could live with.

Behind him, the crowd he'd brought with him could've brought the house down with their raucous applause and cheering. Because of that, he kept the kiss short and sweet, pulling away as he started to laugh.

He held Rose tight and asked, "You haven't eaten, have you? And where's Autumn?" He wished he'd have made Rose get her before he'd done all the strumming and confessing, because he'd wanted everyone important to him and Rose there, and Autumn was a huge part of both of those.

"We haven't eaten," she said. Looking past him, she said, "Come on in, everyone. Autumn's in the back yard."

Lee stepped past her to go get her daughter, because Rose would probably like a few minutes with her parents and sister. Nat had told him that she hadn't seen Rose since May, and she'd talked in a near-non-stop stream on the way to Sweet Water Falls about all the things she wanted to do this week while she'd be here.

He slid open the glass door that led into the back yard and found the little girl swinging in the hammock, a song lifting from her mouth. He smiled to himself as he stepped out onto the deck. Someone joined him, and he turned to find Will carrying Thumper in his arms.

"That was dang near perfect, Lee," Will said with a smile. He bent to put the rabbit on the ground. "She's perfect for you."

"Mm." Lee walked to the edge of the deck and watched Autumn, who still didn't know he and Will were there. "Maybe, but do you think I'm perfect for her?"

"Absolutely," Will said without hesitation. "She's been as miserable without you as you've been without her."

"How do you know?"

Will cut a look at Lee out of the corner of his eye, a smile spreading across his face. "I heard her say it to her mama just now."

Lee nodded, because he'd heard Rose say she loved him. He felt it in the careful way she held his face and kissed him.

Another set of footsteps came outside, and Lee turned to find Travis leading Daddy onto the back deck. "Good job, Lee," Travis said. "She's putting the flowers in water while her mom gets out paper plates. You did it." He clapped Lee on the back, and Lee finally allowed himself to smile.

"I did it."

Daddy limped up beside his three sons, and he smiled out at Autumn too. "Mama and I want to trade houses, Lee."

Lee jerked his attention toward his father. "What?" He expected Will and Trav to protest, to say something. Neither of them did.

"We'll take the cabin where you and Ford live now," Daddy said. "You and Rose can have the farmhouse for your family."

"You don't need to do that," Lee said, glancing at Will for help. His brother only nodded, and Lee wondered if they'd practiced this too.

"We can put the swing out on the back patio," Daddy said. "We'll be happy there, and we don't need all the space in the farmhouse. You two will."

"Ford's only with me on weekends still," Lee said. "We don't need the farmhouse for a while."

Daddy gave him a disgruntled look. "It's decided, son. Mama's already packing."

"Daddy."

"Do you not want the farmhouse?"

"Of course I want it," Lee said, not sure why this had turned into an argument. He curbed the frustration inside him. "Thank you, Daddy." He turned and stepped into his father's arms, glad he had his steady, strong influence in his life.

When he stepped back, something niggled his mind.

"I don't have a back patio, Daddy. You're thinkin' of Will's place." He looked over to his brother again.

This time Will grinned at him. "I'm gettin' your cabin," Will said. "It's bigger than mine, and Gretchen and I can raise a lot of kids there if we decide to stay."

"Mama and Daddy are moving into Will's cabin," Trav said. "And mine will be built before the baby comes."

"So we're all good," Daddy said, and with all of them in agreement, they turned back to the house. All of them except for Lee. He went down the steps while they went inside.

"Autumn," he called, and the little girl lifted her head. Pink and purple sparkles caught the sunlight, and she launched herself out of the hammock when she saw him coming.

"Mister Lee!" She ran toward him, and Lee laughed as he scooped her up and tossed her high into the air. She squealed and laughed, and Lee caught her and hugged her.

"Come on, baby," he said. "Your grandma and grandpa and Aunt Nat are here to see you."

Later that evening, Lee stood in Rose's dark kitchen, kissing her. So much had changed in the past six or seven hours, and he'd never been happier for a shift in his life. "I should go," he whispered just before pressing his lips to the feather-soft skin along her collarbone.

She sat on the island counter, and he stood between her legs, his arms around her back, keeping her as close to him as he could get her.

"You should," she said, bringing his mouth back to hers. She didn't kiss him like she wanted him to go but rather the opposite. Her parents had gone to their hotel an hour ago. His had left two before that, along with his siblings and his son. Her sister slept down the hall in Rose's spare bedroom, which sat across from Autumn's. Even Thumper had disappeared, leaving Lee and Rose completely alone.

Lee had been with a woman before, and he wanted nothing more than to be with Rose, wake up beside her in the morning, and make sure her Sabbath was glorious and full of joy. She matched him stroke for stroke, but he knew it wasn't an invitation for him to stay the night with her.

"What are you doin' tomorrow?" he asked, finally pulling away and getting control of himself.

"I don't know," Rose said, pushing her hands through her hair. "Probably going to the beach. Nat loves the beach." She smiled at him, the happiness in her eyes making him happy too. "Please come."

"Just tell me when," he said.

"You'd miss your family lunch?"

"Of course," he said. "Or you guys could come to it,

and then we can go to the beach after that. Whoever wants to."

"Who's cooking tomorrow?" she asked as if that would be the deciding factor.

"Rissa," he said. "She said anyone was invited."

Rose clasped her hands around the back of his neck. "You're my hero, you know that?"

"Hm, I thought I was just a surly cowboy." He grinned at her, glad when she grinned back.

"Not at all, Handsome." She kissed him again, and Lee let her set the pace as he moved with her, enjoying every moment with the woman of his dreams.

CHAPTER THIRTY

Rosalie called her daughter's name as she went down the hallway. "We have to get going," she said. "Lee and Ford are going to be here any minute." She entered the bedroom to find her daughter struggling with the fairy wings that would complete her costume. "I got 'em, baby."

She dropped to her knees behind Autumn and helped her get her arm through the right loop to position the sparkly wings on her back just-so. "There."

Autumn turned, bumping Rosalie in the face with the pointed tip of one wing. "Oof."

"Sorry, Momma." Autumn glowed with the joy that only Halloween brought to small girls who loved magical fairies and unicorns and glitter. She wore a leotard in bright pink and green, with more bedazzlement than Rosalie thought one garment could hold. Both Shay and Gretchen had helped

Rosalie deck out the costume, and they'd all been there when Autumn had opened the package a couple of weeks ago at the farmhouse during one of their Sunday lunches.

Out of everyone there, only Rosalie and Autumn didn't belong to the Cooper family officially. She hoped Lee would rectify that soon, but so far, there had been no proposals and no mention of diamond rings.

He'd shown up at her house about six weeks ago now, his guitar in his hand and everyone who mattered to her at his side. They all loved him too, so even if he could be distant sometimes, and proud others, and yes, surly, he was still everything in a man she'd always wanted.

He let her pick the restaurants they went to, and he showed up with surprises for her and Autumn just to make them smile. He kissed her like he meant it some-times, and other times, he let her dictate how fast or furious the kiss would be. He never let a day go by where he didn't tell her he loved her, and that meant so much to Rosalie.

The doorbell rang, and then Lee called, "It's us, Rose."

Autumn hugged her tightly and she said, "Go show him and Ford what you are." Her daughter skipped out of the bedroom, calling for Lee to come see her. He laughed with her while Rosalie got to her feet. She peered out of the doorway to watch their interaction, and her heart had never felt so full with the love she saw and experienced between Lee and Autumn.

He would be her father figure, the man who'd raise her, and gratitude that her daughter would have someone like Lee in her life full-time overcame her.

"You didn't dress up," Lee said, looking past Autumn to her.

"No," she said, stepping into the hallway fully. "I see you didn't either."

"You're lucky I'm here," he said dryly. He didn't say he disliked Halloween, though he had in the past. She knew he didn't like it, but he'd agreed to come walk around the neighborhood with the kids.

At the end of the hall, Ford stood in his wizard robes, and Rosalie smiled in his direction. "Let's go get this done," she said. "Then we can have hot ham sandwiches and caramel popcorn."

"That's the only reason I came," Lee said, bending to put Autumn down. She ran off toward Ford, and the two of them disappeared into the kitchen to get her treat bucket. "And to see you, of course." He took Rosalie into his arms, breathed her in, and swayed with her right there in the hallway. "I saw those caramel apples in the kitchen too."

She giggled against his chest. "I bet you did."

"Are those for me, or...?"

"You can have as many as you want," Rosalie said. "Gretchen dropped them off earlier today, while I was at the office."

Lee looked down at her, something serious in his expression. "What?" she asked.

"I'm glad you get along with Gretchen and Shayla," he said. "Rissa too. Mama. Everyone."

"I am too," she said. "Now, if someone would get his act together and ask me to marry him, I wouldn't have to feel on the outskirts of the family for much longer."

His eyes danced with light. "Get his act together?"

"Yeah, that's right." Rosalie backed up out of his arms and started to go past him. "We've talked about marriage, where we'll live, all of that. I'm not sure what you're waiting for."

"Rose." He latched onto her hand, his fingers tight against hers. She turned back to him, surprise darting through her. "Kids. I want to talk about having more kids first."

"Oh."

"Is that something you want? I mean, I've got Ford, and you've got Autumn, and the four of us will be fine. I just...wondered."

Rosalie had fantasized about having a little boy or girl with Lee's shiny, dark red hair. Maybe more like hers, with just a hint of fire in there. "Yes," she said simply. "I'd have more children, Lee." She reached up and tracked her fingers down the side of his face. "Your children."

He smiled softly into the palm of her hand. "All right, then." He kissed her then, and Rosalie could only imagine what it would feel like to be his wife and the mother of his children.

"Dad," Ford said, and Lee ducked his head to break the kiss. "We can't find Thumper."

"That rabbit," Lee said under his breath. "I'm not so sure about him, Rose." He strode away from her, barking questions at his son about the gate in the front door and where the kids had last seen Thumper.

Rosalie stayed in the hallway, smiling to herself, because while Lee acted grumpy about the rabbit, she knew he wouldn't get rid of him. The USS Thumper had been a gift to Autumn from her father, and Lee wouldn't take that from her, even if James lived in California and he hardly ever saw his daughter.

"Found 'im!" Ford called a few seconds later, and Rosalie went down the hall to gaze upon the three people she couldn't wait to live with.

ANOTHER WEEK PASSED WHERE ROSALIE'S LEFT RING FINGER SAT diamondless. Lee's sister was only a few days away from her due date, and she pulled up to the little white cottage-style cabin out at Sweet Water Falls Farm. Chrissy Cooper was throwing a baby shower today, and Rosalie had brought a large gift from her, Nat, and her mother.

"Ready?" she asked her sister, who rode in the passenger seat.

"Can I carry the present?" Nat wore glee on her face, and Rosalie couldn't tell her no.

"Sure," she said. "Let me know if it's too heavy for you." They'd gotten Rissa a set of bumper pads and bedding for the crib, though Rosalie had already been to this house and seen the nursery. It had been set up for a month, but she knew from personal experience that every new mother needed an extra set of everything. Sometimes two extra sets.

"I've got my gift," her mom said from the backseat. They all got out, and Nat collected the big box from the trunk while Rosalie and their mother waited. They started toward the cabin together, sounds of laughter and chatter coming through the open windows. The fields out here had been harvested and replanted with winter crops, and Rosalie couldn't even imagine all of the scheduling and work that went into a farm of this size.

She'd been in Lee's office dozens of times now, as she came out to the farm almost every day after work to see him. He made the trip to town on the weekends to see her, and she'd really enjoyed the accelerated relationship over the past couple of months.

At the door, she simply went in without bothering to knock. It seemed like everyone else had already arrived, even Cherry, who'd made the drive from San Antonio that morning. Lee's older sister spotted Rosalie, and a smile brightened her face.

"Hey, you," Cherry said, coming toward her and embracing Rosalie. "Who's got Autumn today?"

"Lee," Rosalie said, having dropped off her daughter with her boyfriend several minutes ago. "He's taking the kids to the corn maze at the Forresters."

Something crossed Cherry's face, but Rosalie held her tongue. Lee had speculated that Cherry and Jed Forrester had something going on between them, but when he'd asked, his sister had denied it. Watching her now, with her eyes flicking left and right, Rosalie was inclined to believe Lee.

"Is it good?" she asked.

"What?" Cherry blinked rapidly. "Is what good?"

"The corn maze at the farm next door." She shrugged as if she didn't really care, because she really didn't. "I've never been to it. Some are good and some aren't."

"I have no idea," Cherry said, plastering her smile back on her face. "I haven't been to a corn maze in years." She turned away from Rosalie, but not before Rosalie saw the hint of a lie in those deep, dark eyes. "Come get something to drink, Rosalie. Hey, Natasha."

Rosalie loved Cherry, because she didn't treat Nat any different than anyone else. Some people did, and Rosalie didn't like that. But not Cherry. Nat fell into step beside her, already talking about something Cherry probably didn't care about. But the other woman laughed, and Rosalie stopped worrying about her sister fitting in with the Coopers.

Her mother had gone straight to Chrissy's side, and the two of them sat on the couch already gossiping about something. As Rosalie gazed around at the women gathered for the shower, and the soft blue balloons that wafted lazily above the dining room chairs, she felt like she belonged here.

Even if she didn't have a diamond ring yet. Even if her last name still didn't match anyone's here.

She still belonged here.

A couple of hours later, Rosalie walked along the side of the dirt road on the farm, headed toward Lee's. He'd texted during the shower to say he and the kids were back from the movies and he'd love to make her dinner that evening. He'd invited her sister and mom too, but they were taking Rosalie's car back to town to meet her father for dinner.

Though November had arrived, the weather wasn't terribly cold yet, and Rosalie enjoyed the yellows and browns around the ranch. Everything had been so green in the spring when she'd come for Travis's wedding, but the farm in autumn held its own kind of beauty.

As she approached the final curve toward Lee's, the low strains of guitar music reached her ears. Joy moved quietly through her, because she adored Lee's ability on the guitar. She went around the corner and found him sitting on his front steps, obviously waiting for her as he had his head up and his eyes trained on the road.

He smiled but didn't get up, and Rosalie told herself

not to run toward him. She walked, and as she got nearer and nearer, his chords started to turn into an actual song

In her head, she recognized it, though she didn't have all the words memorized. Her heartbeat picked up its pace, and she slowed her feet.

"Forever can never be long enough for me," he sang, and Lee Cooper had a gorgeous, clear, lower-register voice. It was nothing like the lead singer of Train, who usually sang this song.

Rosalie had a hard time breathing in, and she pressed both hands to her still-pounding pulse.

He looked down at his fingers to get the notes just right, and then he raised his gaze to hers again. She saw the little black box sitting on the step beside him, and Rosalie realized he'd staged this proposal in the most Lee-Cooper of ways.

Simple. Pure. Perfect.

"Marry me," he sang. "Today and every day." He stood, his guitar going mute. "Marry me. If I ever get the nerve to say hello at this math night."

She grinned at him, her eyes burning with tears.

"Say you will, hm-mm," he said, taking a step toward her. "Say you will."

Rosalie nodded, her voice catching on itself as she said, "I will, Lee."

He grinned, started toward her and then quickly went back the way he'd come. He grabbed the ring box off the step and jogged back to her. "I love you, Rosalie. Will you be my wife?"

"Yes," she said, her whole body shaking as he opened the lid on the ring box and let the afternoon sunshine glint off the gem inside. The bright gold band held a big, round diamond, and to her, it sure seemed like it could hold all of Lee's love for her.

She looked into his eyes. "Yes, I'll marry you."

He smiled as he slid the ring onto the appropriate finger, and when he looked up at her, he seemed shy and strong at the same time. Her cowboy prince, the one who held all the happiness for her future right there in the palm of his hand.

"I love you, Rose."

"Love you too, Lee." She wrapped him in her arms and kissed him, this surly cowboy who'd refused to clap for her after a presentation. Now, it seemed like all of heaven —and both of their families—applauded them.

"Come on," he said, his voice husky as he pulled away. "Let's go tell the kids."

KEEP READING FOR A SNEAK PEEK AT THE NEXT BOOK IN THE Sweet Water Falls Farm series, **SALTY COWBOY**, which features Cherry, the oldest Cooper sibling! *You can preorder the ebook now.*

SNEAK PEEK! SALTY COWBOY CHAPTER ONE:

Cherry Cooper put on her blinker to turn right about five miles before the turn-off for her family farm. She'd lost her mind, that was all. She could schedule a few sessions with her therapist and drive Jed Forrester out of her head again.

She'd done it before with Charlie, then with a man named Tyler, then Dr. Freeman. Then Jed.

And yet, she turned right onto the paved road that led to the corn maze at Forrester Farms, something she didn't even want to do. She hadn't been to a corn maze in years, and he hadn't invited her to stop by and get lost with him among seven-foot stalks and plenty of straw bales and scarecrows.

Why was she here?

The salty cowboy had told her he didn't want to date

long-distance. *I don't have time to drive to Casper every week, Cherry.*

The words stung at her brain as much now as when he'd texted them back in September. After he'd kissed her, of course. The man had likely gotten what he'd wanted, and he didn't want her anymore.

Cherry hated the self-defeating talk inside her mind, but she couldn't come up with another explanation as to why Jed had been so keen on texting and calling and getting together...and then gone cold.

After he'd said that, Cherry had been so glad she hadn't told Lee or Will about Jed. She didn't want to have to defend him, because he didn't deserve a defense.

"Then why are you here?" she asked, panic starting to set in. If Jed was working the corn maze, he'd see her car. He'd know she'd come by to see him, and that would only fuel his already huge ego.

The parking lot for the maze wasn't big by any means, and a single cowboy stood at the entrance of it. He didn't seem tall enough to be Jed, and Cherry couldn't turn around on the road anyway. She had to go into the lot to then go back the way she'd come, and she watched the man wave her to the right. She went that way, desperate now to get away from this place.

Why in the world had she come here?

Why not? her feisty mind fired back at her. She had every right to visit this public venue. She'd pay the fee, and she'd wander through the dry and dying stalks, and then she might have the strength and courage to continue to her family's farm. Her sister was due with her first baby tomorrow, and while Cherry had already been home more this year than she had in the five preceding it, she wouldn't miss being there for Rissa when she came home from the hospital with her first child.

She parked and got out of her car, tugging her hooded jacket tighter around her and zipping it up. She wore a pair of jeans that hugged every curve and had a thick seam going down the front of them and a pair of trail running shoes that had extra thick soles with a hiking boot grip on the bottom of them. She'd practically dressed for this corn maze, and she hadn't even known it.

She paid the fee to a woman in a make-shift ticket booth with a large American flag flying far above it and moved toward the entrance of the maze. Now that Halloween had passed, the place wasn't terribly busy, but a family had gone in ahead of her, and she walked slowly until she couldn't hear their voices. At every junction she came to, she turned right. Right, right, right, until she couldn't go right anymore.

Then she started turning left, and eventually, she had no clue where she was. The maze had big bridges built into it, so she could go up a dozen or so steps and stand on the bridge and look out over the corn stalks to try to find the way out. She didn't do that, because this corn maze had become a representation of her life.

Always making the wrong turn instead of the right

one. And if she did turn right, she found out later that she should've taken a left. She walked alone in the maze, just as she did in life. Sure, she had friends at work, and friends who lived in her neighborhood, but she knew it wasn't the same as having someone really close to her whom she could count on for anything.

Her mind needled at her, telling her things like, *It's probably time to come home, Cherry,* and *You won't have to see Charlie. You'll be okay.*

She definitely needed more therapy to let go of the broken pieces of her past, to knock out all of the bad tile and replace it with granite countertops or hardwood flooring. All of her siblings were now happily married or would be soon enough. Lee had just proposed to his girl-friend, Rosalie Reynolds, and Cherry had gotten a text last night about their celebratory dinner this upcoming weekend.

She'd taken the whole week off from her academic advising job in San Antonio, and she didn't have to be back for nine more days. So much could happen in a single hour, and Cherry didn't like making plans too far into the future.

Lee and Rosalie had set a date to be married in April, which was an idyllic month in Texas, with plenty of flowers and sunshine, all of which suited Rosalie so well.

At Cherry's wedding, they'd probably be black napkins and zero lace, because she didn't ever think she'd get married. She had, once, but that dream had died a slow, painful death that sometimes still haunted her.

Now, Cherry didn't dream at all. Life was just life, and she didn't want to get too bogged down in thinking about whether it was fair or not—it wasn't—or good or not. Such a thing was so subjective anyway, and she just wanted to do a good job, go home and eat something delicious for dinner, and try to find a way to ease her loneliness.

Once again, she turned left when she came to a crossroads, and she thought she should probably consider returning to the farm where she'd grown up. There was room for her there—or there would be once Travis's new house got built. She could live right next door to her sister and be the best auntie in the whole state of Texas.

As she walked over the hard-packed dirt ground, a voice came over the loudspeaker. "The corn maze is closing. Please make your way to the nearest exit."

If she could do that, she would, but Cherry honestly had no idea where she was. She could be in the middle of the maze or along an outside wall of it. She glanced around and didn't see any bridges in the vicinity, and she wondered what the cowboys here at Forrester Farms did to make sure all of their guests got out of the maze. Did they have cameras that would show her wandering around, panicked and scared?

Humiliation streamed through her, and she picked up

her pace as she approached the end of the aisle. Left or right?

She went left, practically jogging as another announcement to find an exit filled the air. "I'm trying," she muttered to herself. She'd given up praying for help long ago, but now she found herself with a plea in her heart for the Lord to guide her and help her get out of this maze.

Rissa and Spencer were expecting her, and she couldn't *believe* she'd turned off the highway too early.

A bridge came into view, and Cherry hurried toward it. She sprinted up the steps and looked out across the maze. The huge American flag flew above the ticket booth, and it was behind her. Back the way she'd been walking.

Helplessness crowded into her throat, and she swallowed against it. Perhaps the farm had a helicopter that could come pluck her from this bridge, saving her the energy and time of trying to go back the way she'd come. Perhaps she could just start crashing through the dry stalks as she forged her own path and made her own exit.

Footsteps crunched through the dry foliage on the ground below, and then they started up the steps to the bridge where she stood. Her heart hammered in her chest as she watched a cowboy arrive not ten feet from her.

Not just any cowboy.

"Cherry Cooper," Jed Forrester drawled. He didn't smile. He didn't approach. He wore a windbreaker that wasn't big enough to go across his broad shoulders, a pair of sexy dark denim jeans, and his gorgeous dark brown cowboy hat. He heaved a great big sigh and said, "I'll help you out."

Cherry wanted to argue with him and claim she knew the precise path that would lead her to safety. She couldn't say that, because it was the furthest thing from the truth.

"Well, come on then," he drawled in that deep bass voice that followed her into the depths of her slumber at night. He turned and went down the steps without waiting for her to say anything, and she didn't see any other choice.

He'd once saved her from Charlie at Travis's wedding. Over the months since then, his texts and calls had saved her from her dreary, quiet, lonely nights. And right now, he was literally saving her from wandering through this maze for the rest of the evening.

She followed him, reaching the ground just as he went back into the maze. She ran to catch him, saying, "Can you slow down?"

"Nope," he said over his shoulder. "We're closed already, and I've got more work to do before I'm actually done for the night."

Cherry panted as she reached his side. She didn't know what else to say. As they approached a corner, he indicated they should go left, and he led the way. He was taller than her, with much longer legs, and she figured as long as she could see which way he went, she didn't have to walk right beside him.

He didn't want her there anyway. Foolishness filled her, especially when she followed him to the right and then dang near plowed right into him. She yelped and flung up her hands, her eyes slamming shut for some reason.

He caught her deftly, because Jed was sure and strong about everything. He didn't hem and haw over a long-distance relationship. He just said *no. Not for me. Thanks for the past few months.*

"Don't touch me," she said, swatting his hands away from her waist now that she had her feet under her.

"Why are you here?" he asked, not giving her an inch in this small corner of the maze. She'd turned right, and then it immediately jogged left again, but Jed hadn't taken the turn.

"I needed a few more minutes before I went home," she said, not giving herself enough time to censor herself.

"So you came *here*?"

"It's a public place," she said.

Jed searched her face, and Cherry had no idea what he was looking for or if he'd ever find it. He said nothing, sighed, dusted his hands, and took the right turn to go around the small corner.

"Jed," Cherry said, but she didn't know what else to say. *She* shouldn't have to say anything. *He* was the one who'd dumped her. He kept walking, and she followed, and only a few minutes later, they emerged into the parking lot. It wasn't the same entrance she'd used to get into the maze, but she spotted her car off to her left, across the whole dirt lot. Every other car and truck had gone, and another dose of foolishness hit her in the face like a bucket of icy water.

"Thank you," she said as diplomatically as she could, and she started toward her car. If she could make it there, she could get off this farm and bask in her own humiliation without an audience. She held her head high as she walked, and because she was so focused on her goal, she didn't realize Jed had started walking too.

She finally heard his footsteps and turned to see him only a couple of paces behind her. "I'm fine now," she said.

"Do you want to go to dinner tonight?" he asked.

Surprise tripped through her, actually tripping up her feet too. She stumbled, and blast him, Jed reached out and steadied her. Everything in her life had been more stable since he'd whisked her away from Charlie at the wedding.

Everything.

"No," she said, not quite sure what question she was answering. Or even what she was saying.

His eyebrows went up. "You have dinner plans with your family?"

"No," she said again.

"Then why can't we go to dinner?"

"Because you don't want to," she said, frowning at

him. "I asked you if you could do the long-distance thing, and you said no."

Jed's dark blue eyes blazed with fire. "Maybe I made a mistake."

"I haven't moved," she said. "I still have my job in San Antonio."

"I'm aware."

She was aware of how close to her he stood, and how she didn't want him to back up. She hadn't told Rissa or Spence what time she'd be there, and honestly, her sister was used to her arriving whenever it suited her. She absolutely could go to dinner with Jed.

Not here, her mind screamed at her, and Cherry balked once more at the idea. "Where would we go?"

He folded his arms, one hip cocking out. "I suppose you don't want to go anywhere in town."

"Somewhere else would be ideal," she said.

He looked up into the darkening sky. "I can't believe I'm doing this."

"Then don't do it," she snapped. She spun around and marched away from him again. "You're no prince, Jed. I don't need to be saved."

"You're no princess either, Cherry," he called after her.

He was so right, but she didn't stick around to tell him so. She reached her car and yanked open the door to get behind the wheel. She started the ignition and threw the car in reverse. Her car beeped and the seat beneath her vibrated as she started to back up.

She slammed on the brakes, her eyes finally catching up to what the car already knew. Someone stood behind her.

Jed.

Fuming, she unclasped the seatbelt and threw open the door again. "Move," she demanded as she got out of the car. "Right now."

SNEAK PEEK! SALTY COWBOY CHAPTER TWO:

Jed Forrester watched the gorgeous Cherry Cooper's fingers curl into fists. For whatever reason, that action made every cell in his body hot, and he wanted to get burned by this woman. Badly.

She wore a form-fitting jacket with jeans, cute hiking shoes-slash-runners on her feet, and her hair down. It flowed over her shoulders like liquid fire, the kind that burned low at midnight and didn't come from a bottle. She possessed deep, dark brown eyes with a hint of green if they caught the light just right. Jed had only seen that once, and he ached to try to find the ember of emerald in her eyes again.

"We can go to that pho hut in Beeville," he said, not quite sure why he couldn't let her drive out of his life again. In fact, he'd been the one to drive her away last time. It was only several weeks ago, actually, and Jed had regretted his text for weeks now. "I know you like that kind of stuff."

Cherry softened right in front of him, but she kept her chin high and her eyes slitted as she studied him. He supposed he couldn't blame her for not trusting him, though he'd always said things just how they were. He'd never tried to hide anything from her, but that was because he didn't have ultimate control over what came out of his mouth, not because he was so upright and honest.

"Come on," he said, trying on a small smile. "You can leave your car here and everything." He extended his hand toward her. "Come tell me why you're back in town."

Slowly, Cherry approached him, but she didn't put her hand in his. They didn't exist in fists anymore either, and she tucked them into her jacket pockets instead of touching him. "Rissa's having her baby tomorrow."

"Ah, of course," he said. He'd known Clarissa Rust was pregnant, and he should've known Cherry wouldn't miss being there to meet her new niece or nephew. "Boy or girl?" Lee might have told him at one point in the past, but Jed didn't carry details in his brain that didn't matter to him.

"Boy," Cherry said quietly, moving with him as he walked away from her car. "Wait, my car is still running." She jogged back to turn it off, and she returned to his side with her purse in her hand too. "Okay, ready."

He smiled at her, but she barely returned it. He was used to that, as he was definitely the loud, jovial one out of the pair of them. Cherry preferred letting him take the lead, and while she'd smiled and laughed with him over the past several months, he definitely had to work hard to draw those things out of her.

Heck, he'd had to work hard for everything he'd gotten from Cherry. Even getting her phone number had been like pulling teeth.

His chest vibrated in a strange way as he stepped up to his midnight black truck and opened the passenger door for Cherry. She boosted herself up and into the seat in a single movement, which made Jed's mouth turn a little drier than it already was. She looked at him, and Jed could get lost in her gaze for a good, long while.

Move, he told himself, and he managed to step back and out of the way. He closed the door as his phone chimed at him, and he looked down at the notification. His brother had texted, and Jed's heart dropped to his knees.

Corn maze clear? You're feeding the horses in six tonight, right?

Jed couldn't believe he'd invited Cherry to dinner. He'd known he had more chores to do after clearing the corn maze. Had he known the lost customer in the maze had been her, he probably would've sent Chris to go in and get them out.

He tapped to call his brother, and the line only rang

once before Chris picked up. "Hey, so I have a slight problem," he said, glancing over to Cherry and quickly moving away from the window. She wouldn't like being called a problem, and he'd already yelled at her that she wasn't a princess.

In reality, Jed hadn't stopped thinking about Cherry since he'd run into her at Travis's wedding. He'd only seen her once a month, and yeah, he'd wanted more. She'd offered him Casper, and he'd thrown it back in her face.

He looked up into the sky as Chris said, "What kind of problem? The kind where I have to find someone else to go feed the horses?"

"Yeah," Jed said with a sigh. "That kind of problem."

Chris let out a long exhaling breath. "The corn maze is clear, right?"

"Yes," Jed said, glad he didn't have to disappoint his younger brother again. He, Chris, and Easton ran their family farm together, and Chris managed all of the logistics of things while Jed handled more of the big-picture items. He paid bills and made sure they had the men and women they needed to work the fields and handle the animals and bring in the harvest.

He pitched in and helped wherever needed, and he spent a lot of time with a hammer or a saw in his hand, fixing whatever had started to break around the farm. Too bad he couldn't fix himself enough to keep a woman for longer than a few months. Even his marriage hadn't made it out of month six, and that whole relationship hadn't even lasted a year.

Jed shook all of that away as he rounded the back of his truck. He and Cherry had been sort of dating for months now, and he should've said he'd meet her in Casper anytime she wanted. Breakfast, lunch, or dinner.

"What are you doing right now?" Chris asked.

"Can I tell you later?" Jed asked, reaching for the door handle.

"This has Cherry Cooper written all over it," his brother said.

"No," Jed said too quickly. "Why would it? She doesn't even live here."

"Her sister is having a baby any minute now," Chris said in a deadpan. "You must think I'm so stupid."

"No," Jed said again. He turned away from the truck and ducked his head. "Am I that obvious?" He spoke in a low voice, hoping Chris would say no.

"Totally," Chris said. "She probably doesn't think so, but I've seen you freak out about nothing for the past couple of months, and that was about the time you stopped talking to her. Or she stopped talking to you. I don't know, because you won't talk about her."

"Yeah, well, we can't all have amazing wives," Jed said.

"I'll tell Deb you said that," Chris said. "She's feeling less than amazing right now, so she'll probably bring you brownies later."

"Mint brownies," Jed clarified.

Chris laughed and said, "Have fun with Cherry." He hung up before Jed could protest that his "little problem" had nothing to do with Cherry Cooper. He faced the truck again, shoved his phone in his back pocket, and pulled open the driver's door.

"Sorry," he said. "Chris called."

Cherry trained her big eyes on him, her smile slow and absolutely gorgeous on her face. "How's Chris and Deb?"

"They're great," Jed said. "Pregnant again. Deb's really praying for a girl." He smiled and flipped his truck into drive. "I'm honestly surprised they're having another baby after the twins." He chuckled, and Cherry laughed with him. "They're a handful, let me tell you."

"You've talked about them before," Cherry said, looking out her window.

Jed quieted, because Cherry had, and he didn't know how to talk to her when she receded inside herself. He cleared his throat, uncomfortable in the silence with her. "How's work?"

"I'm thinking of getting a new job," she said.

He whipped his attention toward her. "You are? Where?"

"I have no idea."

"I'm sure there's something for you here," he said.

Cherry turned toward him, her arms folding across her midsection as she did. "Is that so? Here? In Sweet

Water Falls, where there is no college for an academic advisor?"

Jed swallowed, not sure where to go with this. Perhaps he should just lay everything on the line. "You could work at your family farm," he said. "Or do something for a college online. Or take a completely new career path." He glanced over at her and turned out of the parking lot. "Didn't you tell me that once? That you wanted a new career path?"

"I can't remember," she said. "I probably did."

"Not anymore?"

"I don't know, Jed."

He frowned at the road in front of him, because if she didn't know, he certainly didn't. He felt too old to be having this conversation. He knew what his life held, and he'd always known. The family farm. Horses and hay fields and hard work. He didn't really have the luxury Cherry seemed to enjoy of picking and choosing the path she wanted to be on.

He drove the two of them to Beeville without much more conversation, questioning every minute of the way what he was doing. He honestly had no idea—and he was far too old to be doing things he didn't understand.

There was simply something about Cherry Cooper he liked and wanted to know more about. He wanted to help her in any way he could, and he didn't understand that either. His father had always told him he had a too-big heart to run the farm, but Jed had embraced that instead of trying to change it.

If there was an animal in pain or in need of something, he wanted to provide for it. He'd set alarms for a foal who'd been born too early and gone out to the stables every two hours to nurse it along until it was strong enough to survive without his help. In some ways, Cherry reminded him of that foal. In other ways, she was powerful and strong in a way that struck Jed as pure royalty. He could picture her entering a room and having everyone bow to her as their queen. She certainly brought him to his knees in such a way, especially after their first kiss a couple of months ago.

He pulled into the pho restaurant parking lot and came to a stop. "This is okay?"

"Yes," she said softly. She stayed put while Jed jumped from the truck and jogged around the front of it to get her door. He opened it for her and stepped into the space. She'd unbuckled, but Jed didn't want her to get out.

The words he needed to say had been building beneath his tongue during the drive, and he had to say them before he lost her again.

"Cherry." He reached up and smoothed her hair back. "I'm sorry about saying I didn't have time to drive to see you." He looked at her earnestly, hoping she could feel how genuine he was trying to be. "I've regretted that text every day since I sent it. Every minute."

She studied his face. "You didn't mean it?"

"I was frustrated," he said. "So I probably meant it in the moment, but no, overall, of course I didn't mean it. I think about you all the time, and I just don't know how to sweeten up and ask you to forgive me."

She smiled at him, and the heavens opened to him. Light shone on her, and all Jed could think about was kissing her. He wasn't going to do that today, because he didn't want her to think that was all he wanted from her.

"You are a bit salty," she said. "Maybe my sister-in-law could send you some of her truffles. They're as sweet as the day is long."

He smiled back at her. "Can we try again?"

Cherry hesitated for a moment, then she reached out and ran her hand down the side of his face. "I've missed you, Jed."

"I've missed you too," he whispered.

She leaned forward, pushing her hand up and removing his cowboy hat. Normally, Jed didn't like it when anyone touched his hat, but Cherry had a way of doing things that he just went with.

Her eyes drifted closed, and Jed's heartbeat fluttered in the large vein in his neck. She pressed his hat to his shoulder blades, bringing him closer to her, and Jed touched his lips to hers in a soft, sweet kiss that he didn't try to accelerate or take to the next level.

The first time he'd kissed her had been explosive, and he hadn't been able to control the way things had spiraled and taken off. This time, he bowed to his queen and let her lead him in the kiss. She only kissed him for a moment before she pulled away.

"What's wrong?" she asked.

He opened his eyes and met hers. "Nothing."

"You're not kissing me back."

"Yes, I am."

She cocked her head to the side, and said, "Give me some of your attitude, Jed."

He grinned at her, semi-embarrassed at his limp kissing. "If you don't like it, don't kiss me," he said.

"I don't want to kiss you," she said. "I want you to kiss me."

Jed ran his hand up the outside of her thigh and along her waist. "We're going to pick up where we left off, is that it?"

"I'd like to," she said, and he liked that she didn't play games with him. She was a couple of years older than him, and perhaps she didn't have time for a relationship that wasn't going anywhere either. "So?" she asked. "Are you going to kiss me or what?"

Jed looked at her, trying to decide if he should tell her what truly ran through his mind or if he should kiss her the way she wanted him to.

～

BOOKS IN THE SWEET WATER FALLS FARM ROMANCE SERIES

Cross Cowboy, Book 1: He's been accused of being far too blunt. Like that time he accused her of stealing her company from her best friend... Can Travis and Shayla overcome their differences and find a happily-ever-after together?

GRUMPY COWBOY

Grumpy Cowboy, Book 2: He can find the negative in any situation. Like that time he got upset with the woman who brought him a free chocolate-and-caramel-covered apple because it had melted in his truck... Can William and Gretchen start over and make a healthy relationship after it's started to wilt?

SURLY COWBOY

Surly Cowboy, Book 3: He's got a reputation to uphold and he's not all that amused the way regular people are. Like that time he stood there straight-faced and silent while everyone else in the audience cheered and clapped for that educational demo... Can Lee and Rosalie let bygones be bygones and make a family filled with joy?

Salty Cowboy, Book 4: The last Cooper sibling is looking for love...she just wishes it wouldn't be in her hometown, or with the saltiest cowboy on the planet. But something about Jed Forrester has Cherry all a-flutter, and he'll be darned if he's going to let her get away. But Jed may have met his match when it comes to his quick tongue and salty attitude...

BOOKS IN THE HOPE ETERNAL RANCH ROMANCE SERIES

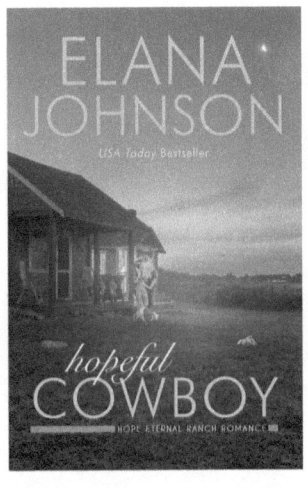

Hopeful Cowboy, Book 1: Can Ginger and Nate find their happily-ever-after, keep up their duties on the ranch, and build a family? Or will the risk be too great for them both?

Overprotective Cowboy, Book 2: Can Ted and Emma face their pasts so they can truly be ready to step into the future together? Or will everything between them fall apart once the truth comes out?

Rugged Cowboy, Book 3: He's a cowboy mechanic with two kids and an ex-wife on the run. She connects better to horses than humans. Can Dallas and Jess find their way to each other at Hope Eternal Ranch?

Christmas Cowboy, Book 4: He needs to start a new story for his life. She's dealing with a lot of family issues. This Christmas, can Slate and Jill find solace in each other at Hope Eternal Ranch?

Wishful Cowboy, Book 5: He needs somewhere to belong. She has a heart as wide as the Texas sky. Can Luke and Hannah find their one true love in each other?

Risky Cowboy, Book 6: She's tired of making cheese and ice cream on her family's dairy farm, but when the cowboy hired to replace her turns out to be an ex-boyfriend, Clarissa suddenly isn't so sure about leaving town... Will Spencer risk it all to convince Clarissa to stay and give him a second chance?

BOOKS IN THE HAWTHORNE HARBOR ROMANCE SERIES

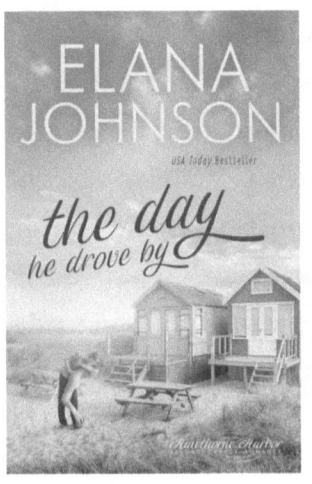

The Day He Drove By (Hawthorne Harbor Second Chance Romance, Book 1): A widowed florist, her ten-year-old daughter, and the paramedic who delivered the girl a decade earlier...

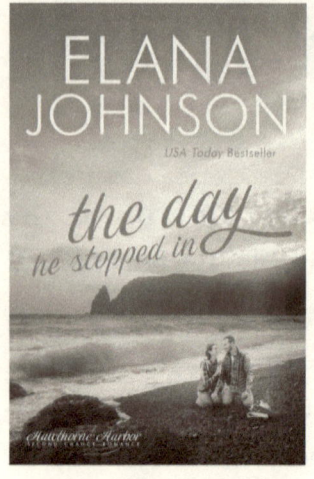

The Day He Stopped In (Hawthorne Harbor Second Chance Romance, Book 2): Janey Germaine is tired of entertaining tourists in Olympic National Park all day and trying to keep her twelve-year-old son occupied at night. When longtime friend and the Chief of Police, Adam Herrin, offers to take the boy on a ride-along one fall evening, Janey starts to see him in a different light. Do they have the courage to take their relationship out of the friend zone?

The Day He Said Hello (Hawthorne Harbor Second Chance Romance, Book 3): Bennett Patterson is content with his boring firefighting job and his big great dane...until he comes face-to-face with his high school girlfriend, Jennie Zimmerman, who swore she'd never return to Hawthorne Harbor. Can they rekindle their old flame? Or will their opposite personalities keep them apart?

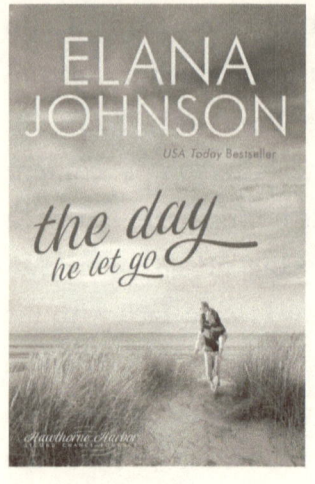

The Day He Let Go (Hawthorne Harbor Second Chance Romance, Book 4): Trent Baker is ready for another relationship, and he's hopeful he can find someone who wants him and to be a mother to his son. Lauren Michaels runs her own general contract company, and she's never thought she has a maternal bone in her body. But when she gets a second chance with the handsome K9 cop who blew her off when she first came to town, she can't say no... Can Trent and Lauren make their differences into strengths and build a family?

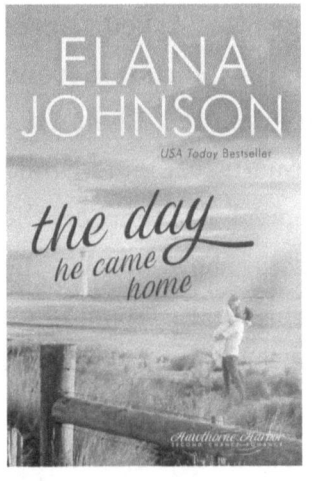

The Day He Came Home (Hawthorne Harbor Second Chance Romance, Book 5): A wounded Marine returns to Hawthorne Harbor years after the woman he was married to for exactly one week before she got an annulment...and then a baby nine months later. Can Hunter and Alice make a family out of past heartache?

The Day He Asked Again (Hawthorne Harbor Second Chance Romance, Book 6): A Coast Guard captain would rather spend his time on the sea...unless he's with the woman he's been crushing on for months. Can Brooklynn and Dave make their second chance stick?

ABOUT ELANA

Elana Johnson is the USA Today bestselling author of dozens of clean and wholesome contemporary romance novels. She lives in Utah, where she mothers two fur babies, works with her husband full-time, and eats a lot of veggies while writing. Find her on her website at elanajohnson.com.